THE DARK WAR

BOOK ONE

ABBY GREENBAUM

Dedicated to William Troha
Fly high. We love and miss you every day.

*I*t's a beautiful day to attack a fellow pirate ship.

The wind blows a gentle breeze that eases the heat of the burning summer afternoon. The sun beats down on the water, illuminating the dark blue sea. The waves are just soft enough for boats to sail smoothly, and there is not a cloud in sight. I changed the sails on my vessel from the usual black and red stripes to plain white, and that's how my crew and I sneaked close enough to climb onto the abaft of Henry Allensway's *S.S. Ghallager* to steal back what he stole from me.

Allensway must have thought we were a regular travel ship. That man really has the audacity to call himself a captain.

Hunched low, I wait for the right moment to give the signal for my crew to attack.

"Nadia," I say softly, motioning my navigator and best friend to me. The other leaders in my crew gather round as well. "I want you to go to the wheel and anchor the ship. Joseph, take John, Adam, and Oliver and go with her to the front of the ship. I want whoever is sailing the ship gone first, then all of the other buffoons. Elliot, keep Ben at your side at all costs—protect him. James and Sawyer, head straight for Allensway. The rest of you . . ." I smile. "Well, you know what to do." Then I raise my cutlass in the air, and the attack begins.

I climb to the top of the lowest sail above me and stand on the poles to watch the fight down below. Discreetly, I unbutton my sapphire blue doublet coat, unruffle my white puffy shirt, and tighten my black belt. I dust off my black tunic leggings and pull up my dark-colored boots. It's time for a dramatic entrance.

It's quite amusing watching Henry the Hothead struggle to get away from James and Sawyer. It's sort of like watching a gazelle try to escape from a lion. I don't even understand why Allensway and his crew are pirates; they're quite horrible at it, and they're actually well-known for being atrocious at what they do. That's why it was such a surprise —and an embarrassment—to learn they'd stolen from me.

Lousy, abhorrent "pirates."

Watching Allensway's crew almost saddens me. The scent of blood fills the air and floods the floors. We truly did catch them off guard, which makes me wonder if they would have been less crappy if they saw us coming, actually put up a fight. They act as if they had never held a cutlass before, as if they were all landlubbers.

Although there's chaos happening all around the ship, my eyes remain glued on Allensway, clumsily fighting my crewmates.

After an easy quarrel, James gets Allensway to his knees. Sawyer holds his hands tightly behind his back, making sure Allensway can't move.

"Please, have mercy. Let me speak to your captain, and I'll—"

"You'll what?" Sawyer asks. "Make her want to kill you quicker? She is not known for her forgiving personality." He laughs at Allensway's incompetence, then looks at James and they both smile.

I jump off the sail and land on my feet, right in front of Captain Allensway's kneeling form. Oh, I remember him. I remember leaving my ship anchored at the docks in Thomalia while my crew and I reveled in a brand new tavern. I remember finding the watchman tied up, my entire vessel torn apart, and Allensway's flag sailing away in the distance. Only one thing was missing, and it took us seven days and a hefty bribe to one of our allies to find his ship. Wisely, it turned out he was on the run. From me.

"You wish to speak with me?" I question as I grab my cutlass.

"Ay, Captain Jones." He nods. "I—I am truly sorry for my actions. I had clearly gone mad. But I'll give it back to you, I swear. Please, please have mercy," he begs as I hold the point of my sword to his neck. He shivers with fear as I speak.

"Mercy? For a thief? I don't think so. You had the audacity to steal from me and now you think you will not be punished?"

"I already apologized, Captain," he replies as my brother, Ben, runs up to us, panting. "What is so significant about a necklace? You already have all of the jewels you could possibly steal."

I nod at my brother. "Look at that, Benjamin. He's challenging me."

James lets out a small snort, already knowing what I'm going to do next.

It's Ben who hesitates. "I don't think—"

"No, no, no," Allensway backpedals. "That is not what I meant. I just—"

"*I know* what you meant," I interrupt. "And it's simply not just a necklace. It's what it compensates for."

"And what exactly does it compensate for?" he asks, his tone shifting as if he's mocking me. Is he getting annoyed with me?

I lean in. "Watch your mouth, Allensway. My actions, my reasons for doing certain things, are none of your business. I think I'm pretty much done here . . . except, I do want to know something. How in the bloody hell did you find my ship?"

Allensway smirks. "The name Alina Ortega ring a bell?" he asks. I tense at the sound of the devil's name.

"Associating with the riffraff, are you? No surprise there. Alina is utterly heinous, and yet even she's intelligent enough not to steal from me, and like me she's a great deal younger than you." I cock my head. "That says a lot, doesn't it?"

He hesitates, reluctance flooding his next words. "I have my reasons for doing things too."

"I don't care what your reasons are," I respond. I stare at him, anger flooding my eyes. He gulps.

"What are you going to do with me? What about my crew?"

I grin at his queries and almost even laugh. I look around at the rest of my crew, still fighting Allensway's remaining crewmates.

"James, tell the others to leave nobody alive. If one person steals from me, everybody steals from me. Therefore, they must all pay the price."

Ben steps forward. "Captain, wait—"

"What?" Henry shouts. "No! Why?"

I eye him carefully. "Because, after all, what's the point of a bunch of living, cowardly idiots?"

"Captain," Ben says. "There is another option. Why don't you just take the necklace and leave him with a warning?" He sounds almost sympathetic.

I chuckle. "Do you not know me by now?" I don't spare any quarter for a thief, especially not after what Allensway took.

My patience grows thin, my blood beginning to boil. If he had stolen anything else, I may have not been so exasperated, so full of rage. But he stole the most important thing I own, and he has to pay for that.

Despite Ben's protests, I carry on.

I raise my cutlass, and with one great, ireful swing, I cleave him to the brisket. Blood pools from the wound, surrounding his body as it thuds to the deck. Allensway will never steal from me, or anyone, ever again. I grab his satchel and pull my ruby necklace from its depths. The sun glints off its jewels like fire, and I place it in my pocket.

Sawyer's steps approach me from behind. "What are we doing with all of the deceased, Captain?" he asks.

I don't look back at the bodies littering the deck, or down at the blood beneath my boots. "They can feed the fish."

2

"Tell Nadia to chart the course for home," I tell Sawyer. "I will be at the wheel."

We leap back onto the *Tigerlily*, which had been anchored behind the *S.S. Ghallager*. I feel better, being back on my ship, like there's a kingship between us. I chose the name *Tigerlily* because it sounds so innocent—not at all dangerous. But once we strike, you'll know you judged us wrong.

As I take the wheel and we get underway, I hold my ruby necklace tightly in my palm. I rub the beautiful stone with my thumb and grin at the memories it brings. I have worked hard for three years to make myself and my crew known. I am the youngest female captain—only nineteen years old— to ever set sail on the deep blue sea. I have been training my entire life for this.

My mother gave me the necklace. It was no doubt stolen, but it's the thought that counts. "It's my favorite thing in the world," she'd told me, "besides you and Ben." She also said that if she were to ever die, she would want me to have a piece of her with me so I'd know she'd always be here. It was my sixteenth birthday present, given to me just days before I saw her for the last time.

My mother had been a pirate too. I never met my biological father, but I never wanted to. Lennard was my stepfather, the most feared captain in all of Olovia, and he taught me his ways since I could walk. Ben and I both grew up with a ship and the sea beneath our feet. A brutal storm took Lennard and my mother down, people said, and my parents drowned at sea.

But I remember everything they taught me. How to sail, how to fight. I don't kill innocents because they didn't; those I kill have either wronged me or my allies. So when Allensway stole my necklace, I had to kill him.

Nobody messes with the *Tigerlily*.

We sail for hours. I search the horizon, growing more and more eager to get back to Olovia, back home.

Nadia comes to my side, holding a spyglass in one hand. "Captain, we will be arriving at the docks in about twenty minutes."

I sigh with relief. I haven't been to North Olovia, Olovia's capital, in five months. We've been sailing around the Southern Seas nonstop since February, but Allensway's ship is the last one that I'd planned to attack. At least for a little while. It's time to head home to take a slight break. My crew truly deserved it.

Our favorite tavern was calling my name. After a long day of spilling blood, a drink sure goes a long way. Allensway had a lot of nerve, but he was the world's biggest nimrod and a mediocre pirate. I consider what Ben had said, too, that maybe I didn't have to kill him. But I did—although

I can never fully ensure that my property remains unstolen, if I let the thieves go they'll come back for more, and beyond that necklace my brother is the one thing that I will always protect.

"Captain," Nadia says, sneaking up on me again. "There is something that you must see." She gestures to the edge of the sip.

"Joseph, take the wheel," I demand as I follow her. Alone, I ask, "What is it?"

"Look." Nadia points north, to where we're heading. We must be only minutes from shore, but now that we're closer everything surrounding the dock is more visible. There, in the sky, is an immense amount of ebony-colored smoke. It almost looks like a storm cloud, only this is much darker and much larger in size. Like a storm cloud, though, it's moving slowly across the kingdom.

It covers the stone buildings of the small city in the shadow of darkness. The usual hummingbirds are no longer flying around the village, and though the streets are normally filled with people, now it looks as if only stragglers are chancing the outdoors.

The longer I stare at the darkening sky above the city, the deeper a perilous chill burrows.

"What is that?" I ask.

Nadia shivers. "Magic," she answers. "It's most definitely magic, but something feels ominous about it."

She's right, though I don't quite understand it. This isn't like any magic I've ever seen.

There are two kinds of magic: sorcery and celestial. Sorcery is possessed by witches and sorcerers. It has to do with spells and it usually comes in the form of light magic. It can be defeated, but only with a magical artifact from the Realm of Magic. Those artifacts are almost futile to obtain, though. Nobody without magic can enter the realm.

But sorcery is still more possible to defeat than celestial magic. Celestial magic is the powers possessed by gods and otherworldly beings. Celestial magic in the Human Realm is quite rare, and though a Realm of Magic artifact can destroy the source of the celestial magic, it can't destroy the magic itself. So even if the being wielding it is killed, the magic still lives.

I've read all about these magics and the gods, hundreds of books across the subject and history. In all my years of being a captain, I've had less than a handful of encounters. I want to assume this is celestial; celestial magic is rare, but this is most definitely not sorcery. Yet there's something so off-putting about it. The cloud is barely moving—not even a centimeter a minute—and celestial magic usually isn't visible, and it doesn't take the smoky form this magic has taken.

The more I study the magic in the sky, the more I finally understand what Nadia was saying, and what I was seeing: dark magic. My heart sinks into my chest at my realization.

Not all magic is the same and not all magic is vigorous. But this? This is something that I have never seen before, and I don't have a clue how someone might go about getting rid of it.

"Who could possibly be behind this?" I whisper.

The war with Gurellia is over; our king and queen signed a peace treaty with them years ago. Tensions still exist, sure, but they've lessened. And judging from the sheer size of the dark cloud, whoever's causing this is greater than any being in any of the nearby kingdoms . . . and possibly the whole Human Realm.

"Should I tell the crew what's going on?" Nadia asks.

"Better not," I reply. "They'll know once they see it. As of right now, it shouldn't do us any harm. No need to worry them."

She nods and sinks into her deck chair. I hear the anxious click of her compass as she flips it in her hands.

Ben comes up from below deck. He runs over, asking, "Have you seen this?"

"I'm not blind, Ben, of course I have," I huff, trying to calm the fear I feel in myself.

He tilts his head to stare at the sky. "What do you think it is?"

"I really don't know," I admit. When I notice him playing with his fingers—a side effect of his nerves—I add, "But I'm sure there is no reason to be alarmed." Behind him, I catch James rushing by. "James!" I call out.

He changes course and stops in front of me. "Yes, Captain?"

"When we dock, I want you to get me information about whatever this may be," I command as I point to the sky above our kingdom.

"Right away, Captain." Before he walks away, he winks at me.

When he's out of earshot, Nadia laughs. "Am I hallucinating, or are you blushing?" she asks as she hands me her compass.

I punch her in the arm. "Shut up."

"I take it you two haven't talked about it yet?" Nadia asks. At my glare, she dances out of reach.

She's overreacting. James and I grew up together, his father having been Lennard's first mate. That means we have a bit of history. We spent a great amount of time together training, and whenever we had downtime. He understood me like nobody else did. He always has.

And maybe we also kissed not too long ago.

As we got older, things between us changed. It just happened. But after we kissed, things had to go on pause. I cannot afford a distraction or another emotional tie, nothing beyond a friend or a mate or my brother. Lennard always warned me about not allowing people to see my relationships, and the best way to make that happen was to not have relationships at all.

Nobody on board knows that I kissed James except for Ben and Nadia. I made all three of them promise they would keep it a secret. It would ruin my whole reputation, and it could put James in danger. At least, more danger than we're already in regularly.

"You know," Ben says, still at my side, staring at the sky. "You are allowed to have feelings."

"I do have feelings," I respond. "I just like it better when people think I don't."

"One day you're going to regret that."

"We'll see." As much as Ben enjoys the thrill of a good ship attack, he has a heart of gold. He's always trying to get me to act more human, to be vulnerable and less defensive. It isn't going to happen. Once I put that barrier up, it's not so easy for it to come down.

I take back control of my ship. As we inch closer and closer to the dock, the people come into view, and I can hear them. Faint screams and arguing. In the distance, the sounds are louder, almost inhuman. People run, their faces petrified masks as they look between the ground in front of them and the sight in the sky. I take a look at the darkness one more time and gulp at the sight.

A chill runs down my spine. Now that we're closer, I can almost hear it. A tingling sensation rushes through my veins, a sensation that the magic is calling me.

"Captain," Adam says, coming up behind me. I shake off

the thought of the magic and turn my attention to him. "Maybe we shouldn't get off the ship. Maybe getting away from ... *that* is our best bet."

"We need more information," I respond. "Once we have that, we can go."

"But if we—"

"Adam," I say sharply, fixing him in my gaze, "I do not feel like arguing with you today. Go help the others prepare to dock."

He looks like he wanted to say more. As I watch him hesitantly leave me alone, I look around at my crew. They all wear the same anxious expression on their faces, although they're doing their best to hide it. Adam's probably right and we shouldn't be here, but I need to get on land and see someone first. Once we know what's going on, we can leave.

We dock. The twenty of us off-board, and together we make our way to the nearest tavern.

But as my boots touch the cobblestone ground, one after the other, I look around at my home village. All of the buildings are either made of stone or brick. There are shops and restaurants lined up along the streets, to the left of the tavern that faces the ocean. They're all empty, or mostly so.

My once warm and sunny home is now slowly being swallowed into the shadow of the darkness.

3

*A*s we make our way to the tavern the few people on the street clear out of the way. They look at me, only me. With disgust or with fear. It would be easier if it was just because I'm a pirate. It isn't. I am not ladylike; I've heard it all: A lady does not kill people. A lady does not wear clothing like that. A lady does not speak like a nimrod.

Let them fear me. Nobody can hurt you if you expect it.

We barge into the tavern, the dimly lit room making me feel at home. "William, we'll have the usual!" I announce to the man behind the counter.

"You're back!" he cheers as he raises the cup in his hand.

I greet him as the rest of the crew sits in their usual seats, spread out across the wide room. William owns the tavern, and he's the only reason we come back to Olovia; his tavern is the only place we're welcome with open arms.

As pirates, we *are* allowed in Olovia, but we're never treated the same as the others who live here. Since we technically don't commit any crimes in Olovia or against any Olovian naval or merchant ships—of that I'm quite careful about—we cannot be arrested, despite many people's wishes. The people look at us as if we're nothing but crap stuck to the bottom of their shoes.

Not William. William basically adopted my mother when she moved to Olovia as a child. She was an orphan before she turned to piracy. By the time she died, we had all become close with him. He's been here for all of us since our parents' shipwreck, becoming like a father to me, taking care of me and Ben, allowing us to move in with him. He always gave my crew shelter while we were training on land.

"How have you been, kid?" he asks as we shake hands and I pull a barstool up to the counter.

"Oh, you know, the usual. Sailing, stealing, attacking ships," I answer.

"That's my girl," he chuckles as he hands me a glass. Before he fills it, he nods to my side and I see James there, waiting.

"Captain, may I borrow you for a second?" he asks.

I nod as I slide off the stool and follow him to a quiet corner of the room, my glass still in my hand.

"I asked some people here about the magic in the sky. It's been here for about four days now. There's a rumor going around that a powerful, unidentified being is trying to wipe out the kingdom," James informs me, almost in a whisper. He leans close to me, not wanting anyone to overhear our conversation.

"Okay, and how is whoever this being is planning on doing that?" I ask.

"The black dust covering the sky has something to do with it. Hundreds of people have already died."

"Why? What does this being want?"

He shrugs. "No one knows."

I don't know how to respond. But I can't keep this to myself. The whole crew saw the magic, the fear. Many of

James moves as if to attack him, but I call for Sawyer to hold him back, though I also consider letting him go. This is getting interesting now, and the prince sounds desperate.

I stand from my seat. "Easy, James. Let the boorish boy pass through."

My crew splits into two sides, allowing the prince to walk through.

Prince Jack of Olovia stands in front of me. Nineteen, like me. Chestnut-brown hair and marble gray eyes. He's dressed in navy and black, his hand resting on his sword belt.

"Look at what the tide washed in," Nadia chuckles.

"Scurvy dog," Adam spits.

"Well, well, well," I snicker. "Look at what we have here, boys. Looks like someone is out of their element."

"I don't care for your comments, Serena. I need to speak with you. Alone," he demands.

"Why?"

"As if she would go anywhere with you," Nadia comments.

"Please," he says, looking only at me. "This is a matter of life and death."

I raise my eyebrows and jerk my head back, my mouth falling a little bit open. Is he being serious right now? From the unwavering steel in his eyes, I gather he is. "I'll just be a moment. Carry on," I announce. I leave my place to sit at an empty table across the room with the prince.

My crew's bewildered stares pierce my back as I sit with the prince. James is pacing back and forth, his sword in his hand. I hear my hearties' whispers, probably coming up with all sorts of theories about what Prince Charming wants to say to me.

"I didn't expect to see you again," I admit. "I'm surprised that you actually came up to me."

"Why?" he asks.

"Why else? Most people are afraid of me. I hope you know I have worked incredibly hard to be unapproachable, and now you're going to ruin my whole reputation," I say, half serious and half joking.

Jack's lips twitch into a grin. "You're not as terrifying as you think you are. Besides, we're not exactly strangers."

"Yes, from when your navy's ships blocked the North Olovian port during the war with Gurellia." A few of my crewmates had a minor . . . *disagreement* with the naval soldiers. Admittedly, we were lucky Jack was there to break up the fight and help us settle on an agreement, but my crew still holds a grudge.

"Why don't you just tell me what you want so you can leave me the hell alone?" I snap.

He sighs. "I cannot do that, actually. I wouldn't be asking this, or even be here for that matter, if I had any other option. The darkness in the sky . . . my parents sent just about the entire royal guard all over the kingdom, the world, to obtain answers and possible solutions. But more and more people are dying as we speak, so we can't wait." He pauses there and leans forward, lowering his voice. "I have a plan, and that's why I'm here. You're a fearless warrior. You've never lost a fight, and I've seen what you can do in a quarrel. You know the ocean like nobody else does." He pauses, then comes out with it. "Serena, I'm asking you to come with me and help me destroy the darkness."

Thinking he's joking, I wait for the punchline. Even without it, I start laughing hysterically. "And how, exactly, am I supposed to do that? Just swing my sword at it?"

"No. But you happen to be a skilled sword fighter, and

since my guards have been sent out to search Olovia and the nearby kingdoms, this is my last resort. I don't think they're going to find anything, which is why I need to move fast. You and I working together may be the key," he says.

I still can't tell if he's serious or not. I narrow my eyes. "And what, exactly, would your *esteemed* parents say if they knew their darling son was working with a pirate crew?"

"They won't know. Nobody will."

"You're right," I concede. "Because I won't do it. Why would you think you need *me*?"

The prince slams his hand on the table. "I need you because my parents refuse to let me take one of our ships out on the water. Or go anywhere, really. You're my only chance to get out there."

I doubt I'm his *only* option. Still, I ask, "What's in it for me?"

"You will be saving the kingdom and quite possibly the world," he answers. Catching the doubt on my face, he adds, "And I'll offer you a reward. Whatever you desire. I know how all pirates love their booty."

"You don't know anything about me, Jack. Not a thing."

"Whatever. Will you help me or not?"

"Do you even have a plan?"

"Yes. If you agree to help me, I'll explain everything."

"Explain now."

He sighs. "The Realm of Magic. We'll sail out to the West Island of the Tammerin Sea, where there's a portal. Because of my royal lineage, the portal will allow us to enter. There's an item there, an orb, that I have assurance might help. I want to use its magic on the cloud in the sky."

"Good plan," I say shortly. "Except I'm not related to anyone of great power, so I won't be able to enter the portal with you." One without magic may only enter the realm if they have magic themselves, are related to someone of great power, or they complete a deadly task. I'm not either of the first two, and I'm certainly not going to do the last.

"Do you know nothing of magic?" Jack asks. "You don't have to be. I have one of the three qualities required for entry, and that's enough to hold it open long enough for you to come as well."

I swallow the lump in my throat, unsure if it's fear or doubt or something else. "And how, exactly, do you know all of this?"

"It's all part of my training. I am required to learn about every kingdom and every realm, and I have spent a great deal of time studying the history of magic."

I'm truly tempted to just sit there and laugh in his face. Again. He wants to use me, my crew, and the *Tigerlily* because he can't get his mommy and daddy to allow him to use his own ship? Not interested. Waste of my time.

But I remember the chill of the darkness, almost as vivid as the cries in the street, and my heart races. I don't need to guess what will happen if the magic continues to spread. If someone doesn't stop this dark magic soon, we may all be doomed.

If I do help Jack, it would be the most dangerous and possibly the most ludicrous thing I will ever do. If I don't, the future of the *Tigerlily*—my crew—would be gone.

I find Ben in the crowd and hesitate. I can't just leave him, but it would be much too risky for him to come. He's only thirteen. Leaving him in Olovia alone was dangerous, and while he gets along with the crew, nobody would take care of him as I do. But traveling to another realm could be just as hazardous.

My crew could attend the journey, but I don't want to put them all at risk like this either. Pirates are one thing; magic wis quite another. What chance do we have against beating magic? We're all only human.

I shake my head. "You're going to have to find someone else. I can't." I stand and try to walk away. Jack grabs my wrist and pulls me back, but I yank my wrist out of his grasp.

"Serena, please. I need you. How much will it take?"

"It's not about the money."

"Do it for the people, then. You will be saving thousands of lives. . . . If you do this, everybody will stop looking at you the way they do. They'll look at you with respect, I can make sure of that. I know that's what you want."

"You do not know what I want," I argue.

"That is what everybody wants." He's trying. He's looking at me as if he can read my mind, see my desires. What a jackass.

But he must know he's struck a chord. He continues, "You see, you and I are quite similar. Half the kingdom loathes my parents, and since I have no power to stop what my mother and my father do, they loathe me too. But when I become king, all of that is going to change. *I* will change things because I just want to be looked at with respect. And you? You're a pirate. An un-ladylike, horrifying, awful *pirate*. So yes, I know what you want."

I scoff. "Listen here, you moronic piece of crap. You have absolutely no right to talk to me like that. You have no idea who I am and what my desires are, and you're making me want to help you less with every word you utter."

"I apologize," Jack says. "That did not come out right. I am not trying to offend you in any way. But I think you know —you know what I am trying to say. I was just saying that we have something in common."

"Look, if you just crawled out of a hat to come here and

insult me, then you're wasting your time. You and I have nothing in common. Nothing you say or do will change that." I pull away from him again, but this time I hear his chair scrape across the floor as he gets up after me.

"What about your brother?" he asks.

I pause in my tracks and slowly turn around.

"I have a younger brother too," he says. "I want to protect him, and you want to protect yours. My brother is part of the reason we're even speaking right now."

I almost forgot about the younger prince. He's not in public often. "How old?" I ask, not recalling anything more specific than that he existed.

"Seven. My parents sent him away to stay with our grandparents in Thomalia."

"Good. Maybe he'll be safe there."

"And besides that," he continues as if I hadn't even spoken, "you owe me." There it is. That smug look on his face.

I scoff. "*Owe you*? Exactly what is it that I *owe* you?"

He walks up to me so we're face-to-face. I stand my ground, feeling his breath on my skin. He says, "When your crew attacked my ships at the blockade, I could have arrested you. Instead, I opened the port for you and allowed you to remain free. Do pirates not have a code of honor about paying back favors?"

Well, he has me there.

It also gets me thinking. "Speaking of that, why *didn't* you arrest us?" *Losing focus, Jones.* But I want to know. And his silence is grating. *Get yourself together.* A seven-year-old does not deserve what is about to happen to his kingdom. Just like Ben doesn't deserve to have his future swallowed in smoke.

"It's my ship," I insist. "If I agree to help you, you follow my rules. You don't control me, you don't try to act like everyone else and try to take charge of what I'm doing."

Jack nods. "Yes, but only until we reach the Realm of Magic. Then we have no choice but to do this together."

I roll my eyes. "Fine. But you still haven't told me what makes you think you and I can actually stop whatever this may be."

"You've had much experience in battle, and since you're a pirate your navigation skills are better than anyone's," he responds, dodging the question. He's obviously buttering me up, and it's obviously working.

But I still doubt Ben's safety. Everyone's safety. "If my crew comes with us, are they entering the realm with us?" I ask.

"No," he says quickly, as if he's already thought all of this out. "They will guard the ship and be prepared to leave. That's it."

"And after this, we're done? We never have to speak again?"

"Trust me when I say *never*," he assures me.

Even if I continue to say no, I assume Prince Charming will continue to pester me until I change my mind. But there's a reward at the other end. And I would be saving thousands of people. And never having to speak to Jack again? That's a reward of its own.

"You have yourself a deal," I say, giving in. As he smiles, though, I hold up my hand. "I need to speak with my crew, though." He nods, and I brush past him to the bar. "William, I need a favor." I lean over the counter and whisper in his ear.

William listens, and then he nods. "Not a problem."

"Thank you." I turn around and sweep my gaze across the room, finding my brother laughing with the others and hating what I'm about to do. "Ben?" I wave him over. "I need to talk to you."

He jogs over, but his grin fades at the sight of the prince still lurking in the tavern. "Is everything okay?" he asks as I pull him aside. "What did the prince want?"

"Yes, well . . . just listen." I take his hand and explain what Jack wants us to do.

Ben's grin returns. "Sounds like a dangerous adventure," he says. "Probably has many toils, traps, and snares, which could involve getting killed. . . ." His smile widens. "I'm in. When do we leave?"

"Well, that's what I wanted to talk to you about. . . ." I trail off, not knowing quite how to break the news. "The crew will be accompanying us, but you're staying here, with William."

"What? This is completely unfair!"

I put my hand over his mouth when he yells, just as everybody looks at us. "Please, don't be upset with me," I plead. "You're my little brother and I love you, which means I cannot risk you getting hurt." I take my hand off of his face.

"But almost getting killed is what we do every day. And if I stay here, what about the magic? It might get to me before you come back."

"Unlike every other day, I don't know what we're up against," I say gently. "I don't know if I will be able to protect you from harm. This is dark magic, yes, but if you stay inside with William, you'll be safe. I need you to stay here, maybe keep a lookout for any signs of the source of the magic?"

"But what about you?" Ben asks. "If I lose you, I don't have anything left either. If I don't go, who will protect *you*?"

I sigh as I grin, warmed by his concern. "I will be okay. I can protect myself," I assure him.

"I don't trust him," he says, glaring at Jack.

"Believe me, I don't either. But in order to keep you safe and for the *Tigerlily* to have a future, I don't think we have a choice."

"If anything happens to you, I will kill him," Ben states firmly.

"And I give you full permission to do so. But, Ben, you have to trust me on this. I will be perfectly okay. Here." I take the ruby necklace out of my pocket and hold it in front of me. "Hold on to this. That way, you'll have me and Mother with you no matter what happens. I don't want to lose it, and it'll give me a reason to come back in one piece."

Ben takes the necklace carefully and puts it in his pocket. "I love you, Serena. Please, be careful."

I pull him into my embrace. "I promise."

He squeezes me tight for a moment, and upon separating he smirks. "Good luck convincing the crew, though."

"Yeah, I know," I groan. I pull away from him and drag myself across the room to a table in the middle. For the second time, I stand on it and raise my voice. "Avast ye!" The crew silences quickly, as if they've been waiting for me to speak. "As you've noticed, I have been speaking with Prince Jack of Olovia, and he has offered us a proposal. An important one. He's on a mission to stop whatever that magic is in the sky, and to do that he needs an object from the Realm of Magic. We're to sail him there, enter the realm, and retrieve it."

"Why would we go anywhere with *him*?" Adam asks.

"This is our payback for him not having us arrested last year when, as I recall, *you* almost got us into a battle with the Olovian Navy."

Adam goes silent, but then Thomas, in the corner, pipes up. "Who cares about a favor? Why should we help him?"

"He's also offered us a reward in return," I tell them. Eyeing the prince in the shadows, and aware we never agreed on a number, I add, "A very handsome reward, actually."

Nadia steps up and speaks. "Sorry, Serena, I don't care how much he's offering. I am not helping the spoiled-rich baby of a prince who can't run his own kingdom."

There are nods and murmurs of agreement, their voices rising until they're bickering among each other once more.

"Enough!" I shout at the top of my lungs. "I know this is usually the opposite of what we normally do," I say. "But I also know that if we don't do this, we won't get a chance to ever set sail again."

In the silence that follows, as they all skeptically look at each other as they decide if they're going to join me on this, I reach my hand into my pocket, forgetting that I gave the ruby necklace to Ben. I want to feel the smooth gems and cool chain, the comfort it would give me. Instead, I grasp air.

Oliver raises his hand tentatively. "What exactly will happen if we say no?" he asks.

"All I know is that you're not going to like it," I answer.

"So, basically, we have no choice," Nadia concludes.

I nod, smiling. "Aye."

That's when Prince Pinhead decides to throw his voice into the ring. "Serena, they have a choice. Whatever choice they make will affect them just as much as it will affect the rest of the kingdom, and possibly the world."

Apparently, his concern about them is all the crew needs to make up their minds. "As usual, I stand with Serena," James says, crossing his arms and shooting Jack a glare that could kill. "She is our captain, and our friend. We should all be on board with her."

"I'm sorry, I didn't mean to startle you. You haven't told us where, exactly, we're going."

"Tammerin Sea," I answer. "We're going to the West Island, the only island in the area we haven't been to." Unless you're going into the Realm of Magic, which people rarely do, nobody goes to the West Island. We always skirt around it. This time, the voyage will be the same but the sight of the island will be very different.

Nadia nods, but she hesitates. "Got it. Is everything all right?"

"Yeah. I just—I want to get this over with."

Nadia's lips curl and she rolls her shoulders back. "I don't blame you. Having the prince around is quite irritating. He thinks he knows everything, and he keeps staring at you. Something's not right; he's up to something. Why'd he come to *you* for help, anyway?"

I look over at Prince Charming, who immediately looks away once he realizes I see him. Keeping my voice low, I explain to Nadia his apparent reason for coming to me: I have a ship and a crew, I'm convenient. But Nadia's accusation gets to me. There are lots of ships to commandeer, so what does he really want from me? I roll my eyes and continue to help my crew get ready to leave the dock.

"James, are we ready to set sail?" I ask.

"Almost, Captain," he answers. I stare at the blackened sky intently, wondering why I continue to feel that pull, why it intensified when that woman took her last breath.

Maybe I'll understand once we defeat it. Because we will; we have to get this over with so I can return to Ben. But if it's not celestial magic and it's not sorcery, what is it?

The crew is still wrestling with the sails. I rest my hands on my hips and focus on them, my frustration bubbling over. "Adam, I swear to the gods if that sail is not tied tighter

I will throw you overboard! Sawyer and Joseph, put your backs into it and help him!"

The prince watches, and he gives them a wide berth as he walks up to me. "You know," he says, leaning in, "there are ways to communicate without threatening people."

"There are also ways to leave me alone," I snap.

"Unfortunately, no, there aren't. I checked. Are you always this bossy?"

"Yes, actually."

"That doesn't surprise me."

I whirl on him. "I'm sorry, can I actually *help* you with something?"

"I just thought you'd want to know what the plan is for after we retrieve the orb. And I wanted to see how you're doing," he replies.

I pull away, my defenses rising. "I'm fine," I say stiffly.

"I just thought you might be shaken up a bit—"

I laugh. "Woah, slow your roll, buddy. One short hour and you already know me so well?" Jack opens his mouth, but I hold up my hand to stop him and step closer. Dropping my voice, I hiss, "This is *my* ship, remember? That means you have absolutely no right to stand there and say anything to me, concerned or not. I already told you, you know nothing about me and you never will. Magic or no magic, don't think you can just read my thoughts and suddenly determine who I am. Is that clear?"

He presses his lips together, but wisely says nothing.

"Now that we have that cleared up, can you leave me the hell alone? That's an order." Even as I say it, I wonder if I'm going too far. He's the prince; I'm a pirate. He's probably used to giving orders, not taking them, and not taking them from scum like me.

But he rolls his eyes at me, and he walks away as if this had been his argument to win, not mine.

Who does he think he is?

My heart beats fast and my pulse quickens. He doesn't know anything about me, and he never will. If tossing him overboard didn't come with such giant consequences I would have done it already. I wouldn't even have thought twice about it. His audacity to come to me sickens me, and already, I'm regretting ever agreeing to help.

"Deep breaths, Serena. Deep breaths," I mumble under my breath.

"We're ready, Captain!" James calls out from the dungbie. I look at the docks one last time before I head to the wheel, wondering if they'll even be here when we get back. Hoping Ben won't die the way that woman died, those symbols burned into his wrists and his last breath a scream.

I don't know if the prince's plan will work. All I know is that if we don't hurry this little "adventure" up, then none of us will be left alive.

6

We move quickly across the dark blue waters as the wind blows in our sails. The breeze brushes my long red hair gently, stretching the strands into the wind. The farther we travel from Olovia, the lighter the sky becomes.

Nadia carries a chair from her quarters and sits right behind me, keeping me company and likely keeping her distance from the prince. Jack has so far followed my orders and is leaving me alone, instead gracing the crew with his surprisingly adept ability to keep a ship in order.

Whether we defeat the darkness or not, I only have to put up with him until we return from the Realm of Magic. After that I never have to see him again. I might die, but it's a comforting thought, although even if the orb the prince talked about can defeat the darkness I realize that it could take a tremendously long time before the magic is completely gone. We don't even know how to use it on the cloud of dark magic.

There are still no clues as to who could be doing this

either. Besides old animosity with Gurellia and expected criminal behavior from, well, criminals inside the kingdom, Olovia is mostly crime-free. In the last few years, we've only had three real threats from sorcerers, and they were dealt with quickly. Then again, sorcery isn't . . . whatever this is. I doubt it's celestial either.

So what is it?

I'm lost in thought when I realize Nadia is speaking to me. "What?" I ask.

"What's going on with you and James?"

Blushing, I say, "Now is not the time for gossiping about boys."

"You're going to have to tell me eventually," she responds. Nadia is a wonderful friend, and she's the best sword fighter in Olovia—better than me, even. While I spend a great deal of time studying swordplay, most of my days are dedicated to learning about astronomy. Nadia mostly focuses on swordplay, aside from navigation. Despite this, sometimes her nosiness scares me, particularly when she wants to turn it on me. I think she got that from her mother, who was like an aunt to me. Like James and I, the two of us grew up together.

"We have much more important things to focus on," I mumble.

James is the furthest thing on my mind. Ben is who I'm worried about. I don't know if leaving him behind had been the right decision. If something happens to him or William, I don't know what I'll do, but I know I'll never forgive myself.

For hours, we sail. I distract myself from worrying about Ben by thinking again about the magic, about what I'd witnessed in Olovia, the symbols on the woman's wrists. The more I think about the markings, the more they come into focus until finally I see them, not entirely clear but enough to understand where I've seen them before. An idea hits me like a ton of bricks.

I look around the deck, finally spotting James. "James, take the wheel." He salutes and takes up the steering, and I run below deck, to my quarters.

I keep a large case of books in my room. There's so many I've only read about half, but many of them are about magic, things I've picked up at different ports and kingdoms during our travels. If I've ever seen those symbols from the woman's wrist before, they'll be somewhere in my collection.

Three books come to mind, my most prized: *The History of Dark Magic*, *Celestial vs. Sorcery*, and *The Tales of Dark Spells*. I tear them from the shelf and flip through them frantically, but I'm disappointed. They're all about the dark sides of celestial magic and sorcery, but they don't have anything about the darkness in the sky or the woman's markings. I turn to the other books, tearing apart my chamber for any scrap of information, looking for some kind of clue.

I almost give up, staring at the books on the floor, some open and some closed, their pages unhelpful. I groan, frustrated, but I remember one more book, one that isn't on the shelf because my mother gave it to me. It was meant for my twenty-first birthday, and I've been saving it. But if it has the information I'm looking for, I don't have time to wait two more years.

At the foot of my bed is a hope chest Lennard had carved for me. I open it up and rummage through, and I find the book at the very bottom. The jacket is black and dusty, and it has no title on it. I blow off the dust and cough as it spreads through the air, then take off the jacket. The cover of the book is black as well, but there is a silver engraving. My chest seizes, squeezing slightly.

The title is in some type of hieroglyphics that carry similar arcs and points as the markings on the woman. I open the book eagerly, but all of the pages are in the same language, something I can't read. I almost give up, frustrated at my inability to decipher the words, but as I desperately turn the pages I freeze suddenly. In the middle of the book, there's a picture of the exact symbol I'm looking for.

Unlike all of the other pages, the writing under the photo is completely in bold. It goes on for three pages, then ends. The rest of the book is blank. I turn back to the symbol, my stomach sinking as I consider why my mother might have a book that contains these symbols of dark magic, why she gave it to me. I could have sworn my mother gave me a note when she gave me the book, and maybe it will explain why, but I look through the hope chest, all of my shelves and drawers, and find nothing.

I guess it doesn't matter at the moment. What matters is translating that book, and I know I have a translation book around somewhere. Lennard gave it to me because it would come in handy while on the seas. I take it everywhere. But though I search through all of the books that I throw onto the floor, I'm unsuccessful in finding it. I have a feeling maybe Ben borrowed it for his own studies and never returned it.

I'm so close to figuring this out.

I need to know what that symbol means, why the magic called to me. Maybe if I can decipher that mystery, I'll understand what's happening to me when I feel the darkness toying with my veins.

I scream and throw a book at the door, not realizing Prince Charming is standing in the target zone. It hits his head and falls into his hands.

"Ow," he says.

I laugh. "I'm sorry?"

"I'm glad you find my pain so amusing," he says, rubbing his head. "Why are you throwing books at people's heads?"

I calm myself and put my hands on my hips. "It's none of your business."

"Actually, it is my business since you hit me in the head with one," he replies.

I consider whether to tell him at all. He'd walked into my quarters without an invitation, sure, but he's the reason I'm looking for the source of the dark magic to begin with. "Fine," I say slowly. "I have been searching for answers about the symbol I saw on that woman's skin. I found a book that might have what I am looking for, but it's in another language and I can't find a translation book." I wait, and though he seems to be thinking about what I told him he isn't providing any answers. "What are you even doing in here, anyway?" I prod.

"I thought you should know that Adam is trying to take control of the ship," he says easily, flashing me that smug grin. "And why didn't you just ask for help? I have one with me."

I ignore what he said about Adam. "A translation book? You do?" I ask.

"Yeah, I always have one just in case I need it. Don't you? I'll go get it." He left, and I nearly follow him but he returns in a heartbeat.

"Why do *you* have a translation book with you?" I wonder.

"You should always carry a translation book when traveling," he says, pointing the obvious jab at me. "My grandfather gave this one to me. It was a souvenir he brought back from his voyage around the world. What am I translating?"

I hand him the book, already opened to the page I need.

The prince frowns. "This is beyond ancient Olovian. It's a very rare language to find, actually. Where did you get this book?" He looks up at me, his eyebrows raised.

"My mother gave it to me when I was fifteen," I say carefully. "She told me not to open it until I turn twenty-one, but I don't know why." Saying it out loud does nothing to calm my growing fears.

The prince takes my answer easily, though I don't know if that's better or worse than the alternative. "This might take a while," he tells me as he sits down at my desk.

"How long is a while?" I ask, impatience shining through my tone.

"A few hours at least."

And he had to choose my room to spend that time in? Annoyed, I exit my quarters and head back out on deck, hoping Jack's jibe about Adam isn't as bad as he thought. But he was right: I find Adam in the middle of the deck barking orders at the rest of the crew, currently in the middle of shouting at Nadia.

"What in the bloody hell do you think you're doing?" I ask him.

He spins around, cheeks going red with embarrassment but covering it up quickly. "Blimey! You nearly scared the jumpin' fish out of me, Captain. You were in your chambers, so I decided to help out on deck." He says it with such confidence I want to slap him.

"Help? By yelling at our hearties for no reason? James is

sailing the ship and everything else is in order. Are you my first mate? No, and there is a reason for that. Go find your brother . . . at the *opposite* end of the ship."

Adam cools quickly, his eyes growing icy. "Yes, Captain," he says sharply. "I . . . apologize." I can tell he wants to say more, but he does the smart thing and walks away. I watch him, making sure he leaves my sight completely. Adam gets under my skin so easily. If he had a true reason to be screaming at my crew, then maybe I would have been kinder.

"He's just a kid." James appears behind me. He and Adam have been building a newfound friendship recently. "You ought to not be so hard on him."

I wonder who's at the wheel, but John's manning it now. "He's not a kid, he's barely a year younger than me," I scoff.

He shrugs. "Still. Are you all right? You seem more tense than usual."

I could write a whole list about the things I'm not all right about, so I hesitate before I speak. "I just want to get this over with, that's all."

"I do too. That magic is spreading faster and faster. What's our time limit?" he asks.

I shrug. I truly don't know.

James continues. "I suppose we'll figure it out along the way. Serena, I have to—"

"James!" Sawyer shouts, interrupting our conversation and waving him over.

James sighs. "Just a moment." He shoots me an apologetic glance before he leaves me and speedily walks to the edge of the ship. I sigh too. There are many things that need to be sorted out.

I wait, but when James doesn't return I take back control

of my ship. Prince Charming won't be done for a while, and I have a lot on my mind. Steering keeps me busy, calms me, but even now it can't subdue that same damn notion that the magic is calling me somehow.

I have to be going mad. There is no other explanation.

Hours pass, and the sun begins to set, making all of my surroundings golden. As the last rays disappear over the horizon, the prince comes out on deck and waves me over. The two of us head back to my room.

Jack picks up the paper the translation is written on, and he hands it to me. I read it aloud: "This symbol of dark magic is neither sorcery nor celestial. It is an unknown type of magic, but is very powerful and dangerous. Each of the symbols represent the digits one through four, meaning that there are four people who can and/or will obtain this dark magic. The darker the symbol is, the proof it is that someone has already wielded its power."

I shake my head. Why the hell did my mother have this book?

The symbols on the woman's wrist—how many of them were dark and how many light? I focus on the vivid image in my head. "Three symbols have already darkened," I say, more to myself than to the prince.

"Why only four?" he mutters.

"That means that somebody else has to take the power next," I continue.

"But who?" The prince turns and begins pacing across the floor. "My guess is that it would have to be a genetic thing if it's that powerful."

"And once the fourth person obtains their magic, what happens then?" I add, my own concern creeping into my voice.

Jack picks up the book with the hieroglyphics and flips through it to the end. "I don't know. The rest of the pages are blank."

I'm more confused than I was when I first walked in here. Knowing what the book says gives us more questions than answers, and the only thing that's clear is that this is way beyond my control. And I hate not being in control of things.

I want to know who else has this magic. If there are really other people out there with this type of magic, then why haven't there been any stories about it? Why isn't it written and known, why can only four people possess it? And what happens once the fourth person is found?

Even more troubling is that this book is in *my* possession. My mother gave it to me, but for what? Why would she have this?

"Why are you making that face?" Jack asks.

"What? What face?" I ask unconvincingly. I shake my head and look away. "I'm not making a face. I want to be alone."

He nods before exiting my room. I spend the rest of the evening with my books, searching for stories of anyone who could potentially have this unheard-of ability.

Nothing. When I start yawning and tire of finding nothing useful, I call it a night. I only get fifteen minutes of sleep in before I open my eyes and can't keep them closed again, thinking about the dark magic, about the few people who contain it.

After hours of restless tossing and turning, I admit defeat and get up, looking to go on deck and do what I always do when I can't sleep: look at the stars. When I was a little girl, my mother taught me all of the constellations in the sky and where all of the planets rest. She always told me that if I were to ever get lost, I only needed to follow the North Star and I'll find my way back home.

But when I walk out on deck, James is already near the railing, taking up the spot I normally lay down in. I hesitate, contemplating going back to my chambers, but I want to finish our conversation from before. Without a word, I lie down next to him, back on the deck and eyes to the sky. James turns his head and looks at me, grinning, before looking back at the stunning night.

The sky is crystal clear, exposing what seems like the entire galaxy. "Couldn't sleep either?" he asks.

"Nope." There's a long pause of silence, then I point up to a glowing planet. "Look, there's Venus."

"Can you still name all of the constellations and planets?"

I chance looking at him, and he's beaming at the memory. "I can," I chuckle. "But now I know more about them. I think astronomy is very interesting."

"That it is. On nights like these it's almost like the galaxy is painting a picture. It certainly shows how small we are compared to other life out there."

"I don't think I've ever seen such a clear night before. It almost looks unreal."

There are a thousand stars above us, the sky around them a canvas of green and pink against the darkness. It's absolutely astonishing, and it finally takes my mind off the dark magic.

"It's certainly one of the most beautiful things I have ever seen," James agrees.

I laughed at a memory. "Remember what we used to do as kids?"

"How could I forget? First one to name all of the constellations we saw in the sky got the biggest of Katherine Jones's famous cinnamon buns."

In her free time, my mother loved to bake. She was quite skilled at it, too, yet she only ever baked for a few people. A baking pirate doesn't exactly have a threatening ring to it.

"They really were good." I nod, smiling at the thought.

He grabs onto my hand. "We can make them again, if you would like."

But his motion pulls me back to the present, to our quest and to everything at risk. "Can I ask you something?"

"Anything," James responds.

"Do you think that this darkness can be defeated?"

"Is that fear in your tone I hear?" he asks in disbelief.

"I'm serious, James. I have to do this. *We* have to do this. Do you understand? For Ben. He is all I have left."

"That's not true. You have all of us. Your crew is your family, even if we aren't blood relatives. Though, I have to ask . . . if you're so worried about Ben, then why leave him with Will?"

I think about my answer carefully. Being honest is the best course here. "Well, I . . . I don't know. Something in my gut told me that he would be safer at home. I suppose I thought bringing him with us would be much too dangerous, more of a risk than the darkness in Olivia. We're traveling to another realm, and who knows what dangers could be lurking by the portal. You and the crew can protect yourselves, but Ben . . . he's just a kid."

"Maybe," James replies. "Though I guess, even if you brought him with us, there is no real escape from the spreading magic, whether he's here or there."

He could be trying to make me feel better, but it sounds like he means it. "James, what were you going to say earlier?"

"Earlier?" he asks. In my silence, he continues. "Well, things between us are, I don't know . . . what are we?"

"I don't know," I admit. I have too much on my mind to think about this, and he must see the worry in my face.

"Hey, we don't have to talk about this right now," he says.

I just nod before he squeezes my hand tighter, and I offer him a grateful smile. He smiles back before we both turn our heads back up to the sky. I'm drifting off, getting too sleepy to get back up and go to my quarters. I must fall deeply asleep before I know it, because when I wake up, I'm lying in James's arms.

Quickly, I pull myself from his embrace and get up to face the sunrise. I take the wheel and order that no one is to disturb me but Nadia. She's the only one who isn't getting on my nerves, who isn't asking the impossible of me.

"Serena, are you okay?" she asks me after some time. "You seem a bit uneasy."

"I'm not," I reply.

"But you are," Nadia insists. "I can see you're nervous about the journey ahead."

"I don't get nervous. I'm emotionless, remember?" I reply defensively.

"You and I both know that's untrue," she says kindly. Then she demands, "Tell me what's troubling you."

The journey, Ben, but the magic most of all. Two days at sea and I can still see it when I close my eyes, feel it tugging at my insides. That book my mother had given me . . . "I want to tell you, I really do," I reply, my voice cracking. "But I can't." I'm afraid of what her reaction would be if she knows what I'm feeling.

"You can tell me anything, you know that," she reminds me.

I hesitate for a moment, then speak, keeping my eyes on the water. "I—I keep feeling this sort of . . . it's the magic. I don't even know if it's a connection, I just feel it, ever since Olovia. It could just be the magic trying to infect me." I pause, then I admit in a whisper, "All I know is that it's freaking me out."

Nadia doesn't respond. When she doesn't say anything for some time, I tell her about the symbols inside the book my mother had given to me. By the time I finish and turn to see her reaction, her mouth is open in shock. "What could that possibly mean?" she asks.

"I don't know. But you can't tell the others, I don't want to worry them. The crew's already skeptical of this whole journey, I don't want them to think we're all going to die."

"My lips are sealed. But now I'm really curious as to who would have this magic too. . . ." She trails off, lost in thought, though it isn't long before she straightens and says, "You're not the only one with resources, though. Remember my thirteenth birthday? I'd been bugging my mother about magic, so she gave me a bunch of old books and scrolls about it. I keep them all in my bunk, if you want to check them out with me later tonight."

I smile at her, and though I think little of our chances of learning anything more about a magic so rare and unknown, I say, "Definitely."

The rest of the day goes by almost painfully slow. The closer we get to the island, the more I lose faith that whatever waits for us in the Realm of Magic will help. We've left the magic behind us, but the farther we get the more difficult it is to ignore.

Finally, the sun begins to set. I pass the wheel to Joseph, and Nadia and I retreat to her quarters, which are outfitted with two bunks, one for her and one for Sawyer. I sit down on one of the chairs at her wooden table, and she grabs about five books from her shelf. She puts them down in front of me and takes five scrolls from a cubby near her bunk. I still have Jack's language translation book, in case we need it.

We settle in, and for the next hour the only sound is the flutter of pages as we turn them. The first four books are completely unhelpful, and I drop them to the floor one by one. I've almost given up hope, my eyes closing with exhaustion. Then I finally find what we've been looking for.

"Wait! This is the symbol I saw."

Nadia stands quickly and comes to my side. "Let me see," she says. She takes the book from my hands and turns it over. The book has a dark purple cover and the author's name is nowhere to be found. "I don't recognize this book," she mutters, then she opens it up and I lean my head over her shoulder to see it for myself.

Unlike the other book, this one is written in a language we can understand. Nadia reads, "Powerful, dangerous, barbaric. Three words to describe the magic my father created. He has gone mad, I'm afraid. Something truly evil, something dark has taken over him. He continued to go on and on about the future of his deranged powers, creating ridiculous assumptions as to what will happen. I can only hope the magic has driven him to madness, and that these predictions are merely from his broken mind, inside of his imagination."

She ends, and I look up at her, perplexed. "Nadia, why would our mothers have books like these?"

"I . . . I don't know." She closes the book again and stares at the cover. "I don't even remember my mother giving this one to me."

"Is there any more information in there?"

Nadia flips through the pages. "The rest of the book just keeps going on about how mad the author's father had gone. There is nothing as to how it was created or what it's called, or who's behind it."

If only there's a way to track down the author to give us the information. But judging by the worn out, crinkly yellow pages, the book is old. Perhaps a hundred years or more.

"Wait . . ." Nadia says. "Okay, you're going to the Realm of Magic, right?"

"Yeah."

"Maybe there's information about it there."

"How? There are only two types of magic known in the world, including the Realm of Magic. How would they have information about this?"

"It's still magic. Someone there has to know something," Nadia replies.

She might be right. But how am I supposed to search for those answers? I agreed to retrieve the orb, then to come right back out. The prince would want to stick to the plan, and though I want to keep searching—though I know something about the information we found is more important than the orb—I'm not sure I want to convince the prince to accompany me.

"Let's go over the books again," I suggest. "There could be something we missed."

Nadia shakes her head. "I think this is all of the information that we're ever going to find. We searched every inch of these books, there is no way we missed something."

Just our luck. The books are easy. They're safe. But

they're fallible, and there are too many unanswered questions. Maybe Nadia's right. Maybe the Realm of Magic is the only place I'll be able to figure something out.

A knock comes at the door, and we turn to see Jack stepping into the room. "I'm sorry to interrupt. We should be at the island at dawn."

"Thank you," Nadia says. Then she looks between us suggestively. "I'm going to get something to drink. I'll be right back." She exits the room, and I begin to put all of the books back where we found them.

"What were you guys doing in here?" Jack questions as he helps me. I swallow my annoyance at his nosiness and tell him everything Nadia and I found—and everything we didn't.

The more I tell him, the more I'm swarmed with a sea of rage and fear. Why would our mothers have these books? This magic that I keep feeling, does no one else feel it too? What is it, and who's behind this? Why?

And why did my mother never tell me anything about it?

I don't realize I've stopped talking, but Jack opens his mouth to reply to me. Yet even as I strain to catch his words, they vanish beneath those darkening waters of my mind. A chill runs down my spine and a raucous ringing sound appears in my ears. My vision blurs and the prince suddenly vanishes from my sight, and all of my surroundings disappear with him.

All I can see is a fuzzy black cloud and a shadow in the middle. My head pounds and my pulse races as I look closer, bewildered and afraid—

"Serena, are you all right?" I hear Jack's voice as if he were underwater. "Serena? Serena, talk to me." I can't respond. It's as if I'm frozen in a trance.

The prince grabs my shoulders. I almost fall coming out of it, but the pinhead's there to catch me.

"What just happened?" he asks, worry thick in his gaze.

I pull away from him quickly, the vision already fading. "I . . . I don't—I think I'm just tired. After all, it is getting late. I should head to my chambers."

Jack grabs my wrist and pulls me back as I attempt to walk away. "You're not fooling me. I know something is wrong. You are not going anywhere until you tell me what happened. I saw the look on your face, I know that it scared you."

I yank my wrist from his grasp and round on him. "No. Just leave me alone, Jack. I'm not scared of anything, or anyone. Nothing happened. Just leave me be."

I make my exit quickly. Of course I'm frightened, but he doesn't need to know that. I have absolutely no idea what I just saw, or what it meant.

Sleep. I just need sleep.

But even after I crawl into bed, every time I close my eyes, all I see is that vision.

After a restless night, I'm woken up at sunrise by Nadia. "Not too far now," she says.

I change into fresh clothes and pull my hair into a braid. I take the wheel, giving Joseph a break from sailing all night. As our ship's navigator, Nadia is already waiting with the compass in her hand.

The wind blows her ebony hair. The weather has gotten much cooler, the air chilling my shoulders. I shiver as we make our way closer to the island.

"James!" I call out. "Have the crew prepare for anchor."

The tiny island grows until I can pick out the details. It looks deserted, but not in an eerie way. Behind the bar of sand at the beach is a whole forest of oak and palm trees, untouched and wild.

"Everything is ready, Captain," James says. "By the looks of it, I'd say we arrived."

7

"Are you sure you don't want anyone else to come with you?" Nadia asks as we anchor the ship.

"I'm positive. I don't want to risk any other lives," I answer with more confidence than I actually have. Entering a whole new realm is highly dangerous, especially since every single person who lives there has magic—and we don't.

"I understand that," Nadia says, "but what if something happens to you?"

"I'll be okay, Nadia. And if we come to any danger, I just have to outrun the prince." I chuckle.

She rolls her eyes and smiles. I stand on top of the ship's railing and grab everyone's attention.

"I'm not sure how long we're going to be gone. But I need you all to be prepared to set sail immediately after our return," I announce before I jump down.

"Be careful," Nadia says to me as she pulls me into her arms.

"I promise," I assure her.

Not too far away, I hear James tell Jack, "If anything

happens to her on your watch, I don't care if I have to get hanged as a punishment. I *will* kill you."

"You don't need to worry about that," Jack responds. Then he turns to me. "Ready?" he asks. With a single nod, we're off on the rowboat.

My boots make a deep hole in the golden sand when I hop off the boat. The cool breeze blows back the few hairs hanging out of my braid, and the palm trees seem to be dancing.

"So how, exactly, does an island turn into a portal?" I ask as we head toward the forest, my ship shrinking with the distance.

"It doesn't. The portal is on the island. There's a specific tree that if you place your hand on, it lets you in," Jack says without even looking at me.

A specific tree. Great. "How do you know all of this?"

"As future king, my parents wanted me to have a thorough study on magic and the Realm of Magic. So they brought in Elias to teach me about everything. In fact, he even gave me the map to find the orb." Jack pauses, his hand on a branch. "You do know who Elias is, right?"

I stick out my tongue in response. Elias is the greatest sorcerer to ever live. He's incredibly famous all throughout the Human Realm, which I imagine leads him to working for many of the kingdoms from time to time.

"And why would Elias give you that map?" I ask nervously.

"Well, I was at his hut for our training session a while back. I saw it in his bookcase, and he told me I could keep it."

"Huh." It sounds a bit too convenient that the sorcerer just happened to give Jack the map to the orb just before he actually needed it. "So . . . which tree is it?" I ask. "Look around, we're in a forest." There are lots of trees, and none of them look special.

Jack sighs and finally looks at me, his look earnest. "Have faith in me, please? I know what I'm doing."

He's all I have to go on, so I grudgingly continue behind him. The quiet between us grows incredibly as we make our way deeper into the forest, where the light is fainter and the ground much more difficult to see.

When Jack breaks the silence, it's like lightning striking. "You know, you're really good with them. Your crew, I mean."

"Oh? Thanks," I reply.

"I really mean that. They listen to you, look up to you. People don't exactly love my family."

"Really? I hadn't noticed."

Jack grimaces. "Ha ha. I just . . . I envy you. How can anyone trust me to be king if they see my family so poorly? My parents aren't bad people. But the kingdom doesn't see it that way." He pauses like he wants to say more, then looks at me and shrugs.

I can hear the pain in his voice, and it makes me consider him differently. Nobody but Nadia and Ben have ever actually been real with me when we talk. It's an unusual feeling, to have a stranger do so now. Especially because it's coming from the prince.

"Why do you think that is?" I ask. I have my own reasons for not loving the royal family, but I'm also a pirate.

Jack thinks for a moment before speaking. "There are certain . . . issues the people want my parents to deal with, but they haven't done anything about it. I don't think they will."

The way he says "issues" . . . I know exactly what he means. The people of Olovia loathe pirates. They loathe the idea of pirates. It's a sentiment they share with Gurellia.

Pirates are part of the reason the war began. There are too many disagreements between our kingdoms, but pirates . . . they're the biggest one.

But pirates are just one issue, and we don't even prey on royal ships, or Olovian merchants. There have to be more reasons, better reasons, why people hate the king and queen. Though, Prince Pinhead does get me thinking: If the people truly hate me—*us*—then why has the royal family continued allowing us in Olovia for so long? I mean, I'm not complaining. But still.

I don't press the prince. I just roll my eyes at him, and I think he knows that I understand.

We keep walking through the forest of trees, for minutes or hours. Everything looks the same, but the prince finally comes to a halt in front of a large tree with bare branches. "Oh, look. Here it is," he says. I look around us; this is the only dead tree we've come across.

Jack places his hand on the dry bark, and he holds out his other hand for me to take. I look at it and back at his face, then I reluctantly grab his hand. In a flash, a bright golden light comes out of the tree and pulls us inside.

Within seconds, it spits us out and throws us on the ground. I yank my hand from the prince's and rub my head as I sit up. We're in another forest. We actually made it into the Realm of Magic . . . I think. Everything looks the same.

"I'm pretty sure this means we're here," Jack guesses, standing and brushing the dirt from his clothes before starting out without me. I climb to my feet and follow him toward a break in the trees that definitely hadn't been there before.

"Yeah," he says in awe. "We're definitely here."

I follow his gaze, and the sight takes my breath away. The Realm of Magic looks like Olovia, but that isn't what astonishes me: This realm is brighter, and there is an atmosphere I can only describe as elated.

There's not a cloud in the sky and the sun beats down on us. There are birds—lots of birds—each singing a similar sweet song above us. A light breeze—a warm one—brushes against my cheek. The forest leads out into a village that looks like the one back home, from the cobblestone pathway surrounded with shops and places to eat to the stone and brick walls of all of the buildings.

The mundaneness of it all is what surprises me most. I was expecting something more . . . magical.

The closer we get, the more I find what I'm looking for in the details. Everybody looks at peace—even before the darkness the people of Olovia were harder, angrier. There are kids all around us practicing their sorcery magic in the streets. They hold spell books, each incantation resulting in a glowing purple light erupting from their hands.

Sorcery magic is actually kind of pretty, when you see it up close like this.

As we walk along the street, we come across a small building that makes me stop in my tracks. I can't see what the walls are made of: It's covered in vines and daisies, braided so neatly it doesn't look natural, more like someone had purposely done this. I can't look away. It's beautiful, and it reminds me of my mother, who absolutely loved daisies, almost as much as she loved rubies. For a moment, I almost forget why I'm even here.

Then Jack taps my arm. Heat rising to my face, I follow him. Once the village comes to an end I spy a giant white marble castle in the distance, but Jack leads us in the opposite direction to retrieve the item we need.

As we leave the village behind, the prince takes his map from his brown leather satchel. "We're going to the northern woods, where there is an old tower. The orb rests inside," he says. He points forward, and we enter another copse.

After that, there's pretty much silence. We occasionally share a look, but what do a pirate and a prince really have to say to one another?

"Can I ask you a personal question?" the prince blurts out.

Wary, I reply, "Depends."

"Why did you decide to become a pirate?"

"Why do you care?"

"I was just curious," he says. "You don't seem fully content when you're with your crew."

I stop in my tracks. Earlier he told me I was a good leader, and now he's saying this? "Okay, Prince Charming. You're clearly as dumb as a bag of hair, so let me break it down for you, since this is the third time I've had to tell you: You have absolutely no right to make assumptions about me, especially when it comes to my crew and the *Tigerlily*."

He holds up his hands, but he keeps walking. "All right, I'm sorry. Believe me, I don't want to be here with you any more than you want to be here with me. But I'm trying to make the best of this. I just figured that since we're in this together, we should have at least some understanding of one another."

We come across another small village that looks similar to the first. There must be a whole string of them buried in these woods. I think about the prince's words, unsure how to respond and trying not to feel guilty, now, for my outburst.

"I became a pirate because I wanted to continue my parents' legacy. My mother and stepfather died in a shipwreck a little over three years ago. Until then, I'd been training my whole life to take my stepfather's place as captain."

After a brief pause, the prince says, "I'm sorry. I had no idea."

"Why would you?" I snap, my voice shaking. I take a deep breath, not wanting to break down here, in front of Jack of all people. "Let's talk about anything else."

"Sure. What were your parents like?" he asks quickly.

Not exactly the change in subject I was hoping for. I would have preferred to just walk in silence. But he seems genuinely curious.

"My mother was . . ." I struggle for a single word to describe her. "She was amazing. She and I were very close. She was one of the best female pirates to ever live. Lennard, my stepfather, taught me everything I know about piracy, so I spent quite a lot of time with him as well. He was a kind man."

"What about your real dad?" Jack asks softly.

"Lennard was my real dad," I shoot back. "I never met my biological father. My mother always said what an awful man he was and that she didn't even want to remember him. She wouldn't even tell me his name." I lift myself over a fallen stump, scraping my hands. Then I huff, "What about your parents?"

Jack hesitates before answering, like he's wrestling with what to tell me. "My parents are complicated. My father never wanted to be king. His family ruled Olovia, and my mother's family ruled Elstedin. My father's older brother was supposed to take the throne, but when he died, my father was forced into marriage with my mother to unite the kingdoms. Even though they actually fell in love, he just wanted a normal life. He's an incredible artist, did you know that? He wanted to travel and perfect his trade. I suppose that's partially why he's not very great with the people. He never wanted to be king, and he doesn't love what he is doing. It's much too obvious."

"What about your mother?" I question. "Did she want to marry him? Be queen?"

Jack shrugs, but his voice brightens. "My mother didn't want to be married either, but she's the youngest of four sisters. She wanted to rule, to make a difference in the world, so when her mother told her about my father, she agreed to marry him. She always said that it worked out because it was love at first sight, but sometimes I wonder if she's forcing herself to love what she's doing. She doesn't always seem content. Maybe because she knows my father's unhappy, even if she's exactly where she wanted to be."

"What about you, then?" I ask, watching him carefully, "Do you want to become king?"

"Yes," he answers quickly. "I want to help people."

With that answer, for a moment I think I might actually warm toward him.

We step beyond the last of the villages, back into the trees, and there's a sudden stop in my movement. A chill runs down my spine and my head starts pounding. The ringing sound in my ears, the one from the ship, appears again, and this time my palms start to sweat. I can't move. My sight blurs and my heart races, and I close my eyes. This time, I don't only see the cloud of black dust—I see myself standing in front of it, my arms forward and my palms flexed. I'm talking to somebody, but I can't hear or see who it is.

The vision freezes, and a rush of pain floods through my body, reaching through all of my veins. My breath catches in my throat, and I can't breathe as the vision replays. I struggle against it, panicking as I try to get it out of my head, the pain like barbs under my skin.

"Serena!" I finally hear Jack shout.

The vision disappears. I take a giant gasp for air and open my eyes, finding myself staring at the sky. I must have fallen and not realized it, because I'm in the prince's arms and he's holding me up.

He helps me back to my feet. I press my hand against the trunk of a tree for support, but he remains close until I stand back up straight and the dizziness passes. "That's the second time that has happened to you," he says. "What was that?"

I stare at him. I don't know how to explain to him what I felt, what I saw the first time and what I just saw now. "I . . . I don't know." I don't *want* to explain what happened. After all, we might have talked about our parents and shared a trek in the woods, but I don't trust him and I'm pretty sure the feeling is mutual.

"Has it happened before we met?" he asks. When I shake my head, his eyes grow more guarded. "What do you think this means?"

"I don't know," I repeat.

He looks at me like he doesn't believe me. "If it happens again, I think you should see someone. Are you all right, though?"

"I'm fine," I snap. "And I don't need to see anyone. I am perfectly capable of taking care of myself."

"I know you are, but—" He must know already it's a losing battle. He shakes his head. "Never mind. Let's continue then." He leads the way, though there's no mistaking the extra looks he casts over his shoulder as we walk.

"Something you want to say?" I ask.

"It's okay to be frightened by this. In fact, if you weren't that would be quite unnatural," he says.

"Right now we don't have time to be frightened. We have to focus on the task at hand."

"I know we do, but I can clearly see how you feel about this. All I'm saying is—"

I stop where I am and groan. "Okay, I get it! Yes, I'm terrified! There, I said it! Blimey, has anyone ever told you that you're a royal pain in the ass?"

He laughs. He actually *laughs*. "Once or twice," he says between breaths. "But I'm just trying to help you."

"Then stop laughing," I snap. "Why do you even care what happens to me?"

"I'm not saying that I do," he claims, and he keeps moving. "You're a pirate, after all. But I'm not inhuman, I can clearly see that you're not used to confronting your emotions."

I grit my teeth and bite out each word. "I said it before and I'll say it again: You have no right—"

"—to make assumptions about you," he finishes, smirking.

"You said it yourself, you don't care what happens to me. So why bother helping?"

"Okay, fine. I'll stop," he says, though he doesn't answer my question.

The quiet is sweet, though. As we make our way farther into the woods, where there are no villages to break the cover, the trees around us seem to grow taller. Their colors change too. Some of the trees have bright colors, such as red, yellow, and orange. There's one tree with violet leaves; I have never seen anything like it in my life. But my favorite is the cherry blossom tree, right in the middle of the woods, growing in a place it never could have grown in the Human Realm. Blue jays and cardinals sing as they land on the branches of the pink and white leaves and brush the blossoms. It's stunning. It gives me something to focus on other than the deepening silence between the prince and me.

In that silence, I think about what Prince Charming mentioned, about those certain *issues* that his parents refused to deal with.

"Why is it that the king and queen allow pirates in Olovia?" I can't help but wonder out loud.

"Why is that so important to you?" Jack asks. "You're allowed there, isn't that enough?"

"Not really. I want to know the reasoning behind it," I state firmly.

Jack chuckles. "My father would serve my head on a silver platter if he knew I was telling you this. But, since you probably won't drop the matter until I tell you, here it goes: He never told me her name, or what happened to their relationship, but before he became king, my father used to travel a lot while he perfected his art. He met a girl in Thomalia, and he instantly fell for her, and she fell for him."

"And?" I press.

"And she was a pirate," he says. "They were together for a while, though I don't have a real timeline. That's all I really know about it, all my father ever told me. I assume becoming king and marrying my mother is what ended it, and I assume he allows pirates in Olovia because of the girl he met all those years ago. He had a soft spot for her and I suppose because of that, his view on pirates is different than the people's."

I nearly trip over my own feet trying to wrap my head around Jack's story. I cannot imagine King Archer being in love with a pirate. Who would be idiotic and desperate enough to fall for him?

"So what's your opinion on pirates in Olovia?" I find myself asking.

"Well, you and your crew aren't *in* the kingdom most of the time. As long as you don't commit any crimes in our kingdom, I don't mind, and there are no charges I could bring against you, anyway. Though I will say, I don't agree with all of the customs of piracy."

I concede that much to him. Our lives are completely different: I grew up at sea. He grew up in a castle. I learned to sail a ship and fight and kill, and he learned to run a kingdom.

"If you feel uncomfortable in Olovia, then why go back?" Jack asks.

I'd thought it would be obvious. "We all have a connection to the kingdom. We grew up there, and also there's William, the owner of the tavern near the docks. He's like my surrogate father. He took care of us when we were training on land, took us in after our parents died. I don't know what I'd do without him." I hesitate, then add, "You know, I find that whole story about your father hard to believe."

"Yeah, I did too. I still do," he admits. "It's odd to picture him being with someone else besides my mother."

"Prince Pinhead, you seem to keep mentioning the concept of love at first sight. Do you honestly believe in that?" I ask in disbelief.

"Prince Pinhead?" he asks. I raise my eyebrows at him, encouraging him to continue. He sighs. "I think it can be true. Don't you?"

"Seriously?" I scoff. "First of all, love is an illusion. Second of all, love at first sight is merely attraction. You can't be in love with someone by just looking at them."

"Okay, the part about love at first sight I get, but love in general being an illusion? How do you figure that?"

"Actually, I . . . I don't even know what love feels like. But love is overrated," I admit. "You can't depend on anyone but yourself."

"What about your parents? And James?" he asks.

I bristle thinking about James. I don't love him, I don't think I ever will. But maybe at one point, I thought I did. "My mother and my biological father are a perfect example of how love is just an illusion. I don't know the full story of what happened to him, but I know enough. He just disappeared. And as for my mother and Lennard, that's more . . . complicated," I tell him.

"How?"

"Well, they never expressed their feelings toward one another. I never saw them actually act however the bloody hell couples are supposed to act." Just so he wouldn't try bringing James up again, I add, "And for the record, I don't know where you got such a ridiculous rumor about me and James from."

"Technically I didn't get it from anyone. I saw you two on deck earlier."

Damn it. "We're not in love. I don't know what love feels like. I don't . . . I don't actually know how I feel about him."

"Well, I'm sure you'll figure it out."

"What, like it's easy? And how would you know? Have you ever been in love?"

"Yes, actually. But it didn't end well."

"Why not?" I goad, snickering. "She got bored of Prince Charming's oh-so-irresistible charm?"

"Maybe. Her name was Mallory, and she's our head knight's daughter. She was the most beautiful girl I have ever seen. I planned to marry her, since I could choose whoever I wanted. But one day I caught her kissing the Duke of Thomalia. He was visiting Olovia for the Adarian Fire Festival."

Adara is the Goddess of Fire, and every year winter Olovia has a festival in her honor as a thank you for giving us fire to keep us warm during the harsh Olovian winters. Apparently, it's a place where other things—and people—warm up too.

"I'm sorry," I reply, realizing as I say it that I mean it. "That must have been awful."

"It was. But I'm over it now. It was two years ago, almost."

"It happens to everyone," I offer. "Nadia had eyes for Joseph once, but when it ended I saw how much pain she was in. I hope I never have to go through that."

"I doubt you ever will," he says. I take it as a compliment.

We fall back into our easy silence, the journey noiseless other than the brush beneath our feet as we walk side by side. Then the tree line ends, only there's no village in front of us.

It's a tower, faded purple paint cracked along its surface and an enormous hole in the front of the roof. In this part of the forest, the sun is blocked out by the tall trees and the wind whistles an eerie tune. There are no blue jays or cardinals here, just crows that continue to caw. My hand settles on the handle of my cutlass.

"The orb's in there?" I ask uncertainly.

Jack nods. "The orb's in there."

8

*W*hen we open the worn wooden door at the tower's front it almost falls off its hinges. Our feet echo in the narrow hallway. It's dimly lit, and though the tower appears abandoned there are paintings of people I don't recognize on the walls.

The hallway empties to a gigantic room that makes me stop in my tracks, and makes the pirate in me want to whoop with joy. The room is long and lined with piles of gold on the floor that are ten feet high. An enormous hole in the roof lets the sun shine through it like a spotlight. Jewels and treasure chests dot the room, resting between the piles of gold. I'm so tempted to take some, to steal it for myself and make this trip even more worth it, though I know I need to focus on procuring the orb. Jack must have the same thought; he eyes me warily as my gaze wanders the room, my eyes catching on the twenty-foot miniature mountain with the orb on its peak.

Even from below, the orb looks like it's a galaxy in a ball. The colors are bright—pink, green, purple, and blue swirling together and shining incredibly.

I take one step forward and regret it. Fifteen spiked traps pop up out of the ground.

The prince pulls me out of the way. "Watch out," he warns me.

I'm not shaking, but I can't deny those sharp spikes gave me a fright. Just one of them could have killed me. "There are probably hundreds of traps like these around here," I realize.

"Just be careful and go slow," Jack replies.

I let him go first, following close behind him—only to almost burn my feet when I step on the wrong tile and fire lights up the floor.

The pinheaded prince actually *lifts me up* and carries me out of the way. I shove him away from me, his touch making my stomach somersault.

"Okay, scratch that," he says, breathing heavily. "We need to move fast."

"You think?" But I only take one more step before a spear flies at me from a chamber in the wall.

I catch it on instinct, the point an inch from my nose and my whole body leaning backward. "I'm going to go out on a limb here and say that most people who tried have never successfully retrieved the orb before," I venture. Now the length of the room makes sense: It's like one giant, deadly obstacle course. If I squint, I can see what I'm pretty sure are a few skeletons on the other side of the room. I kneel warily and pick up a handful of gold coins, then toss them ahead. The next trap is a floor that falls away to more spikes. With it sprung, we dodge it and go around safely.

Then I take one step too many and the ground disappears. I fall through a trapdoor, screaming as I drop at least twenty feet below the surface, tucking and rolling and having the breath knocked out of me when I hit the dirt hard. The prince shouts my name and I grunt with pain. It takes a moment for my head to stop throbbing and to fully regain my composure.

I sluggishly peel myself off the ground and look around at the pitch-black darkness.

"Jack?" I call out. The door above me closes. "Hello?" I whisper. "Hello!" My voice echoes as I shout.

I walk forward, trying to understand my surroundings, trying not to let my fear get the better of me.

The feeling comes upon me in an instant. It calls me. It's right there in my veins. I spin around, my heart racing, the air harder to breathe.

"No!" I yell. I jog forward, hoping I would be able to see something, anything.

I take a breath of relief when I find myself in a thin hallway with lanterns hanging on the grimy brick walls. At the end of the hallway, there are two places to turn: left or right. I hesitantly make my way down the dim hallway, and I jump when I hear a faint noise. I grab my cutlass and turn around to make sure I'm safe. There's nothing here with me.

I turn back around and near the end of the hallway, and I hear the same noise again, only this time it's much clearer as to what it is. And it's much, much closer.

With one final, magnificent roar, a large creature appears before me—the body of a lion, the wings of a phoenix, and the head, powers, and scales of a sea serpent making it large enough to scrape the top of the room. A Flipperfore. My mouth falls open at the mythical creature.

Flipperfores are said to be the guardians of the castle of Arnav, the God of the Sea. Thanks to my life on the sea, I know the tales of Arnav the best out of all of the gods, but never in a million years did I think Flipperfores actually exist, let alone that I'd see one in front of me. The myth is that they reside in the deepest, darkest parts of the ocean—where no human can travel to, or even survive.

But apparently, the Flipperfores can. I stare at the creature, absolutely frozen. When it charges at me, I roll under its legs to its other side. It hisses and growls, and it scares the bloody hell out of me. I swing my cutlass at it, and though my blade slices through its scales, it barely makes a scratch.

It knocks me to the ground with its razor-sharp claws, tearing through my doublet coat and leaving me with a massive scratch on my upper arm. I hop to my feet and charge at the heinous creature. It raises its giant paw and smacks me down again, knife-like claws raking down my back. I cry out, the pain like fire from shoulder to waist, blood soaking into my coat and shirt and dripping down my skin.

The creature beats its wings and glides through the air, landing on top of my body. A disturbing amount of slobber flies out of its mouth when it roars in my face, its breath reeking of human blood. I gag at the odor, my vision blurring and darkening.

Its love for human flesh is crystal clear, and I'm about to be its next meal. When it rises up on its hind legs, about to deliver a final blow, I dodge its bulbous head and kick it in its stomach.

I struggle to my feet and lunge, finally able to give the creature a small gash on its arm. But it seems to hardly feel it. Its glowing amber eyes fill with rage, and I know that it will keep coming at me until I'm dead.

I continue swinging my cutlass but I can barely give it a nick. It keeps flying around me, dodging my blows and throwing me into the wall with its bulky claw. One of the flaming lanterns falls with me. The Flipperfore bolts over to me and grabs my arm in its mouth, teeth like daggers sinking into my skin, scraping against bone. I scream.

But I'm holding something too. The lantern I knocked down is in my grasp. With my free arm, I throw it at its head. The flames lick at its skin. The creature roars in pain, releasing my bloody arm from its mouth. It knocks the lantern away, but the Flipperfore's whole cranium is on fire.

The creature crashes to the floor, howling and scratching at the embers and flames. It can't see me. I take the opportunity, grab my cutlass, and stab it in the heart.

Then I dart down the hallway, my instincts telling me to turn right. I don't care if the monster is dead or not, I just need to get out of whatever hellhole I've fallen into. I keep running, every twist and turn vanishing into more darkness. My body hurts, blood pumping from my wounds. It feels like I'm running for miles, and I can hardly see anything in front of me.

When I come to the end of the long hallway, I trip over a step, relief flooding through me when I see a spiral staircase in front of me. I don't know where it will take me, and that doesn't even matter. I just need to get out. It feels like the walls are closing in on me, and I press against them with my hands, following it up. When I reach the top of the staircase, I shove open the door. It feeds out through the back wall of the room of gold.

I stumble into the light from the darkness, charging into the center of the room and looking around. Prince Pinhead is still here, caught in a net, and the orb is still on the peak of the rocky mountain.

"Serena!" he calls when he sees me. "What happened to you? I tried to go after you, but I took one step and this net—"

His mouth moves, but the rest of his words are drowned

out. By the time I reach the net, I feel faint. I stop moving, my limbs like jelly. This time, there is no cloud of smoke.

I see myself in a white room. A shadowy figure carries me, and I'm trying to break free but I can't. It's suffocating me. I gasp for air, the illusion feeling like reality.

"It's not real," I whisper. "It's not real, it's not real!" I scream it in my head as the ringing noise returns. I clasp my hands over my ears, trying to drown it out, and clench my eyes tightly to rid myself of the vision.

Both fade. I return to reality coughing, finally able to breathe.

I take a deep breath and drop to the floor to cut the net that the prince had managed to get stuck in. He'd stopped fighting it; now, he stares at me. "You had another one, didn't you?" he asks. I ignore him, grabbing my cutlass to cut the rope. "I already tried using my sword. The rope is too thick to cut."

I ignore his comment on the vision. Instead, I drop my cutlass and look around me. If steel won't cut it, something else must. There's an emerald on the ground a few feet away from us, the edge sharpened. I grab it. One press to the rope and the strands came apart. I lift the heavy net off of his head and my legs fail me. I plop on the ground to my stomach, finally taking stock of my injuries. My arm is killing me and so is my back. My skin is smeared with dirt and blood.

The prince kneels beside me and pulls a canteen of water from his satchel.

"Oh, please don't," I say. "I don't need—"

He doesn't let me finish. "Stop being stubborn for two seconds and let me help you."

I'm too exhausted to argue. Jack uses the water to clean my wounds before he rips a piece of fabric from the end of his shirt and wraps it around my arm. He carefully dabs my back with another piece of fabric, though it hurts much more than my arm.

"Thank you," I say through gritted teeth, the stings lessening.

Jack gives me a moment, then he helps me up and nods his head toward the tip of the mountain.

I stare at the orb. It's mocking us as it sits on its peak. As I stare at it, wondering if it's worth it, after all of this, to defeat the darkness—wondering if it will even work—that's when it comes to me. These visions, my paralysis, it only started when I came into contact with the darkness in Olovia. If the orb works, maybe we could use it to figure out what is going on with me.

"We need to get that orb."

"We just nearly died trying," Jack reminds me.

"I'll take that chance again," I say, and I take off for the mountain.

"Be careful!" he calls out as I begin to climb. "I wouldn't put my foot there if I were you!"

"Ignoring you now!" I yell back. My muscles groan and my wounds scream. But I won't let this tower defeat me.

Then again, maybe it won't be the tower. I'm halfway up when I hear footsteps bolting into the room. "Freeze!" a voice echoes. In my surprise I slip, and I slide down a few feet before being forced to jump off of the mountain, nearly breaking my ankle as I land. Without a chance to see who's coming, the prince grabs my arm and runs.

"Where are we even going?" I ask.

"Anywhere but here!" He skirts around the edge of the room and through the hallway, putting us in front of our pursuers and nearer the door. We crash through the door of the tower and into the trees.

"I don't think this is the way back to the portal!

"It doesn't matter right now!" he shouts back. We continue our escape, but we're trapped once we hit a dead end at the forest's edge. Jack panics, searching the wall of stone. "We're done for now."

Our pursuers' footsteps catch up to us. I spin around. They completely surround our perimeter. Silver amor, the same helmets on their heads, revealing relatively young faces.

I grab my cutlass from its sheath and meet them. I cannot risk any obstacles standing in our way. If it's the only possible way to defeat the darkness, we need to go back and get that orb. They're interfering, so I'm ready to fight.

Jack copies my stance, pulling out his own sword. Then we run toward our pursuers and attack.

9

---

*O*ur pursuers are clearly quite experienced fighters. But then again, so am I. Swing after swing, I beat back the man I'm fighting.

"Where did you learn to fight?" he asks, breaking away and panting.

"My stepfather taught me," I reply with a grin. "Lennard Jones, the most infamous pirate ever to live." I lunge forward and swing.

"Indeed?" He dodges my swing. "I don't want to hurt you. The queen requested that you see her immediately."

I attempt to stab him and miss, stumbling to the other side of where we're standing. "Why should I believe anything you say?" I ask, chasing him. "How does the queen even know me?"

"I understand why you would be reluctant to trust me," he says, parrying my next blow, "but you must know that if I was going to kill you, I would have done so already. My magic would have made this fight quick."

If you have magic, then why use swords?

I pause a distance away, circling him, wondering if he's

telling the truth or not. If I agree to go with him, he could just kill me, anyway.

"I don't believe you." I'm tiring much more quickly than I should. My injuries won't let me keep going for much longer. I eye him skeptically. "How does the queen know me, and how does she know I'm here?" I ask. "How did you even find us?"

The man lowers his sword. "I will explain everything if you just come with me."

But he still hasn't given me a good enough reason, or any reason, and I can tell that he's getting annoyed with me.

Suddenly, he knocks my cutlass out of my hand. No sword. There's just a block of ice on the ground near its hilt. Magic? But he used ice. *Ice.* Neither sorcery nor celestial magic could affect the elements. How is this even possible?

I stare at my sword, my mouth agape as I look closer and realize the entire weapon is covered in a thin sheet of ice as well. I've never seen anything like it before in my life. I look over my shoulder at Prince Pinhead. He was handling himself well, but now he's lying on the ground with the same expression on his face that I had on mine. The soldier he was fighting has fire coming out of his hands. I would have thought I was hallucinating, but it's most definitely real.

"What kind of magic is that?" I ask, trying not to allow my fear to shine through.

"It's elemental magic," the man I'd fought says. "Just come with us and you will find out whatever you want to know."

I step away from him. "Tell me how the queen knows me and how she knows we're here."

The man looks to his colleague, then nods. "When the

two of you entered the portal, we received energy signals of dark magic. Unheard-of dark magic."

"That's impossible," I say. "And even if it wasn't, if it was unheard-of then how would you even recognize it?"

"We don't know, but I have never felt an energy signal that dark before," he says gravely.

I agree slowly. I need to know what this energy signal has to do with us. "Fine. I'll go."

Prince Pinhead finally climbs to his feet and comes to my side. "Well if you go, I don't have much of a choice. If I show up to the *Tigerlily* without you, I'm dead meat."

"Prince Jack." The man bows his head suddenly.

"You know who I am?" Jack asks, surprised.

"We know every kingdom in the world, and who rules them," the man replies. He finally removes his helmet, revealing his features. He looks maybe twenty-five years old, and he has blonde hair and sky-blue eyes. Not terrible looking, really.

"My name is Ian, and I am Head Knight to Queen Iana of the Realm of Magic. It is my job to know about the outside world in case they make their way into our realm. Now come along, Queen Iana is expecting you."

We hesitantly follow the few soldiers back on the path to Queen Iana's castle. There aren't many of them, but I don't trust them one bit. If Ian truly is going to kill me I suppose he would have done it already, and before bowing to the Olovian prince. Besides, I have never seen a castle up close before, and now that we're headed to one I'm actually quite eager to see one for the first time.

But my eagerness is interrupted by a wave of perplexity. Elemental magic? How had that been kept a secret from the rest of the world? I mean, I'm sure some people know—secrets can't be kept that completely—but nobody in Olovia knows. I'm also upset that Ian froze the sword that my mother gave me, and he hadn't offered to unfreeze it. It's in its sheath now, hopefully thawing enough that it will soon have a sharp edge again.

I do have another one in my chambers on the ship, but it's just not the same.

Jack echoes my concerns, leaning in and whispering, "It's not just me who is totally confused, right?"

"It's definitely not just you," I reply. He nods at me.

I jog up to Ian, the prince trailing behind me. "Why hasn't the majority of the Human Realm's population ever heard of other types of magic?"

He shrugs, but I see the grimace on his face. "Well, you know how non-magics are. And people in general. They tend to fear the unknown. Celestial magic was never questioned, since it's the powers possessed by the same gods the people worshiped. Sorcery has always been common, for many centuries. Other types of magic are more rare. A long time ago, there was a misunderstanding between someone with elemental magic and someone who knew sorcery. The person who possessed elemental magic was just a child. She didn't know how to control her powers.

"She killed a beloved sorcerer, accidentally, and was burned at the stake because of it. It happened again, and again, elemental magic users who couldn't control their powers becoming criminalized. After a few more cases like that, other kinds of magic have been seen as deadly, dangerous, and unpredictable. Most importantly, it was uncontrollable. It became a sin to the gods to even mention the magic. So in the silence, all of our history was thrown away and forgotten. Even royal families like yours, Prince Jack, were not allowed to have access to that knowledge. Centuries passed, and over time the world just forgot about it."

Even with the explanation, it's exceedingly difficult to wrap my mind around. Celestial magic and sorcery are also as strange as elemental magic, but we know about those.

"So you have ice, he has fire," I say, pointing to the other soldier. "What does Queen Iana have?"

"Queen Iana is quite spectacular. She possesses the lightest type of sorcery magic, and she has a form of elemental magic—ice, like me."

"Two?" Jack exclaims. "How is that even possible?"

"Genetics," Ian answers simply. "Or sometimes it can be a gift from the gods."

"Just out of curiosity, can anyone obtain magic?" I ask.

"Technically, yes. But it's quite rare. Most people are born with it or are gifted it."

"Ian," one man calls out.

"Excuse me." Ian nods to each of us, then moves ahead to see what his soldier needs. The prince and I share a look that's part excitement, but mostly nerves.

We finally come to the castle gates. Up close, the castle seems to be a thousand feet tall. I have to crane my head all the way back to see the sun reflecting off the bright white marble building.

The gates in front of the castle are made of real gold, and there are two guards on each side. Inside, we're met with a gigantic courtyard with two white stone fountains and a beautiful garden surrounding it. There are roses, daisies, and tulips alongside baby pineapple bushes. We walk along the gray stone pathway between the greenery, approaching the large wooden double doors to the castle. Beneath the branches from the garden, the sun is completely visible and shines its warm rays down on us, my hair catching the light and burning even more red.

I'm actually almost blinded by the light. There's so much of it.

But I can't look away. Everything is absolutely breathtaking, the flowers more colorful than I've ever seen and the water from the fountains sparkling.

"This is the most beautiful thing I have ever seen," I admit.

"It's the second most beautiful thing I have ever seen," the prince mutters.

I look away from the grandeur and at him instead. "What's the first?" I ask.

He doesn't respond.

We remain silent as we approach the door. The guards open it for us, and we enter the foyer.

If I thought the courtyard was beautiful, this is something else. There is a ginormous glass staircase in the center of the giant room, and two large windows that make the staircase glimmer like the waters outside. Portraits cover the baby blue walls, and in front of us is a large red velvet throne on the landing. This must be where the queen greets visitors, and in my torn, bloodied, and dirty clothing, I'm completely out of place.

Two men come down the stairs quickly.

"Presenting, Queen Iana Orlendada of the Realm of Magic," one of them announces. The guards line up on either side of her throne, their swords resting in their hands.

The queen appears, moving down the stairs gracefully, wearing an emerald green dress with long sleeves. She's escorted by a man who is not dressed in a suit of armor, making him difficult to identify. I wonder who he is to her as he leads her to her throne.

But that thought is only brief, my attention returning to Queen Iana. She wears an emerald stone hanging off a silver chain around her neck, and her crown is golden, resting on top of her long, curly, chestnut-colored hair. Her eyes are ocean blue and she has matching emerald earrings hanging from her ears. Her pale skin is absolutely perfect, flawless to the point she looks like she's glowing from the inside. She sits down on her throne, swiftly and neatly, and she grins at us as she motions for us to come forward. The man who escorted her down the stairs stands behind her, his face emotionless.

I bow before I speak. It seems like the right thing to do in this situation, even though it makes the aching pain in my back from the Flipperfore burn. "It is an honor, Your Majesty."

I wait for Jack to do the same, but I then peer over at the prince. His eyes are glued to the young queen, mesmerized by her beauty. My throat burns at his ogling, and I step on his foot.

The queen nods to me, then shifts her attention to Jack. "Prince Jack of Olovia, welcome. Who is your friend?"

She asks him this without taking her eyes off of me. She looks as if she's studying me—truly, thoughtfully studying me. So I answer for Jack. "I wouldn't exactly call us friends. I'm Serena. Serena Jones." I bow my head again.

The queen's smile grows, the closest I think she can get to embarrassment. "Forgive me for staring. Your features are familiar to me, but I'm afraid I can't place them. Have we met before?"

"No, Your Majesty." I'd remember meeting someone like her.

"Hm . . . Well, I'm sure it will come to me later. Now, Ian has told you why you were brought here, yes? I was not sure which one of you it was, but now that you're here in front of me it is clear which one of you radiates the dark magic that alerted us to your entrance through the portal." She stares at me with great intensity in her eyes. "Miss Jones."

Her stare, once curious, now burns. It sends a chill down my spine and the light shining through the immense window darkens, as if time is standing still and the walls are about to close in on me.

I feel my face begin to pale, and I swallow a lump in my throat. "What? That's not possible."

"Oh, it's more than possible, dear. I can feel it inside of you," Queen Iana replies, her eyes narrowing.

No. She has to be mad. I don't have any magic in me.

"You're lying," I say, my voice sounding small. "Take it back." But there is only silence. I look to the prince, who stands next to me, and though he looks confused he also looks as though he believes her. I panic. My anger flares in me, hot and wild in a way I haven't felt before, and I need to let it out. "*Take it back!*" I yell, my voice echoing, its tone and power something I've never heard leave my mouth.

Jack pulls me back, and I realize I'd stepped toward the queen. "Woah, easy, tiger," he says softly, though kindly. "What's with you?"

I'm panting. Fear, pain, exhaustion—it all swirls within me. I don't know what's happening to me. "I . . . I'm sorry. I don't know what came over me."

In a flash, a look of petrification comes over the queen. A look as if she knows what's going on, like she has seen this before. She inhales, and she says loudly, "Get her out."

At her order, the guards move toward me. I step back as they approach. I pull my cutlass—thawed, thankfully—into my hand and back away, ready to defend myself, to run away from this realm and back to my ship. Back where things make sense.

But before the fighting has a chance to begin, Jack jumps

in front of me, shielding me from Queen Iana's guards. "Wait! Please! I'm sure you've heard about the darkness in the sky. In Olovia. That's why we're here. We're only here to get the orb, we want to use the orb to destroy it."

The guards pause and turn to Queen Iana, who looks bewildered at Jack's exclamation.

She motions for the guards to stand down. "I was actually planning to speak with you about that. My guards informed me they found you trying to steal the orb. Is that truly the reason why you want it?" she asks, doubt in every word.

The prince puts up his right hand. "I swear on my grandfather's grave."

She tilts her head, considering, but from the way her eyes soften she sees the honesty and sincerity on the prince's face, and hears it in his tone. She stares at him for a moment, looking as if she's considering her options.

"All right," she says, waving to send her guards back to their positions. "You should have come to me before you attempted to steal my orb."

"We apologize." The prince bows his head. "With all due to respect, if you care so much about the orb then why leave it unguarded in such a worn-down tower?"

She leans back in her throne. "I have a guard. My Flipperfore usually attacks when someone's foot crosses the threshold. But today, I suppose, was not his best day." She motions pointedly to the wraps around my arm while the prince's face screws up in confusion at the mention of the monster. "I keep the orb in the tower because it is much safer there. Nobody goes in those woods, especially not so deep. And I cannot keep it here with me. My magic is purely light, but the orb possesses both light and dark magic. It is much more powerful than me. It would destroy my powers."

Jack nods. "Thank you for not being angry. We just thought that the orb was our only option. We read about this dark magic in an old book, and the only information we gained was that four people are going to obtain this magic, which we don't understand."

Queen Iana's eyes widen, her fear creeping back in. The prince and I share a look.

"Your Majesty," he says carefully, "do you know something about this?"

She remains speechless for a moment, her eyes wide but unfocused, as if she's remembering something. "I can't . . . no, I really shouldn't . . ." she sighs, closing her eyes and pressing her fingers to the bridge of her nose. "I will tell you what I can."

We wait. When she speaks, she speaks softly. "The man behind it, the man you're looking for, is called Tellerous."

10

"Who the hell is Tellerous?" I ask.

"He resides in the Dark Realm," Queen Iana says. "He rules over the people there, but he has an ambitious goal to combine all three of the realms together, and to rule them all as king."

I shiver. I have only ever heard about the Dark Realm in old legends and stories. It's where dead people reside, and those who are alive but being punished by the gods. I didn't know it actually existed. But then again, I've been learning about all sorts of things I never knew were real.

"And how do you know him?" Jack asks.

The queen drops her eyes. "He is an old friend of mine. We met many years ago at a school for magic training called Renayhemm, on the very remote island of Magia. He came across a prophecy that led him down a different path than the rest of our fellow students . . . a darker path."

"What kind of path?" I prod, thinking of the dark magic hovering over Olovia, the woman's screams. "How does he think he can rule three realms?"

"There are a lot of people in three realms," the queen

continues. "Tellerous has a plan to lessen the population, to weaken them in order to obtain better control, hence the awful deaths that you have seen in your kingdom."

"What exactly can his power do?" the prince asks.

"Just about anything. His magic is even rarer than the ones you've seen here. Cretion magic. One of his early, early relatives chose the name, and only three people have had this magic, but soon it'll be four. I believe you know this already. It looks like sorcery, save the color it emits is much darker—black instead of violet. It is limitless: it can create, destroy, make anything the wielder wishes disappear and reappear . . . it can also be a dangerous weapon against people, and depending on the person it can give them other abilities as well. This specific dark magic is much more sinister than most forms of dark magic. It looks the same, but it is much more wicked and tenacious."

The prince begins pacing, which I'm coming to realize is something he does when he's upset, or thinking. "So what's the prophecy?"

The queen smiles softly, as if he's asking the right questions. "In Tellerous's family, the first man to obtain the magic also created it. The magic gave him a vision, and he predicted that only three of his direct family members will have the genes dark enough to carry the magic, to hold it until the magic will reach its full abilities. It gets stronger in every host, but in the fourth and final host it will fulfill its full potential. I'm afraid I don't know what happens to the fourth person once the magic is inside of them. It was prophesied that it would be Tellerous's child who gets the magic next, only nobody knows who they are."

"Does the magic still stay in the others once the next person in line gets it?" the prince asks.

"Yes, but it's just not to the full extent that it was before the next person obtained it. The previous host is weakened, but can still wield it."

I have been quiet so far, mostly. The more I hear, the more I want to disappear. Something isn't adding up. She told us I radiate dark magic, and I want to think it's because I'm infected with it, that maybe in Olivia it had attached to me somehow.

But the visions, the pull. It's so promising, and I'm almost eager to follow it. I have to ask—

"Queen Iana . . . am I . . . ?" I can't say it out loud, but she must hear the fear shining through my tone, and though her gaze is gentle, almost pitiable, her voice goes flat.

"I don't know."

My shoulders tense up. The knots tighten in my stomach and my heart is about to beat out of my chest. But it isn't until I feel the connection to the magic—that pull, that whisper—that tears begin forming behind my eyes. They begin to water, to burn. But I force myself to hold them back. I refuse to cry in front of people. I had almost forgotten the feeling.

The pinhead prince is staring at me. Maybe he pieced together what I've been trying to ask; maybe he doesn't want to know. "Are you sure there isn't anything more you can tell us?" he asks, his question aimed at the queen.

"I am afraid not," she says coldly. "Now, I must send you on your way. I have said too much already. I will give you permission to use the orb, but you must bring it back. The orb is one of our most prized possessions. It belonged to Lucinda, the Creation Goddess, who offered it as a gift to my people when we were forced to go into hiding from non-magics and sorcerers. If you destroy it, I am afraid I can no longer show either of you any kindness."

As if kindness was what I'd received today. I remain silent, but Jack promises, "We will do our best to keep it safe."

I can see the hesitation in her forced smile. "I know you will try."

11

$\mathcal{W}$e bow to Queen Iana one last time before quickly making our exit. I tell myself to breathe, but it isn't working. Processing the queen's information is not easy, and it leaves me with a terrible, horrible feeling that I know who the fourth person to obtain the dark magic is going to be—and Queen Iana knows too.

But what if I don't *want* the dark magic?

"Would you slow down?" Jack grabs my upper arm and pulls, turning me around to him.

"We don't have time to talk," I reply. "We need to get the orb, and then we need more answers about Tellerous and who his child is." My voice shakes. If Queen Iana is right, we already know one of those things. I step away from the prince, but he blocks my path.

"Just leave it, Serena. We don't need to know who he is, all we need to do is destroy the magic in the sky. That's the only reason we're here, who cares about its history?"

I wait for the punchline, but I'm mortified to realize he's serious. "How damn stupid can you truly be?" I ask him. "Surely, the soon-to-be King of Olovia would have at least an ounce of common sense? The cloud in the sky may disappear, but Tellerous will still be here. The *dark magic* will still be here. It's him we have to destroy."

Fear flashes through his eyes. "And why do you suddenly care?" he asks, shaking his head. "I hired you to get the orb. That's it. Sure, Tellerous will be a problem still. Going after him would mean not just saving Olovia, but all of the worlds. But let's just say that I, and probably a lot of other people, don't have you pinned down as the saving-humanity type." He leans in. "So tell me, selfish pirate, what would be in it for you?" Even his insult falls flat against the uncertainty that slips into his voice.

"Yes, I'm selfish," I admit. "But you can't stand there after hearing everything Queen Iana said and deny that I need answers. And I think that you do too. You know deep down that destroying the cloud won't guarantee Olovia and the Human Realm's safety. I don't like it any more than you do, Prince Pinhead, but we have to keep going. And you still need me."

All of that's true, but there's more that I don't dare say out loud. I need to keep going because something's happening to me—the vision, the magic, the sudden rage I acted on in the queen's castle. I have the right to know what it is. There are so many things—so many worse things—that I could be doing this for. I don't care if it means I have to spend more time with his royal pain in the ass. I need to know, and maybe I need him too.

Jack stares at me for a moment, never breaking eye contact. Like he's waiting for me to break first. I dare not look away, no matter how much I want to.

He rolls his eyes. "Fine. You're coming along, but once we get off this island I'm calling the shots. We'll go to Elias. Queen Iana wasn't telling us everything. Maybe he'll be able to tell us more." He sighs. "You know you can call me Jack."

Glad that he'd backed off, I relax and follow him back into the woods. "Where's the fun in that?"

The tower is less imposing when we walk up to it a second time. Since all of the booby traps had been sprung—and clearly not set again—we walk right back up to the small mountain, and like last time, I begin climbing it. My foot only slips a few times, but I make it to the top swiftly, my memory shifting back to a summer some time ago when I climbed a mountain in Belevina. That had just been for fun; I envy that time. How long it will be until I can be so carefree again?

At the peak, the orb sits waiting. The sunlight from the hole in the roof makes the colors in the orb shine incredibly bright, and even standing at the edge I can feel its power. I press my palm to its surface, ready to grab it and go.

As soon as I make contact, a sharp pain rips through me, like I'm being stabbed in the chest. My vision blurs, the ringing sound returns—a thousand times more strident than it had been before. I remember Iana telling us of the power in this orb, the light and the dark, and the power it holds to destroy her magic, and I wonder if this hadn't been a big mistake.

Through the ear-splitting sound, I hear hundreds of faint screams that make my head hurt even more. My heart pounds and my palms grow slick. It's like there's already magic moving through my veins, hot and heavy and burning through me.

I stumble away and slip from the rocky mountain. That's when I start to scream.

Time stands still. It's like all the air has been sucked from the room. I can scream, but I can't breathe. I'm coughing and gasping for air as I fall, and all around me all I can see is that cloud of black dust, only it's moving faster now.

It's not real. *It's not real.* But as much as I tell myself, it doesn't do me any good. I fall and I fall, as if I'm trapped in my own personal hell. The falling, the burning, the lack of air, the *black dust* all feels too real. It feels as if I'm dying.

Maybe I am dying. I hear the prince's voice along with all of the other screams, but his is louder, though more muffled.

Everything goes black.

I'm not unconscious. I'm awake, but I can't see or hear anything. My eyelids are too heavy, but the feeling fades after a few minutes. When I open my eyes I can't move my body. My head is in the prince's lap, and he hasn't noticed that I regained consciousness.

When he notices I'm awake, I look away.

"Oh, thank the gods. You're alive," he says. "Otherwise your crew would throw me overboard."

I try laughing, but it comes out as a cough that hurts my ribs even more. "*Hilarious.* What happened to the orb?" I try sitting up and look around, realizing I'm still in the prince's lap.

He holds up his left hand and shows me the orb in his palm. "When you fell you took it down with you."

It really is quite small, but the feeling it gave me when I

touched had been agonizing. He offers it to me, but I shake my head. I don't want to touch it. These visions are getting worse—this last one could have killed me, if the mountain had been any higher. The pain lingers, this last vision the most painful thing I have ever experienced—and I was once stabbed in my stomach, which also bled a lot. Not to mention the Flipperfore's knife-like teeth and claws that sank into my skin not too long ago.

When I'm ready, Jack helps me off the ground. "Are you all right?"

"I am now," I answer, wanting to leave it at that.

He keeps his hand on my arm and lets me lean on him as we leave the tower. "Come on, let's get you back to the ship. You should rest for a while." But he doesn't let go. As soon as we enter the woods, he asks, "What did you see this time?"

"Just a cloud of black dust coming toward me." I answer. "Same as the other times."

He's quiet, but the look on his face means he was deep in thought. Or maybe afraid to say what he's thinking. "Serena, what Queen Iana said, and the reason you want to find Tellerous . . . You don't think that—"

"Can we please talk about anything else?"

"Of course." But he just can't stay quiet. "The most painful thing that ever happened to me was when I was ten years old. I was playing outside the castle and I tripped and fell and cracked my head open."

At least he's changing the subject. "Another pirate stabbed me once, in the stomach." I press my hand to where the scar sits. "Alina Ortega . . . but that was almost three years ago, the only time I almost lost a fight. I'm much more skilled now with my cutlass. Would have bled out if it hadn't been for James."

"You keep dodging it, but you two seem to have history."

"Of course we have history, we grew up together." At his pointed look, I add, "James was my first kiss."

"I thought you said you've never been in love."

"Oh, it is definitely not love. Like I told you, love's overrated."

"I disagree. If you find the right person, it can be really magical."

"You mean Mallory?"

Jack hesitates. "Right, yes. Mallory." But he sounds unsure of himself.

I sigh. "I don't know. Maybe I'll find out one day. You know, assuming I can live long enough to do so." The way things are going, it's not likely.

"Shut up. We'll make it through this, and we'll save the Human Realm."

"First of all, never tell me to shut up again or you won't be able to say anything to anyone anymore," I warn him. It feels better to threaten him. "Secondly, we'll see."

"You're not like most girls."

"I'm going to take that as a compliment."

"That's how I meant it," he insists. "I just . . . want you to know that I admire the fact that you aren't afraid of what everyone else thinks. You're tremendously brave, and you have the courage to say what you feel, to a prince like me or a queen like Iana. Not many people do."

I look at him uneasily. No one has ever said anything that kind to me before. I stutter out a "thanks," not really knowing what else to say. "Hey, Pinhead, it's my turn for a question. You said that Queen Iana's castle was the second most beautiful thing you have ever seen. What's the first?"

He reddens quickly. "I don't recall saying that."

"Oh, but you did."

"No, I didn't."

Is he challenging me? "Stop being a pain in the ass." I playfully punch his arm.

He grimaces, and I wonder if I actually hurt him. But then he laughs. "Yeah, I'm the pain here."

I roll my eyes and smile, and our conversation trails off.

But that's my first mistake. Once it's silent between us, it's clear that whatever's inside me isn't going away. I can hear the magic whispering something to me inside my head. It's trying to say something to me. The tingling in my veins appears and my eyes trail to the prince's pocket, where the orb is. A lump appears in my throat. My body craves it, but my head refuses it.

Without our conversation to distract me, suddenly every worry that I had comes back. The lump in my throat grows, and I realize it's not the magic—it's me. My eyes sting. This feeling isn't going away, and as the magic in the sky grows, it will only get stronger. I clench my fists, trying to make the tingling stop. I feel like a magnet, like there's another force pulling me.

We need to get to Elias fast.

I don't realize when we're at the front of the realm again. "Serena?" the prince asks, prodding me. "Hello?" When he finally catches my attention, the magnetic feeling disappears.

"I asked you a question," he says. "Did you not hear me? I asked what you're going to tell the crew."

"Oh, um . . . I don't know right now. I haven't thought about it." Though now I have something else to worry about. This trip was supposed to be to the Realm of Magic and back. I don't think they'll take kindly to an extension.

"You may want to decide, because we are almost to the portal," Jack warns.

"I'll figure something out," I assure him.

I'm actually relieved when I see the dead tree take shape in front of us. I just want to get out of this realm, where my problems had multiplied. Once I am back on the ship, I want to be alone. I want to lock myself in my cabin and bawl for as long as I want to. I want to speak with Nadia.

The portal spits us out again, and the rowboat is waiting for us on the shore. Jack rows as quickly as he can to get us back to the *Tigerlily*, and I sigh in relief once I lay my eyes on my beautiful vessel. "They have returned!" I hear Franklin cheer.

We've returned.

12

We climb aboard as my whole crew gathers to greet us. Nadia forces her way to the front, shouting, "You're back!" when she sees me. She pulls me into her embrace and squeezes me tightly. When I wince, she notices the wounds from the Flipperfore. "Oh gods," she says, her grin falling, "what happened to you?"

Before James or anyone else can get to me, I yank her arm and take her to my quarters where we can be alone. Everything comes spilling out, and Nadia, ever one to take things in stride, puts her arm around me and listens as I tell her everything I learned in the Realm of Magic and cry my fears into her shoulder.

When I finish, she's quiet for a moment, then she says, "This doesn't make any sense, Serena. You don't think that you're—"

"What? No," I say quickly. "No, I can't be."

"But Serena . . . you don't know who your biological father is," Nadia says, ever logical. It's one of the reasons she's my best friend, why she's the only person who I can truly confide in, besides Ben. She takes my hand and squeezes it, but it doesn't comfort me. I want her to be wrong. *I* want to be wrong. "I'm sorry," she continues. "I don't even know what to say. That's a lot of information to take in. Though, I've got to ask . . . what are you planning to do about it?"

I shake my head. She hugs me tighter and rubs my back as I continue to sob, and I'm grateful for her company and our privacy. I can't have the others see me like this.

I take a moment before sitting up straight. "The pinhead and I decided to continue our journey," I tell her finally. "I need answers, so we're going to the sorcerer Elias. I'm going to give the crew a choice, whether they want to continue or not."

"Well, I don't know about the others, but you can count me in," she tells me.

I manage a thin smile, at least a little relief flooding through me. "Thank you."

"In fact, I am not leaving your side. I will be your left-hand girl. We will do this together."

I let her pull me into another hug. "I love you," I mumble into her shoulder.

"I love you too," she replies. I roll my eyes. Ever since the darkness appeared, I have been sharing more feelings with people, more over the past three days than I have in an entire lifetime.

Once I calm down, Nadia hands me the canteen of water sitting on my desk. "Where is the orb now?"

"The prince has it."

"You should get it from him. If you truly want to protect it you should hide it while you're not using it."

"Yeah, you're probably right." I rub the wound on my arm. I've bled through the makeshift bandage Jack had given me.

Nadia reaches for my arm. "Let me help you."

I turn away from her. "I can do it myself."

"Oh, don't try me right now," she warns.

I roll my eyes and hold out my arm hesitantly, allowing her to dress my wounds. Jack had done a decent job, given we hadn't had any salves or real bandages. Even Nadia looks impressed. When she finishes, there's a knock on my door that makes the two of us jump.

"Joseph is sailing us back to Olovia," James says through the closed door, though I sense him lingering once we've received the message.

"Anything else?" I ask.

"Actually, yes . . . Nadia, can you give us a moment?"

"This isn't really a good time, James," Nadia tells him.

"It's fine," I say. "I can talk for a second. Just give me a moment." I sniffled one more time and wipe off one last tear.

Nadia helps me change out of my ripped, bloody clothes and put on a new white shirt and a burgundy doublet coat. I yell for James to come inside, and he walks into the room and stands in front of the bed. Nadia looks between us and hesitantly exits the room.

"Have you been—"

"Shut up." I stop him and get to my feet, stretching my stiff arm and my back, testing the wounds. "What do you want?"

"I figured that since we're on our way back, you have less to think about. I mean, it's over, right?" He waits for me to answer, but I can't. He continues. "I've been wondering for a long time, and I think I've been patient, but I think we need to talk about . . . what is going on with us?"

"There's nothing between us," I tell him irefully. My hands curl into fists, his question infuriating me beyond what I should have felt. *How selfish can he be?* The thought comes from nowhere.

"But what about what happened with us on your eighteenth birthday?" He asks, disappointment heavy on every word. "Or last night? I thought that was why you made me your first mate."

I remain silent. I can't trust myself to speak.

"It's the prince, isn't it?" he asks. Then he laughs, envy and disbelief creeping into his voice. "It's so obvious. The way you two were looking at each other when you got back to the ship."

I laugh too. "How in the bloody hell did you come up with that conclusion?" Me and Prince Pinhead? Never in a million years.

"Then what has changed if it's not him?" he demands. "What happened in the Realm of Magic?"

For once I'm at a loss for words. I actually don't have the answer to that question, because I have a feeling he doesn't care about the magic, or the orb, or anything we'd learned about Tellerous. He wants to know something deeper, something I'm wondering myself.

"I don't . . ." I sigh and try again. "I can't answer that question," I tell him truthfully, trying to dial myself back. I have never truly lashed out at James before. The fact that I'd done so now, that I want to do it again? It makes me anxious.

James exhales. "I get it," he says. And he walks away.

"James, wait!" I call out. He doesn't even look back, just disappears down the corridor and up to the deck above. I remain frozen in my chambers. What did I just do? Why do I have to ruin everything? I may not have feelings for him, but he's still important to me. He needs to know that.

"James, please." I run after him, catching him on the stairs. "I have lost enough people, I can't lose you either."

He turns around, and before I can stop him he pulls me close to him and kisses me.

But him kissing me doesn't help anything, it just makes me more confused than before. The first time we kissed, I felt a deeper connection between us. Now, I don't even know what I feel. It definitely isn't the same. Just empty.

One more thing that I have to figure out.

I pull away. "I just need time to figure things out. Can you please give that to me?" I ask. James runs his hand through his hair and nods, looking like he hadn't even entirely planned that kiss himself. I step toward my chambers, but that's when I see Nadia at the top of the stairs, looking down at us.

She follows me back to my quarters. I sit down next to her and tell her what happened, even though I know she'd seen the whole thing.

"Oh, the plot thickens," she responds, raising her eyebrows and giggling.

I bury my face in my hands. "I can assure you, this is nothing to celebrate. Now I have one more thing to add to my list of tasks."

"Honestly, I always thought you and James were meant to be. But even so, you just need to follow your heart and think carefully. Nothing's ever as simple as it seems when it comes to matters of the heart."

"I can't think about this now," I tell her as I stand up. "I have to go tell the crew what we're about to get ourselves into. Give them a choice." I shove open the door and walk out on deck to the front of the ship.

"Avast ye!" I shout. "I need everybody here, now!"

They all stop what they're doing and gather around me, huddling together, their eyes passing over my bandages as they listen.

"The prince and I have decided to continue our journey," I tell them. I inform them of everything we learned in the Realm of Magic, the orb and the darkness and Tellerous. Everything save the detail about *me* radiating darkness.

"There are too many unanswered questions," I finish. "We're sailing back to Olovia to consult with Elias. He might know something we can use. Now, this is something I have to do, but I am giving you all a choice. You may come with us, or you can stay on the ship. I don't know what will happen after we see Elias. We may have to venture out again, and if that's the case you can either stay in Olovia or journey with us.

"I can't make this decision for you," I finish. "It's too dangerous."

There is a moment of silence, and everyone looks at me as if I have three heads. I see all of the hesitant faces among them, the fear and uncertainty. This isn't what they signed up for, and I know that.

Then, James raises his cutlass into the air and nods his head. Soon after, the whole crew raises their swords and cheers as they clink them together. I grin at them, not realizing until now how much I depend on them.

The cheers die down, and Adam pipes up, "So what's the plan then?"

I balk. All I know is we're going to Elias. Who knows what might happen after that? "We haven't gotten that far yet," I admit. "Let's get to Olovia first."

The pinhead and I will come up with something . . . I hope. My whole crew's decision to come with us really boosted my confidence, but even after we speak to Elias we need a way to either find Tellerous or make him come to us.

I force a grin on my face, hoping to exude confidence.

As I step away. Jack grabs my arm and pulls me aside.

"Before you make any more announcements, you might want to have an actual plan first," he reminds me.

"And we will," I say, not completely convinced. "I told Nadia everything, and I am sure the three of us can come up with something."

"Probably . . . Just—I don't think you should give them false hope."

"I'm sorry, aren't you the one who told me to have faith?" I recall.

"Yes, but I'm just worried about your visions. I noticed you didn't tell the crew about those, but they might affect all of us just as much as you."

Grudgingly, I see his point. "What was I supposed to say? 'We have no idea what we're doing and we're leading you into a blind war'?"

"No, I know," Jack says. "Just be careful about what you say to them from now on. For their sake, and for yours."

I don't want to admit he's right, but I've been so eager for some bit of hope, something to pull me from my despair. Jack steps away, leaving me alone, and as my fear crests the tingling in my veins returns. I stand on the side of my ship, staring into the glittering ocean and inhaling the salt of the sea, doing my best to rid myself of this feeling.

I don't have the chance. "Serena!" Nadia yells, nearly swallowed by the shouts of, "Captain!" from the back of the ship.

I spin around and see the ship bearing down on us. A ship with white sails, but this is no travel or merchant ship. I run to Nadia's side and take her spyglass, and I curse when I look through. I don't need to see the flag with two crossed swords; I only need to see the all-female crew and the girl standing at the edge, a smile aimed at me.

Alina Ortega. And she's about to catch us.

13

"*H*ow did she even find us?" I shout. I don't wait for an answer; I bolt into my chambers to get my cutlass, and by the time I return, there she is.

I don't know how she found us, but she must have hung back while we were at anchor. It's the only way she could have caught up to us so quickly.

110 pounds of pure ignoramus. She's the one who hired Allensway to steal my mother's ruby necklace. We've known each other for years. After my parents died and I was trying to find more people for my crew, I started with the orphans on the streets. Alina was one of them. She wanted to be in my crew, and though she was skilled there was something lacking in her. Or maybe it was her attitude, the way she challenged me—just like she did when I cut her loose. She lost, which confirmed to me she wasn't worth my time. Not my best moment, probably.

After she lost, she created her own crew. And she'd made it her mission to come after mine. I am the best female captain on the sea, and I have the best crew. She thinks she can take that from me. Only one year younger than me, the only other female captain on the waters, an all-female crew. She has all the makings to be great, but she has always come second.

There's no outrunning her. Already her crew is working on docking the *Tigerlily*, but while my crew engages them, Alina is for me. She swings herself on board and stands in front of me, grinning maliciously as she holds her cutlass in one hand and twirls the end of her short, golden locks in the other, as if we were catching up and not about to murder each other.

"What are you doing here?" I spit, circling her.

"Miss me, S? I've been traveling the realm for the past six months. I've been so busy beating your record I hadn't gotten to stop and see if you got my message."

"Allensway's dead," I tell her. "And as to your claims on my record? Doubtful." I laugh. "Very doubtful."

She lunges at me. I step aside and meet her blade with mine, and we break away.

"Why don't you just tell me what you want?" I demand as I dodge her swing.

She cuts low. I jump back. "I want that orb," she growls.

"How do you even know about that?"

"Oh, trust me," she purrs, dancing away, "you'll find out very shortly. Don't spoil the fun, S."

"Never." I swing my sword and cut the side of her arm. Her confidence wavers. I grin. I'm still a more skilled swordswoman than she is, and she knows it.

More importantly, she thinks I have the orb.

Across the deck, my eyes find Jack. The orb is in his hand. He must not have had time to hide it, and while my crew engages hers, he has his own opponent to worry about.

Use it, you brainless prince!

Alina follows my gaze. She kicks me in the gut, knocking

me back, and takes off. Jack doesn't see her before she tackles him to the ground and wrestles the orb out of his hands.

"I got it!" she shouts. I leap for her and pin her down, pressing her face into the deck with one hand so hard I hope she gets splinters. Her grip on the orb loosens, and I take it from her.

It's too easy. She just laughs at me while I stand. She doesn't even fight back. In fact, once she gets back to her feet, she just walks away.

"Alexia," she calls out, her eyes on me. "Bring him now." As if on cue, the fighting around us quiets. Her crew pulls back, though they don't leave my ship. One of her mates brings someone onto the ship, a small figure that makes my chest tighten and my knees weaken. He has a bag over his head, but I recognize him even before they reveal his face.

Ben.

He shakes his head, squinting against the sudden light. His hands are tied behind his back, and there's a bandana over his mouth. I almost call to him, but Alina holds her sword up to his throat.

He stills and meets my eyes. He looks absolutely horrified.

My brother is in the hands of my enemy.

"If so much of a drop of blood exits his skin, I swear on my mother's grave, I will end you," I nearly growl. "All of you."

Alina's red-lipped grin widens. She knows she has me. "You're not as frightening as you think you are," she laughs.

Nadia runs to my side, chest heaving. I take her arm to keep her from lunging. "Give him back," she demands.

"I'd love to," Alina says. "I will call off my crew and give little Benjamin back to you without even a scratch . . . if you give me the orb."

I glance at the prince, but he's no help. He has a little brother too. He nods at me, like he won't be mad if I make the wrong choice.

"I can't do that," I reply hesitantly.

"Fine, then." Alina presses her sword into Ben's neck.

"Wait!" I yell. Alina stops. "Why do you even want the orb? How did you know we even have it?" I ask.

Her mask flickers. There's urgency there, beneath the carefully exuded certainty. "I've been spying on you, in Olovia," she says. "My hearties heard your oh-so-inspirational speech about journeying to get the orb. Really, S, you should be more careful about who hears your plans."

"Then you know we need the orb to defeat the magic that threatens the kingdom," Jack offers.

"That's what *you* need the orb for," she hisses. "If it's strong enough to save the kingdom, then it's strong enough to heal my sister."

The revelation silences me. All the years I've known Alina, I never knew she had a sibling, or any living family.

Alina's grip on her cutlass tightens, and she holds it to Ben with renewed dedication. "If you must know, my sister was struck with the dark spell," she says softly. "But it didn't kill her, it's keeping her unconscious. I need to help her."

There's a lot to unpack there, but I keep getting hung up. "You have a sister?"

"Unlike you, I don't parade my siblings around," she says. Her conviction is dropping, her voice a whisper that's desperate and angry. "She's only eight years old. She doesn't deserve to be in pain."

Nobody does. "I understand that." I drop my cutlass and hold out my hands. Harmless. "I don't want to be the reason your sister is dying, but the whole kingdom is dying. I need this orb."

Alina nods and presses her lips together. "So be it, then."

A line of blood appears on Ben's throat.

"Stop!" the prince shouts before I can. "Listen—"

"Alina," she helps him.

"Alina, you don't seem completely unreasonable. Serena's telling you the truth, we're on our way to defeat the darkness right now. If we can do that, it will free your sister, but we need that orb to do so. Please, just give Ben back and we can all leave in peace. I'll even give you compensation for your troubles," he offers. "Collateral, if you will."

Alina looks to me, then to him, her eyes narrowing. "Why should I believe a word you say?"

"You can trust me, Alina. I have my whole family and an entire kingdom I want to save. You can believe me. We want to do everything we can to save our people, and that includes you and your sister," Jack pleads. "Please, just call off your crew and release Ben so we can talk."

She stares at him thoughtfully, her gaze always trickling back to me with a disgusted look in her eyes. I can't take waiting. I drum my fingers anxiously against my leg as she takes her time, the unrest in my crew growing. The longer she stalls, the more worked up they'll get.

Her thoughtfulness curls into an unsettling grin.

"You know, I could always come with you," she says. "I don't believe that Serena, of all people, could do something so selfless. She won't give it to me."

I start to object, but she raises her hand. "I need that orb, and the only way to ensure I get it is if I come with you."

"No," I explode. "No way in hell that's happening, you boorish, heinous, bi—"

"Yes," the prince says suddenly.

I hit his arm. "What part of 'no' did you not understand? You have no idea what—"

"Do you want Ben to stay alive?" he asks. I hesitate. "Then let me talk." He turns away from me, turning on all of his stupid, princely charm. "Alina, as long as you release Ben, you and your crew may join us to ensure your sister's safety."

I tighten my grip on the orb as Alina glances over at me. At the moment, I can't tell who I hate more, Alina or Jack. Why the hell would he assume I would ever want to work with Alina Ortega, of all people? I hate her with every fiber of my being, and I'll get Ben back another way, preferably ending with my cutlass through her heart.

Alina seems to consider Jack's offer seriously, and before I can object she says, "Deal." She shoves Ben away from her and I catch him. "I'm not bringing my whole crew. I can't have all of us associating with the riffraff."

I hardly hear her. I untie Ben's arms and legs and he pulls off the bandana, and though he's trying to say something to me I hug him tightly. I never want to let him go.

"Hey, hey, hey . . . you're okay now," I whisper in his ear, trying to calm him down. I look daggers at Alina over his shoulder.

She meets my gaze coldly. "Alexia, tell the others to stand down!" she shouts.

I hate her. Rage builds in me and I hold Ben tight as he turns back around and Nadia embraces him. I'm more than angry at Alina, and at the prince plague. He doesn't need to know she's my enemy. This is my ship, and he promised me it would be my rules.

While Alina speaks to her crew and mine mills uncertainly, I pull the prince plague aside. Shove him, really. He's lucky I need him for this, otherwise I'd let him swim with the sharks.

"Are you out of your mind?" I nearly shout.

"I did you a favor," he shoots back. "She was going to kill him, do you get that? She was going to kill *your brother*. I know how much you love him, Serena. Her sister is just a little girl, and what about my brother? We could use a few extra people in case things go horribly wrong."

I don't want sense from him. I don't want the plan and what-ifs and his lack of consideration. "You're unbelievable. Besides nearly *killing me*, you have no idea what she's done to me." I storm off into my chambers.

We would have saved Alina's sister, anyway. She doesn't need to come. I refuse to speak to that girl and I have the scar to prove why I don't need to.

I slam the door so hard it sounds like the wood cracks. It's happening again. I'm furious, and when I'm furious, I'm only *furious* . . . but this anger, this rage . . . it's more powerful than anything I have ever felt before. I close my eyes and see red. I clench my fists and a storm rages in my skull.

Every time my emotions spike, it's there. After what Queen Iana said, I know it's the dark magic amplifying everything I think and feel. Nobody wants to get on my bad side when things are normal. Now? Ill-tempered doesn't quite describe it.

Nadia comes into my room, opening and closing the door and otherwise acting like I'm not throwing a fit. "Hey, I know you're peeved, but you should actually be thanking Jack for saving Ben's life. I don't think there was another way out of that situation."

"I could have killed her," I reply. "You remember what she did."

Nadia holds her hands out in supplication. "I know that,

and believe me, I still loathe her. But what if what happened to her sister happened to Ben? You would do the same thing. And once this is over, you never even have to see her again. Just like the prince said."

"I can't work with her," I say. Every time I look at her I get angry, and every time I get angry, that same sensation rushes through my veins. I can't allow it to take over me.

After my parents were killed, after Alina and I quarreled, our crews came into contact with each other a lot. I often thought she planned it that way, and knowing she'd sent spies to watch me in Olovia only added to that theory. She spread lies about my parents, about their deaths; she nearly killed me.

I don't know if I can ever forgive her for that. But seeing the way Nadia's looking at me, I suppose I can *try* to be in the same room as her.

Who am I kidding? Jack and Nadia are right. I suppose there was no other way that she would give me my brother back. But taking him in the first place is what ticked me off the most. Almost killing me is one thing, threatening Ben is another.

The heat in my veins surges. I need to stay calm. If I don't, I fear I'll have another vision.

Nadia's patient with me. She takes my shoulders and squeezes gently. "I'm going to make sure nobody's killing each other. Come out when you're ready."

What goes unsaid is that I'm acting like a little girl. I'm angry and upset and emotional. At this point, I can't even tell if it's the darkness or just me anymore. I suppose it's a little bit of both.

Alina's joining us whether I want her to or not. I should probably apologize to the prince, since he saved Ben, but I'd much rather continue yelling at him.

I take a few deep breaths before exiting the room and returning to the deck. Then I wish I hadn't. I almost stumble when I see Alina standing close to James, smiling and laughing and putting her hand on him briefly. Even more horrid is that it looks as though he's flirting back. It makes me sick to my stomach.

What could they possibly have to talk about so soon after she threatened to kill my brother?

Looking at them makes me want to puke out my insides. Maybe it will make my decision about him a little bit easier, but there's no denying the jealousy that flares within me.

"Are they saying anything important?"

I jump when the prince appears behind me abruptly. Since he's here, I grit my teeth and spit out my apology. "I was just coming to find you actually. I'm . . . sorry," I said. "For snapping at you. Even if I had every reason, because she is the most odious person on the planet, and you're going to find out one way or another. But . . . thank you for saving Ben."

"You're welcome," he says, looking relieved. Then he nods to Alina and James, still getting cozy with each other. "And if you have feelings for him, you might want to tell him before it's too late." He sounds almost sorry to say so.

I consider that maybe James isn't flirting with her, but Alina's trying so incredibly hard with him. I roll my eyes and walk past them, looking for Ben, who seems to have been swallowed by the rest of the crew.

"Hey, you're here!" Nadia says as I take position at the front of the ship. "Feeling better?"

"Definitely," I lie. I place my hands on the ship's railing, trying to hide my sudden dizziness as I lean out over the sea. Nadia's voice is drowned out by a sudden whisper in my head. *Find me.* It isn't a vision, just words, over and over again, that pull appearing, making my head spin. The winds of the ocean carry the voice on its breeze. I listen to it speak, trying to recognize the voice, but I can't stop it. My body aches like it's starving.

I shake my head. I want the voice *out*.

"Serena, what's wrong?" Nadia asks. She takes my shoulder, but this time physical contact doesn't break the spell. "Serena, you're scaring me." I try to reply—try to do anything—but I can't move. I can't stop the whisper in my ears, can't shift my focus away from it. "Somebody!" Nadia shouts. "James!"

But it's not James who comes. "Oh no, not again." It's Jack. "I got her." He pulls my arm over his shoulder and we're moving, the prince taking most of my weight as he and Nadia guide me back to my room. The door slams loudly, and I know we're alone, and the quiet and familiarity of my bedroom is enough to silence the voice and pull me back to reality.

I blink, catching my balance on my table and falling into a chair. "Another vision?" Jack asks.

"Not quite," I say, and I explain what happened.

Nadia looks at the prince, then at me. "Wait, you've been having these and you never told me?"

"I didn't tell anyone," I tell her. "I'm sorry. I couldn't. I have no idea what these are or what they mean . . ." I remember what I was on deck for. "I was looking for Ben. Can you find him for me?"

Neither of them look like they want to leave. Maybe I look miserable enough, though. They exchange glances and exit the room.

Minutes later, Ben's here. He knocks softly before entering and sits down beside me. "Hey, you wanted to see me?"

I hug him fiercely. "I'm just glad you're safe," I say.

"I'm all right," Ben says, false bravado sneaking into his tone. "I knew she wouldn't hurt me." He isn't telling me something. I want to press him, but he's old enough to tell me in time, when he's ready.

Just like I'm ready to tell him everything. "I need to tell you a few things."

He's quiet, as I tell him of our journey into the Realm of Magic. About Tellerous, my visions, and the feeling of my connection to the darkness. He's my brother; out of everyone on the ship, he deserves to hear this first.

His brow furrows as he listens. He refuses to meet my eyes when I finish, and then he says, "What that queen said, about you and the magic. Does that mean—"

"I don't know. But we are going to try to figure it out," I assure him.

"You're going to need this, then." Ben pulls our mother's ruby necklace out of his pocket.

I grin at the sight of the red stone and tuck it back into my own pocket. "Thank you."

"I'm sorry I wasn't there with you, Serena, to find that information. That must not have been easy to go through."

I muss his hair. "Aren't you sounding mature." He knocks my hand away, but that smile is there. "Well, the important thing is that you're here now. Want to tell me how Alina even got to you?"

He snorts. "How else? She came storming into the tavern and threatened to kill me if I didn't tell her where you were. She told the truth, about the spies. They sent her a letter telling her of your journey." He pauses, looking down at his lap. "Serena, there is something that I must tell you about that. I was waiting for the right time and I guess this a good a time as any. You see, Will did his best to protect me—and I don't think anyone did it on purpose. I think it was more of a reflex, but . . ." He exhales heavily. Something is weighing on him and he can't say it.

I'm not sure I want to hear. "Go on," I prod.

"Will is gone," Ben says quickly.

My heart stops. "What do you mean, gone?"

"Will tried to protect me from Alina, but she—she . . ." Ben's voice grows soft. "Serena, Will's gone."

14

I'm still not quite sure what he's saying, but as it sinks in I struggle to determine the exact feeling making my heart crumble.

"I'm sorry, she did what?" I hear myself ask.

Then I'm off my bed and bolting through the corridor, up the stairs to the deck. I search for Alina among the crew as Ben shouts behind me, but I hear none of what he says. I'm enraged. Crushed. William was all I had left. He was the reason I picked myself up after Lennard and my mother died.

She's easy to find, still talking with James. Neither of them notice my approach, and I only know I've hit her when I feel the sting across the back of my hand.

Alina goes down. I hit her again, dropping on top of her, tearing at her hands covering her face. "How could you do that?" I scream. "You murderer!"

Hands take my shoulders and suddenly the prince is holding me back. The whole crew has flooded the deck to see what all of the chaos is about. I squirm in Jack's arms, still screaming as the few crew members Alina had brought on board pick her up and place themselves between us. My vision blurs with tears and I wish I'd been able to grab my cutlass.

"What the hell was that about?" the prince shouts, trying to get me to hear him over my cries. He wraps his arms around me, and just like that, I weaken. My anger fades to grief and I let him hold me, close my eyes so I won't see Alexia or Alina, or the regret thick in Alina's eyes.

"Alina killed William," Ben whispers in the prince's ear.

Nadia must have been close enough to overhear. "Everybody back to what you were doing," she demands. "Now!"

And I know why. If the rest of the crew finds out what happened, they'll tear Alina and her comrades apart in two seconds flat. I wouldn't be able to stop them. I wouldn't want to. Reluctantly, they all leave us.

"Come on," Alexia says to Alina, "let's get you cleaned up." She makes sure to give me the dirtiest look.

"I want her off my ship," I finally say.

"I'm sorry, Serena," Jack says. "I truly am sorry. Alina knows we have the orb, and I don't think we have a choice but to keep her on the ship. You know she'll just take the orb and go. But I truly am sorry."

I stop listening. I'm too busy thinking of ways to get away with pushing Alina overboard to retain whatever he's telling me.

I look up. Judging by the position of the sun, it's only the middle of the afternoon. How long has it been since we sailed from the Realm of Magic? I almost lost Ben, I found out I might have a genetic connection to the Cretion magic, and I've lost the last parent I had. I can't keep losing everyone I care about.

"Is it okay if I just want to be alone for a while?" I say, my voice thick. I feel like my mouth has been filled with cotton.

I shrug the prince off before he can answer my question. I see Ben whispering to Nadia, and she's about to storm off when Ben pulls her back.

Jack's wrong. We can get rid of Alina. Since he clearly isn't going to let me do so on my own ship, I'll wait. As soon as this is all over, I will hunt her down like a dog and kill her, no matter what it takes.

I didn't even get to say goodbye to Will.

Sure, he was on the older side. I knew he wouldn't live forever, but if he was going to die it should have been from natural causes. He wasn't a pirate, that had never been his life.

I close the door to my quarters and crawl under my covers, burying my face into my pillows. The more I sob, the more the connection to the magic in my veins grows, which just makes me sob harder. This pain . . . it's my fault Will's gone. He's gone because of me, because I thought I could keep him and Ben safe. Because he let me into his life— because I let him—he's gone.

When we get back to Olovia, I'll have to dry my eyes and push all of these emotions aside. But for right now, alone, I will allow myself to be angry and disheartened.

I lay in bed until the tears stop, then I slide out and dig through my hope chest. There's a small box inside, and inside is a silver pin made in the shape of a lion. William gave it to me the day after my parents died. He'd said it was his mother's, and she'd given it to him before she died. It symbolizes bravery, and strength, which Will always said I had.

Seeing it, holding it in my hand, I no longer want to cry. It's just like the first time he'd given it to me, when the pain of my parents' death made me want to curl up in a ball and never see the light of day again. But he'd shown me this kindness, and I knew that what I needed was to be strong. It was up to me to take care of Ben, who had only been ten at the time, and all of the crew members' children whose parents were no longer there. They were my family now; they were my crew. What they needed was a tenacious leader to train and guide them, so that's what I became. I learned from the best, so I became the best. In order to uphold our parents' legacies, I worked diligently with the other kids for months and months before they were ready to go into battle.

That was what William had given me. In that moment, that silver lion, and in every moment since.

He was so proud of how far we've come, and he'd be proud of what we're about to set out to accomplish. I place the silver lion back in the box and kiss the top of the box before placing it back in my hope chest, burying it carefully under all of the other items in there. If he were here, he would tell me to push through the pain. He would tell me he died honorably.

Not that it justifies anything. But now, I need to push him aside—no matter how difficult that may be. Now, we have a job to do.

Alone in my chambers, I pull myself together and wipe off all my tears. I crack my knuckles and my neck, take one more deep breath, and leave my room once more. It's time to discuss the matter at hand.

"Joseph, keep it steady," I say to him coarsely when I find him at the wheel. Sitting thoughtfully in her navigator's seat, Nadia looks at me like she wants something to do too.

"Nadia, grab Ben, James, Alina, and Jack. Meet me in the study across from my chambers."

"Even Alina?" she asks softly.

I hesitate, breathing deeply as I say, "Yes. Even Alina."

Then I go to the study, clear the large table in the middle, and I wait. Jack is the first to arrive, followed by Nadia and Ben and James. Alina's last. When she walks into the room, I catch sight of the scratch on the side of her cheek and the small bruise on the side of her head, along with a black eye and cut lip. I straighten smugly. She sits down at the round wooden table in front of a bookshelf nearest the door, trying to ignore the daggers shooting out of my eyes and into her stupid face.

But I need to get a hold of my anger. If I lash out, I'm afraid that my visions will come back. Or worse. Although it's not easy, I bite my tongue. If she's going to stay, she's going to help us.

"Tellerous is coming for Olovia," I say. "We need to stop him before it's too late. Our first stop is Elias, in Olovia, and we're hoping he can tell us more about Tellerous and the Cretion magic, but once that's done we need to be ready. If we could ambush Tellerous somehow, then I think that might be our best option."

"Is there even a way to locate him?" Ben asks.

"There must be," Nadia says. "He may be all powerful, but he is still a person. He has to be somewhere."

The prince jumps in. "Queen Iana told us he resides in the Dark Realm, but we don't know how to get there. Up until a few hours ago, we didn't even know that was a real place. Even so, he's most likely not there. He's trying to cast his spell, make it stronger, and he's looking for his child."

"Well, isn't his location obvious?" Alina chimes in softly.

"How do you figure?" Jack asks.

"Think about it," she says, leaning forward. "The spell he cast is over Olovia, hence the enormous cloud of magic in the sky If he's looking for his child, the best way to draw them out is to use the magic, and he'll be there, waiting."

I shake my head. "It's too obvious. Besides, what if his child isn't in Olovia?"

Her eyes roll into the back of her head.

"No, no she may have a point," James says. "He may not be there now, but he will definitely come to see his handi-work. We just need to figure out when."

"And just how would we do that?" I shoot back. I'm not imagining it. James is backing Alina up. They're sitting close together. Is he just trying to make me mad? I want to tell him what Alina did; it's so hard not to. I cross my arms. "Just because the magic is there, that doesn't necessarily mean his child is."

"We don't know who his child is or where in the realm they could be," Jack adds, backing me up.

"But we need to start somewhere," James says.

"Then why don't I say what we're all thinking?" Alina stands and turns to me. "James filled me in, and you're all dense if you keep denying it. The answer that you're searching for is obvious: he's looking for Serena." She smirks. "I saw you on deck. You went so still and nobody could revive you. I saw it before, only my sister hasn't come out of it yet."

She's the third person to say it out loud. Only, she said it in a full sentence, and it sounded worse. I sink deeper into my chair and look around at the others who wear the same expressions on their faces: doubt, concern, fear, confusion. Nobody will look at me, and I know they silently agree with her. Knowing that it could be true is crushing.

I feel it before it strikes. It's familiar now, when it hits my body, when my heart begins to race and my eyes widen with fear. I swallow it quickly. "Someone please say something," I whisper. "Someone disagree with her."

They all look around at each other.

Jack rises and begins pacing. "Okay, you know what? Let's not jump to conclusions. We'll wait to see what Elias has to say. He'll know."

"Oh, don't worry, S, it's a good thing," Alina says, recovering some of her sass as the world crashes around me. "After all, the apple doesn't fall far from the tree. We won't even have to wait to see Elias, we can just use Serena as bait, and we'll know then if she's Tellerous's daughter or if she's just dying."

"There's just one flaw in your plan," I snap.

"What?"

"Everything!" I slam my hand on the table, and the whole structure shakes. "I am not Tellerous's daughter—"

"You're in denial—"

"—and even if I was I would not be using myself as bait," I continue. "He'd take me before you'd even get the chance to ambush him."

"You don't know that. And it's the closest to a plan we'll get." She leans forward, resting her elbows on the table, one arm folded over the other.

I stand, my chair crashing to the floor behind me. "Do you forget *he has magic*? You are such a—"

"Enough!" Jack yells. Nadia, James, and Ben shrink back in their chairs, too, as if they're the target of his outburst. "I get it, you two hate each other, and you have every right to. But right now we have more important fish to fry. Alina, we're not using Serena as bait or doing anything else until we hear what Elias has to say, and Serena? You don't have to disagree with everything she has to say just because you don't like her."

We're quiet a moment, but I see the look that says Alina isn't going to let Jack get away with yelling at her, and I'm going to let him get away with interrupting me.

"Actually," Alina says, "it *is* a great idea because—"

I groan. "Oh, shut up! We already ruled out—"

"You are always—"

"Me? Oh no, I'm not the one who—"

"Oh, will you *stop screaming at each other, for the love of the gods*!"

Alina and I both pull back, staring at Nadia in the corner of the room. I've never heard Nadia yell before. Or use that tone. It rattled the ship and sent a chill down my spine, but once I'm quiet I hear my pulse rushing in my ears and I wonder if it's best if I bite my tongue for the rest of this meeting. I remain quiet as the others continue, their conversation fading as Alina's accusation repeats itself over and over in my head.

I never knew my father. My mother always said he was an awful man. But I can't make myself believe that an inconsequential pirate like me is the daughter of a magical madman, and all on the say-so of a queen I've only met once.

I force myself to look around the room. If I speak again, I'll go off on Alina. Looking at her isn't any better, because it looks like James has moved closer to her. I cross my arms tighter and look away.

I know that I said that I need time to figure things out, but I didn't think he'd find someone else, especially if that someone is Alina Ortega. It's worse than betrayal. If he wants to get to know her, of all people, he should talk to me first. Even so, it doesn't bother me as much as I thought it would. I don't want them near each other, but I'm not angry so much as confused.

"Serena, are you even listening?" Alina asks, her voice cutting through my attention.

"Hm?"

"I was in Olovia last. The darkness in the sky has now stretched over a little more than half of the kingdom. As I was explaining, that's why I've been assuming that means Tellerous is there."

"Well, we're going there anyway. We'll figure it out then," I remind her, half-hearted bitterness in my voice.

I'm going to puke out my insides. I excuse myself to get some air and go straight to the wheel. "Joseph, I'll take it from here for a while. Go take a break."

"Sure, Captain," he says. "You all right?"

I nod and grab onto the wheel, the tug of the *Tigerlily* and the sway of the waves at my fingertips. Staring into the ocean, looking for the horizon, actually settles me. The calming sound of the waters and the gentle breeze encompassing me like a blanket makes me relax.

After some time, Jack joins me, wisely keeping his distance. "We have some ideas now, at least," he says, standing behind me. "We decided to think about it on our own and come back if we have any ideas. That includes you."

"That's great," I reply drily.

"You have every right to feel the way you do. But you know we don't have any other choice than to work together."

"I know that," I reply. "And I told you. Didn't I tell you who she was when you let her on my ship? Why do you think I left the room? I can feel it, Jack. I can feel the darkness and it keeps on getting stronger. I'm trying to not allow it to influence me, but it's not that easy."

"I know," he says. I look at him. "I see it in you. You did the right thing, leaving. And if it makes you feel any better, after all of this is over I'll look the other way if you get your revenge on her."

I chuckle softly. "That actually does help."

Jack grins at me before he walks away. I almost call out to him, not wanting him to leave, or at least not wanting him to leave me with a strange, tingly feeling in my stomach. It's not the magic; at least, I don't think it is.

Soon after, Nadia pulls up her chair and sits down beside me, her compass in her hand.

"I'm sorry I screamed at you," she says, not sounding sorry at all.

I smile. "I forgive you."

"It's all I could think of to make you guys stop fighting."

"Don't be sorry, I get it. I should be the one apologizing. We were being inconsiderate to you guys." I sigh. "It doesn't matter. I don't plan on speaking with her, even if she is on the ship with us. I just want to get this over with so I can finally kill her."

15

---

*A*fter sundown, I give the wheel back to Joseph and do my best to try and fall asleep.

But it's another sleepless night. Shocker. It doesn't take me long to give up and steal out of my chambers to lie on the deck and look up at the stars. Nobody else is on deck but Joseph, and the quiet and the rush of water around us is so peaceful. I think of William. Whenever my parents would go on a journey that I was too young to go on, they left me with Will. He taught me how to read, and I took my first steps in front of him. He gave me a home after I lost my mother and Lennard. He didn't care that my parents were pirates, or that I would become one too. He was just a good man.

He saw the best in me, even when I didn't see it myself. He was the only reason I always came back to Olovia. I always knew he would be waiting there for me whenever I returned from a voyage, and now, even knowing that he's not there, it doesn't feel like he's gone. I realize I don't want to return, to dock at Olovia and not find him in his tavern.

I'm lucky that I even got to have him in my life.

I hear Nadia's light steps before she sits next to me. "Hey, I figured you'd be out here," she says, looking up at the sky with me. "You've never been the best sleeper, ever since we were kids."

I blink, remembering. "I could always hear my mother crying in her sleep," I admit. "She had nightmares every night."

"Really? I never heard a thing. What were the nightmares of?"

"She never told me. She loathed talking about it, and her feelings in general."

"I know someone else like that."

Ignoring the jab, I add, "I wish I knew what was going on with her. Things that seemed so normal just aren't anymore. The secret of who my biological father was, the nightmares, that book she gave me . . ." I sigh.

Nadia makes a humming sound. "I was a heavy sleeper. Well, except for the year my father died. My mother cried then, too, but every time I checked on her she'd force herself to stop."

I turn my gaze from the stars to Nadia. She doesn't talk about her father often. He died when we were ten after contracting Hillenonia, a lung disease. I remember that year more vividly. Nadia and Sawyer both were quite different then, getting used to their father being gone.

"How often do you think about them?" I ask. "Our parents."

"All the time," she replied. "Being at sea isn't always easy. Being home isn't either. There are so many painful memories everywhere. And not just of them, the entire crew."

"Then why do you stay at sea?" I wonder, not really knowing the answer.

"Because our hearties are all I have left. My parents taught me that your crew is your family, and that we must always follow the code and stick together. And then there's Sawyer. He's always loved the idea of being a pirate, even more than me, and he wanted to stay. So I stay too. How you feel about Ben is how I feel about Sawyer." She pauses, and then she elbows me playfully. "Besides, how could I leave my best friend behind?"

I sit up and lean against her, my head on her shoulder and my arm looped through hers. "I truly am glad that you've stayed. I don't know what I'd do without you, especially now."

"Me too. Serena?" Her voice wavers.

"Hm?"

"I'm sorry about Will. I wasn't as close with him as you were, but he was always kind to me and Sawyer. I loved being in that tavern, around his good energy. It made things even better whenever we would come home from one of our victories. I wanted to kill Alina when Ben told me, but I realized I wouldn't have done it for me. I was about to kill her for you." She looks down, and I can't tell what she's feeling. Pain and grief, yes. Sadness. Regret?

"Yeah, I know what you mean," I say. "I will kill her."

"I never had a doubt. Scurvy dog," Nadia spits.

I lift my head from her shoulder and move so I'm sitting directly in front of her. "Nadia, do you think that what Alina said is true?"

She rolls her eyes. "You'll have to be more specific. Most of what comes out of her mouth is bull crap."

"What she said about Tellerous," I say in almost a whisper. "And about me."

She holds her breath for a moment, looking at her lap

again and pulling at the hem of her shirt. "Um, I really don't know. And I don't think we'll know until we find Elias. He knew where to find the orb and that it might help, and though we have to be ready that he may not have all the answers we need, we may be able to figure out something from whatever he does tells us," she answers.

I stare at her. She tried to dodge it, but she can't lie to me. She agrees, even if she won't admit it. It's the uncertainty that scares me, hers and mine. All of these emotions are jumbled up in my head, and they keep adding up. Heartbreak and rage and bewilderment—it's all too much. I used to have my parents for this, then when I lost them I had Will. I don't know how to handle this without them.

I drop my head into my hands, the weight in my chest pulling me down. I think it's the magic, at first; I prefer it to be the magic. But my lack of breath, the hitch in my throat —it's not magic. This is pure panic.

"Hey, it's okay," Nadia says, pulling me into her embrace as the tears start and don't stop. "Breathe, Serena. Breathe. Come here."

I want to stop so badly. I hate crying. It makes a mess, and it makes me feel so helpless. Especially since this isn't just crying—it's bawling. It's loud and snotty and my face is a waterfall. And I hate myself for it. Will once told me that shoving your emotions away will only make things worse in the end, that everything I shove away will bubble up to the surface and explode. I never believed it. It never happened to me before. But here we are. Guess Will got the last laugh.

What happened to my humanity switch? On and off. This uncertainty isn't me. My body physically hurts from the pain, and I don't mean the wounds the Flipperfore left in my skin. My shoulders ache from sobbing, my throat burns from gulping in the cold night air. I remain in Nadia's arms until I'm able to stop blubbering, her tight embrace the only comforting thing I have. Eventually I stop, but we remain locked together in silence under the stars, leaning against each other, the only rocks we have.

I feel better when we call it a night. No more certain, but more at peace.

Four hours later, Sawyer wakes me. It's dawn and time to relieve Joseph. I sluggishly roll out of bed and pull my coat on over a fresh shirt. I brush through my hair and replace the bandages on my arm and back.

The golden sun rising in the early morning sky shines brightly, nearly blinding me as I walk out on deck. The water shimmers like a thousand diamonds, a spectacle I'll never tire of and never want to look away from. Next to Queen Iana's castle, it's one of the most beautiful things I've ever seen. For that moment, and for a short while after, everything is calm.

Until Adam comes on deck, irritable and shouting and complaining about the state of the deck and the knots holding the rowboats in place. Barking orders, taking control of the activity on deck, demanding tasks that had been done to be redone. I glare at him, my hands tightening on the wheel as my temperature rises. That's James's job as my first mate, not his.

"Adam!" I scream, my gaze never leaving the horizon, my hands glued to the wheel. "I swear on Arnav's honor if you say one more word—"

He silences and scurries off. I exhale but the anger remains. One day, words won't be enough. One day, I won't be able to abstain from physically harming him. Or anyone, given the way this connection to the magic is strengthening.

After the exchange, Ben joins me at the wheel, hands in

his pockets, eyes scanning the sea. "You know, you are doing the right thing."

"Not throwing Adam in the brig?" I ask.

He laughs. "Keeping your anger in check, not hurting Alina." He grows serious, then. "Will died trying to protect me. It's all my fault, Serena, and it's the worst thing I've ever seen . . . experiencing it, watching it . . ." He sighs. "I know that it must not have been easy, keeping yourself from her. I wanted to let you, then I wanted to kill her myself."

"Take that back right now," I say sharply. "Ben, you did absolutely nothing wrong, and avenging Will is not your responsibility."

It hadn't occurred to me how Ben might be handling this, witnessing the closest thing he had to a father die, all because of Alina. My hatred flares anew, at Alina and at my own thoughtlessness.

"I wasn't there to protect you," I hear myself say, "and I'm sorry. I should have brought you with me in the first place. That makes his death my fault." Ben is silent, and I bump him with my shoulder. "But what's important now is that you're safe."

"You know, I really do consider you a hero," he says.

"Now I think you went a little too far," I chuckle.

"No, I disagree. I know how much you love pirating—the traveling, the jewels, the fighting . . . keeping Mother and Father's legacies alive. But I also know you're not really a bad person. You're risking your life to save the world. I just want people to see that."

"That's really sweet, Ben," I say slowly, testing my response, uncertain how to say what I want without tearing him down. "But you know, I am perfectly content with the way people see me. I don't need approval from others. I don't need to be a good person. I just need you."

Finally, Ben looks at me, grinning, and he throws his arms around me while I keep hold of the wheel. And I realize I'm actually grateful that I have him on the ship now, despite what happened to get him here.

For a split second, everything's okay.

16

The vision hits me in a flash.

I have no warning. I'm on deck with Ben, then I hear the roaring sound of a thousand whispers, a thousand tiny needles stabbing into my ears. The ship disappears —*Ben* disappears.

I see the same black cloud again, but this vision is much different than the others. The cloud charges into my body, courses through my veins, tears into my insides. I can't stop it. I can't breathe as my heart struggles to pump the particles from my body, straining and stretching. My hands slip from the wheel and I have a moment of clarity as the ship rocks and swerves against the winds. The last thing I see is Ben grabbing the wheel.

I fall to the deck, my vision darkening, my veins searing. The presence of every person on the *Tigerlily* presses in on me, but I can't see or hear them. I grit my teeth, the scream building in my throat. I try to snap out of it but I can barely even hear myself in my own head over all of the whispers. My hands press to my ears, squeezing, and I can't hold it any more.

I scream.

With that cry, everything goes black.

I'm not unconscious. I can't open my eyes, I can't move. I'm weak, but I'm still able to hear everything around me.

I just can't move or open my eyes. I'm scared, but I can't ask what happened. People surround me, the air thick and warm with their bodies, their voices.

I hear Jack's voice—"We need to get her to Elias"—then Alina's—"We won't be back in Olovia until tomorrow." I strain myself, trying to use every muscle in my body and directing every last bit of strength into my vocal cords. Nothing happens. I can't move, and I can't speak.

But I am moving. I recognize the feeling of the prince's arms under me. The warm sun vanishes from my skin and the prince places me on my bed. Nobody speaks, but I don't think he ever even leaves the room. Not when Nadia insists on remaining—her voice shaking and full of fear—not when Alina, Ben, and James join them and their little conversation offers no answers.

"What can we do?" Ben asks.

"We can use the orb," Alina suggests.

"But we don't even know how to use it," Jack reminds them.

I could have lain there for a thousand years. Unable to move, unable to even sleep, impatience tugging at me to stay awake, to listen, to try to make a sound. Nothing happens.

Time, in that state, is strange. So many thoughts rush around my head, but none of them take shape. I spend twenty-four hours chasing them, until I hear my hearties mention with relief that we'll be docking in five minutes.

As Prince Pinhead carries me off of the boat, I hear the crew talking about the sky. Whispering, really. The darkness has finally reached the ocean's edge. The air is cooler, and there's panic in the streets like I haven't felt before. I can still hear the agonizing cries of the people—louder, sharper, more often. The prince's grip tightens around me as he walks forward.

I don't need to see anything to know we need to speed things up if we're going to defeat Tellerous. If Olovia is any indication, unleashing this spell on the world would be disastrous, and if that happens it'll be too late.

"We're making our way to the Olovian woods now," Jack says softly. He narrates what's happening, every move they make, describing the town and then the trees. I can almost feel him staring at me the entire time he's carrying me in his arms. "Serena, I don't know if you can even hear me, but I promise you that we will help you." He sighs and lowers his voice. "Actually, maybe it's a good thing you can't hear me. I have a confession to make—"

"Jack!" Nadia interrupts him. "Come on, you're falling behind. I know you're carrying a whole person, but honestly, the girl is as light as a feather. Hurry it up, we're almost to Elias's hut."

I want to know what he was going to say. I try to ask him, but I suppose it will just have to wait.

"Is this it?" Ben asks.

"That's it," Jack confirms.

"It looks so . . ." Alina struggles to describe it, and even if it's *Alina*, I want to know what it looks like, where we are.

"Not like I imagined a sorcerer's house to look," Nadia finishes kindly, though her voice betrays her lack of impression. She coughs and says, "Ben, James, Alina—stay out here with the rest of the crew. This shouldn't take too long."

"But I want to—"

"Ben, I don't want to hear it right now. You either, Alina," Nadia snaps.

Someone knocks on a door. "Elias?" Jack calls. A creak indicates the door opening, and I know we're inside when the scent on the air changes. Nadia and the prince continue to call out his name.

The voice comes from nowhere. "I assumed you'd come." The sudden sound of his voice makes my heart race. Nadia takes my hand, out of surprise, maybe; there's a lot of anxious energy radiating from her. The prince's demeanor hardly changes; he's comfortable since Elias is his tutor.

"My friend," Nadia says, "she—"

"Fainted from a vision?" Elias asks.

"How did you know that?"

He chuckles. "I know many things. I predicted Prince Jack here would use the map to find the orb." Jack makes a sound, but Elias cuts him off. "That is why I gave it to you, after all. Now come, lay her down right here."

"Can you wake her up?" Nadia asks.

"Give me the orb."

The last time I touched the orb, I fell off a mountain. I'm not sure what to expect this time, but the power washes over me immediately. This time, the magic is warm, light even. It's gentle on my skin, but even so it's restrained, something binding it, keeping it from its true form. Elias, maybe?

I think I understand now why Queen Iana kept this object far away from her castle. And why she chose a Flipperfore to defend it. When the magic touches my skin, I feel so powerful, a rush of energy flooding my veins like lightning.

I gasp and open my eyes finally, eager for the light and to see everyone hovering over me. They help me sit up, and I look around, realizing I'm lying down on a table directly across from the door that looks like it's made from a tree branch. Next to the door is a little breakfront with sculptures on the visible shelves. There's a spiral staircase right next to us and a white door above the landing. To the right is a large bookshelf against the gray walls and a sofa to sit on. To the left is a door that leads into another room. Nadia didn't know how to describe Elias's little home. I'd call it charming.

I shift my focus to Elias. He's the definition of a sorcerer, the model for stereotypes. Dark brown robes, long white beard, a bald head. There are wrinkles under his amber eyes and he holds the orb in his hands with ease as he leans in and studies my reaction.

Like a spell has broken, Nadia wraps her arms around me. "Oh, thank the gods you're okay."

Jack looks ready to collapse from relief. "Thank you so much for waking her," he says to the old man.

"Of course." Elias helps me off the table and back onto my feet, steadying me when I lose my balance. "Now, Serena, is it? Tell me what you saw."

My head is still spinning, but at Jack's encouragement I tell him everything I can. Four visions—five? "Each one continues to get worse and worse."

"And do you see anything in these visions?" Elias asks.

I nod. I explain seeing myself, the cloud of black dust, or both in the same vision. "Can you tell me what that means?"

Elias places his hands on his hips and stares down at the floor thoughtfully. After a few breaths, he then jerks his head up. "What did Queen Iana tell you about Tellerous?" he asks.

"Only that he's behind the darkness in the sky, and the prophecy about the fourth to receive Cretion magic," Jack offers. "Oh, and that she went to school with him. . . . You knew him, too, didn't you?"

Elias leans against the table and folds his arms. He nods thoughtfully. "That is quite true. The three of us were at Renayhem together. I had just become a professor there when I met them. Tellerous was a teacher in training, and Iana was still a student learning how to control her magic. We spent many years together. The three of us became quite close."

"Not to be rude, but what does that have to do with me?" I ask, ready to finally understand what has been happening to me. Ready, I think, to find out if Iana's assumption is true.

Elias props himself up and points his finger upright, shaking it with a gleam in his eyes. "I was about to get to that, young lady. Queen Iana is correct, and the prophecy was foreseen by one of Tellerous's early relatives, the first one who obtained this unnatural magic. The prophecy states that Tellerous's child will be the fourth—and final— vessel of the magic, and also that this child's abilities will be even more powerful than Tellerous's, and more than one-hundred times as deadly." He looks around at the three of us, and like Nadia and Jack, his gaze settles on me. "You have figured it out by now, haven't you?" the sorcerer asks. "Why, Serena, you look just like him. Surely Queen Iana told you . . . ?"

I shake my head. Not because Iana hadn't already warned us, but because I want to reject what Elias is about to say out loud.

"Serena Jones," Elias says softly, almost kindly, "you are Tellerous's child, and the child the prophecy speaks of."

17

I had known this for a while. I didn't want to believe it, but hearing Elias confirm it puts me over the edge. It hits me like lightning. I hear him as if through a bubble, wanting to both deny it and succumb to the relief that floods through me that I don't have to use up any more energy doubting what I know to be the truth. The visions, the connection to the magic, the darkness Queen Iana felt in me. Even why my mother had the book in which I found the information about the dark magic.

But even having confirmation—knowing we aren't just guessing anymore—a feeling of panic fills me. Tellerous is my father. *Tellerous is my father?* How could my mother keep something like this from me? Tears threaten to form in my eyes. I have always wondered about my father, but now that I know the truth, I wish I was still oblivious. Envy overtakes me when I think of Ben. Envy that Lennard was his biological father and not mine, that Lennard was normal and human and my father is a magical mass murderer. It feels as if I've just been punched in the gut. Utterly betrayed. What happens to me when I obtain the magic? Why did Tellerous wait until *now* to cast this darkness?

So many questions, but all that comes out is, "How?"

"I know this is a lot to take in," Elias says. "But unfortunately, it is the truth."

The prince places his arm around me. Normally, I'd elbow him in the gut for it, but I'm too lost in my own thoughts to even move. Nadia moves forward, closer to Elias.

"So what the hell do these visions mean?" Nadia asks, almost as freaked out as I am.

Elias puts his hand on his chin, deep in thought as he walks the length of the room. "It is my assumption that these visions are Tellerous trying to send you a message. Either that, or the darkness itself is trying to warn you, somehow, with possible events of the future." Then he shakes his head. "No, Tellerous has always been highly clever, whether coming up with a way of teaching or if he had a plan. He is most definitely trying to tell you something. It wouldn't surprise me if this spell he cast, the darkness, was meant to help him find you and make contact. But Serena, if these visions continue to get worse, I am afraid your predicament goes beyond him sending a message, something much worse." He hesitates, and he looks at me like he's waiting for permission. I nod. "The progression of these visions seems to indicate that he is trying to-to *infuse* the darkness into you."

I feel sick to my stomach at his explanation. My legs wobble and the room spins and I think I'm ready to pass out.

"What do you mean?" Jack asks. He looks at me and then back at the sorcerer. "How?"

Elias stops moving, coming to a stop right in front of me.

"Well, I believe he is trying to speed up the prophecy. Technically, quickening the events is not against the rules of magic. But if this is the case, these visions will continue to mess with your mind, your body. These are painful, yes?"

I nod.

He sighs. "The pain will also get worse. The darkness would appear as a respite, and so the pain could subject you to giving in to the darkness."

I shudder at the thought. Worse? The visions could get *worse*? I don't know how much more of this I can take. I should never have gone with Jack when he showed up at the tavern; I knew this would turn out to be something more than I thought. I hate the idea of a prophecy, the idea that someone could be deciding what my life is supposed to be, and I refuse to accept my fate as someone else laid it out for me.

"Is there any possible way that we can stop the visions?" Jack asks.

"Unfortunately, there is not," Elias replies. "I understand that she is fighting them, but soon they may be too powerful to be stopped."

I finally speak up. "You said that the darkness could be trying to send a message or a warning to me. What kind of warning?"

"I believe it is trying to warn you about the power. You felt it all of those times, did you not?"

"And if it can't be stopped? What happens to me when I get the magic?" My voice shakes, my heart about to beat out of my chest.

"Then Tellerous will take you to the Dark Realm," Elias says. "The spell he is trying to cast, to combine the realms? He needs to combine your magic with his in order to accomplish it."

I remember what Iana said, about the previous hosts being weaker, and suddenly my anger toward my father becomes hatred toward myself. I've been having visions for days, but now I know why Tellerous is waiting so long to come after me. He's waiting for the magic to take me.

"Does he know where we are?" Nadia asks.

"Most likely." Elias shrugs. "Once she is connected, he'll be able to find her anywhere. But he will not come for Serena directly until a certain portion of the sky is filled with darkness. Timing is everything."

Nadia points her finger at him. "If you know him and what he's planning, then why can't you just stop him yourself?"

Elias rolls his eyes at Jack. "I would have thought Prince Jack could have figured that one out. Have you learned nothing from our tutoring sessions?" he scolds. "Prophecies are not to be taken lightly. It is against the rules of magic to interfere with a prophecy. There is a gruesome punishment given by the gods if one not associated with the prophecy attempts to get in the way. We must wait for it to play out, one way or another." He sighs and looks away, and suddenly his age seems to show on him. "Even if it wasn't against the rules, it would be futile for me to try to stop him. Dark magic is much more tenacious than light magic, much stronger than sorcery."

I fold my arms to contain the heavy weight that settles on my chest, and to stop trembling. If Elias, the most powerful sorcerer ever to live, can't stop Tellerous, then who can?

"You said my visions will keep getting worse?" I ask.

"Sadly, yes. And I must warn you that these visions will become more and more painful as Tellerous moves closer to enacting his plan. I am not certain what you will see, but you must brace yourself for what you will feel."

Great. Just when I thought things couldn't get any worse. I want to kill my father. I *need* to kill my father. For the sake of the kingdom and the realm, and all of the other realms. And for me.

Because I'm already a killer. I don't need dark magic to help me. Allensway, the Flipperfore, dozens more from my years at sea. If I fall under the influence of dark magic, what might happen? What about Ben? Nadia? My whole crew?

I place my hands in my pockets and tangle my fingers in the ruby necklace. It calms me as I process everything Elias has told us. I wish my mother had told me about this years ago.

Elias continues to speak. I watch the prince instead. Whenever he looks at me, my stomach flips. Nadia elbows me when she realizes I'm not paying attention.

"What will happen to her once she gets the magic?" the prince asks.

"Well, it depends," Elias says. "Every person is different when it comes to magic. Even if a prophecy predicts they will have it, nobody can say for sure to what extent or how it will manifest." Elias moves back over to the table.

This teetering into the unknown used to be something I loved. I loved the idea of adventure, new and exciting surprises every day. I loved fighting and the adrenaline of survival. But now? This unknown fills me with unease.

"So how can we stop him?" the prince asks. Suddenly, I'm grateful he's here.

Elias holds up the orb. "This orb will help, but it won't do much besides weaken his power a little bit. I do not know if you can kill him, but you'll need his own weapon. If you can get him to that point, it has to be just Serena."

I press my finger to my chest, "*Me*?" I ask. "Just me?"

"Yes. You're the only one who will have the power to do that. Anyone caught in the crossfire will likely not survive the encounter."

He must be joking. No. Sure, I want to kill him, but alone? There is no way I can kill my father on my own. Up until about ten minutes ago, I didn't even know he *was* my father.

Don't give in to the darkness. Kill my father. Save the realms. That's a lot of pressure to put on a teenage girl. But I've been feeling the pressure since the moment we stepped foot out of Iana's castle.

Nadia grabs my hand. "How is she expected to do that alone?"

Elias shrugs, unconcerned. "She will know when the time comes, and then she will have to decide."

Honestly, seeing Elias has just made everything worse, and it's leaving me even more confused.

Elias straightens and nods to Nadia and Jack. "Now, if you please, I must speak with Serena alone for a moment."

"But we—"

Elias points Jack to the door. "Get out."

They hesitantly leave as I switch positions with the old man, nervously leaning on the table, anxiously awaiting what Elias has to say.

"Now," he says softly, whispering as if wary of anyone eavesdropping, "there is something that I purposefully left out of the information that I gave you, something you alone should know. There is a bit of a catch that comes with obtaining the Cretion magic. The prophecy states that you are destined to receive the magic, but as I mentioned, what happens next is up to you. There are two possible outcomes. Since you are getting the magic at its full power, it could be more hazardous to you than the previous vessels." He leans in, then, and he whispers the rest into my ears.

I stand there listening, frozen with fear. "Are you saying it'll kill me?"

"I truly am sorry, but there is no way of knowing."

"If that's true, then why didn't Queen Iana tell me?" I ask, my throat completely dry.

"She takes non-interference with prophecies extremely strictly. Her son tried to interfere with a prophecy once, and she witnessed firsthand his horrid punishment." He puts his hand on mine. "I meant what I said, Serena. The prophecy is about you, and you are alone."

But if that's true, then what happens to my crew? And Ben? My sweet little brother.

"So, what now?" I ask, tears in my eyes.

"You must find Tellerous and kill him. I do not know his exact location, but I sense that he is indeed in Olovia.

"But that isn't all." Elias's tone shifts into sorrow. "You deserve to know the whole truth. It wasn't just Tellerous that I knew, Serena. Not long ago, your mother came to me for help when she realized the time drew closer for your father to begin to cast his spell. I informed her that nobody could interfere with a prophecy, but she still was determined. She loved you so much. The last voyage your parents embarked on was to Magia. Renayhem was their destination.

"In the deepest, darkest depths of the Sovereign's palace lies the Enchanted Emerald. It was a gift from the Terrain Goddess Rosalind when the very first Sovereign who ruled the land saved her son's life. This enchanted stone was said to hold even more power than the orb. Your mother read about it in an old book, wanting to use it against Tellerous. I warned her against it, but she had already made her decision. All I could do for her was give her a map."

"The storm," I breathe.

He nods gravely. "Tellerous figured out your mother's plan. He created the storm that sank their ship."

No.

No, no, no.

My father killed my mother. *My father killed my mother.*

Rage courses through my veins, an uncontrollable, tenacious fury that's going to make me explode. I clench my fists, trying to keep my composure as a tear runs down my cheek.

"Thank you," I manage as he hands me the orb.

"No need. When you use the orb, place your finger on the brightest star in order to activate its power. And wait, there is one more thing I must give to you." He digs through a drawer in his breakfront until he finds what he's looking for. He takes out a tiny brown bag tied with a single rope.

"These are called Dissometers. You can put them around your neck to protect you from magic when you fight. You and your friends will need these."

"Thank you," I say again, my voice growing shaky.

"You are very welcome. I wish you the best of luck, Serena." He puts his hand on my shoulder. I force myself to smile before he holds the door open for me to leave. "And remember: You alone will be able to kill him."

18

___

When I exit Elias's house, it becomes clear that he lives in a tree. Not what you'd expect from a sorcerer, like Nadia said, but I respect the fact that he's different from everyone else in Olovia. I step outside and into the forest, and my fear grows as I look up through the tall oak trees at the darkened, night-like sky.

What am I going to do? The weight of the world is on my shoulders. I have never been under this kind of pressure before. I raided and fought and traveled for *me*, nobody else. And not being in control of things is the one thing that I despise most, especially when it comes to my own life.

But most of all, this is a kind of a terror that I have never felt before. And not only that, but I'm fuming with rage and filled with sorrow.

Any decision I make won't just affect the people I care most about, but the entire kingdom, and quite possibly all the realms. I can barely breathe as I consider everything Elias told me. The more I panic, the more I the darkness closes in on me. I try to breathe, to calm myself down, but it isn't any use.

There are too many things that can go wrong, and one incorrect move can cause my father's plan to succeed. And if Elias is right, there isn't much chance of defeating him, anyway.

But as I drop my gaze and see my crew watching me, expectant, I throw my shoulders back. I have to act confident, especially around them. I have to protect them, which means I can't let my guard down anymore. I can't think about what could happen, because it would make me break down.

"There you are," Nadia says. "What did he tell you?"

I don't respond. I *can't* respond. I pace while my crew watches, trying to think, mumbling curse words under my breath as silent tears assault me once more. Ben says something, but his words are blocked out.

James comes up to me and places his hand on my shoulder.

I shrink away, smacking at it. "Don't touch me!" I cover my mouth. I'd spoken in the same tone that I used in Queen Iana's castle, and it still wasn't on purpose.

"Serena, calm down, it's just me," James says. "What did Elias tell you?"

"I am not telling you a thing. Go be with Alina, you guys deserve each other," I respond with a combination disgust and annoyance in my voice. But again, I don't know where it comes from, how the hurt I'd wanted to keep in keeps pouring out of me.

"What? No, it's not like that at all," he says, hesitating. "You know I care for you."

Something inside of me doesn't believe him, though his genuine tone should convince me otherwise. I ignore him— ignore everyone around me—and keep walking back and forth as I try to calm myself down.

"Serena, can you please tell us what happened?" Ben begs.

"Captain," Adam adds, "could you stop being stubborn for once and just—"

"Enough!" I yell. They all quiet down. I sweep my gaze around them and know I owe them the whole story. "It's true," I say. "Tellerous is behind all of this, and he's my damn father. He needs me to take in the magic in order to create a spell that will combine all three realms together, and then destroy them." I laugh, not meaning to give them the *entire* truth. But it comes out anyway. "Oh, also, he murdered our parents, sank their ship three years ago. And according to Elias, I am the only one who can stop him." I turn to Adam. "So, excuse me for being *stubborn* and not knowing how to act after that!"

I don't tell them about the last part Elias told me. Nobody needs to know that. I step back and stare at the surprise on my crewmates' faces. Alina wears an "I told you so" look, and Adam almost looks furious. But fear hides behind his eyes. All of their eyes.

Breathing deeply, I add, "And whatever Elias told me last is none of your business. It's for me to hear only, and it's nothing you should be concerned about."

"Serena," the prince says, "if you don't tell us then we can't—"

"Just stop trying to play the role of the hero!" I holler, my arms flailing. My chest aches. That burning sensation is returning, the darkness infecting my vision. My crew takes a step back from me, sensing the powerful anger coursing through me.

"The magic is affecting her emotions," Nadia says to no one in particular.

I myself take a step back, breathing hard. It *is* the magic, but I have no control over how the magic might play around with my feelings. "I-I'm sorry," I stutter. "I can't—I don't know how to stop it," I tell them as more tears pour down my face.

"It's all right," Nadia says. "We just need to—"

Every bit of movement and conversation comes to a halt, all at once. I'm not listening to Nadia, I'm staring at the sky behind her. Everyone turns around and watches the black magic shooting straight up into the sky, like lightning coming from the ground.

"That's the West Woods," Jack says. "But nobody ever goes in there."

Dark magic, the West Woods. That's when I know where Tellerous is.

Something looks to be going right.

I toss the orb to Jack and explain how to use it as he shoves it in his satchel. Then I head west.

"Serena? Serena!" Prince Pinhead yanks me back.

"Where in the bloody hell do you think you're going?" Nadia questions, concern written all over her face.

"To meet my hellish father."

"This could be a trap," Jack argues.

I don't care. At all. I just want to meet my father, then see him dead.

Sawyer joins in on the conversation. "Tellerous killed all of our parents. I'm with the captain on this one, we need to go after him. Now."

"I want to avenge our parents," Joseph agrees.

Within seconds, it's like the chaos from that day in the tavern. Everyone speaks over each other, bickering about what we should or shouldn't do. I glance over at Ben, who still seems to be at odds with all of the information that I'd shouted out at everyone.

We don't have time for this.

"All right, that's enough!" I yell. Their voices continue to rise. "Everybody shut up!" Finally, I catch their attention. "As captain, I am making the executive call!" I holler. "If you want justice for our parents, we're going to the West Woods now, before it is too late."

My whole crew cheers. Alina goes quiet, rolling her blue eyes at me. Her two crewmates look apathetic.

Jack takes my arm and pulls me aside. "Justice or vengeance?" he asks.

"Doesn't matter," I reply. "As long as Tellerous dies, nothing else matters. Nothing."

Tellerous is going to pay for what he did to my mother and Lennard, for what he's doing to me now. Even if it's the last thing I ever do. And according to Elias, it very well might be.

Elias's words linger through my mind as I lead the way through the darkened forest, cutting away at low branches and vines with my cutlass. Two outcomes, neither of which look good for me. I debate whether or not to tell Ben. At the very least, Nadia. But this is a secret that I should probably keep to myself. If they know, they'll do everything in their power to stop it—stop me—and that would put them in grave danger, risking the wrath of the gods.

The crew's nervous energy radiates behind me, everybody anxious and ready to finally meet the man responsible for this ludicrous journey in the first place. But as we travel deeper into the forest, I have an unsettling feeling in my stomach. This is the first time I'll be meeting my father, the man my mother hated, who murdered her—and yet I'm nervous too. I'm not sure if I'm nervous that I won't defeat him, or nervous just to be in the same room with him.

It's bewildering and infuriating that even though I want to kill him—even though I *have* to kill him—I'm curious about him. What he is going to be like? Guilt tears through me for wondering about it, but I can't help myself—especially since we're almost there. The magic here is stronger than it has ever been.

The blood in my veins flows violently, ready to meet the magic waiting for me, to invite it inside of me. My palms cramp around my cutlass and my bones tingle. My steps quicken, the pull on my body even stronger, like there's a rope connecting me to the magic. How much longer can I attempt to fight for control over the darkness? It's already toying with my body—my emotions. I saw the fear on my crews' faces. Only the gods know what else the magic will try to take from me.

The West Woods nears. As we approach, I stop everyone and give every member of my crew a Dissometer, though I contemplate leaving Alina, Alexia, and Freya defenseless without one. But there's one for every person, as if Elias had known exactly who would be coming along.

"Be alert and aware of your surroundings," I tell them. "We have no idea where Tellerous could be lurking."

We pick up our pace, quietly trotting over the lightless path of dead trees and prickly bushes. Ravens fly overhead, an omen of death, and there is a cold, grim breeze that whistles an eerie tune as we swat gnats out of our faces. The prince plague takes out the orb and uses it as a light source, catching up to me at the front so we can see what's ahead of us. I hear the impatient mumbles of my crew behind me as the prince and I are forced to slow over the increasingly rocky terrain, walking with more caution.

The faint calls of owls in the distance add to the spine-chilling sound of the ravens' caws. I nearly trip over a thick tree branch, gripping the prince's shoulder as a result. To keep me from falling, he wraps his arm around my waist. I stare at him for a moment, wondering at the feeling of sparks where his hand grips me. I only pull my gaze away when I feel James's heated stare.

I ignore it. I let go of the prince and hold onto Ben's hand, pulling him to my other side. He's trembling, and I feel horrible. I don't know what to say—*I'm sorry my father killed your father?*

"Are you sure you want to come?" I ask. "I can send you back to the ship with Sawyer or James."

"No, I'm coming," he replies, an anger like I've never heard festering in his voice. "He killed our mother, Serena. My father."

I nod, unsure how to take the way Ben said "my" father. Sure, Lennard was his biological parent, but Lennard was the only father I knew. He was my father too. Not my stepfather. He was all I had.

Ben must sense my unease. He squeezes my hand a bit tighter.

The feeling of the Cretion magic intensifies. I walk in the direction of where I most closely sense it, and I know we're near the moment a burst of energy rushes through my body. I gasp, but I don't have to explain what happened—what makes things clear to Ben and the prince and the rest of the crew is the stench of smoke filling the air.

I rush forward until I hear the sound of the crackling fire and echoes of unfamiliar voices. We come up to the edge of an old gray cave covered in vines, pause in our tracks, and slowly peer through the entrance. I don't see much besides the dying embers of a fire and the shadows of the strangers.

As they speak, I hold up my hand to signal my crew to stay put.

"Let me make sure I'm getting this right," a heavy, powerful voice says. "I sent you to the Realm of Magic for two things: I needed that orb, and even more, I wanted my daughter. You came back without the orb *and* without my daughter." The fire crackles so loud I jump. "*You* came back without her! *I told you,* she's much more important than getting the orb *and what did you do*? You did not follow orders. I *told you* she was there, why would you leave the island *knowing* she was there?"

The next voice is weaker, frightened. "I-I'm sorry, sire. Kelvnick told us to just get the orb, since not enough time has passed. By the time we were caught by Iana's soldiers, the girl was gone."

"*Kelvnick*? You only take orders from me, is that not clear? I want Kelvnick's head on a platter for his incompetence! I need my daughter, anyway, you idiots!" Something crashes. I flinch, realizing *this* is my father. When he speaks again, his voice is calm, frighteningly so. "Luckily for you, we still have time. Meet me on Southwest Hillins Island. Because of your screwup, I have to take care of a few things before we can proceed. Heed me: The next time you disobey me, I will banish you to the Outlands of the Dark Realm for an eternity."

I don't want to just stand here like a fool anymore. It's now or never. I close my eyes and ready my breath, my grip on my cutlass deadly.

"Serena?" the prince whispers uncertainly. "Serena! Stop—"

He killed my mother, he killed my mother.

I bolt into the cave without thinking twice about it.

Normally, I would come up with an excellent strategic

plan. But I don't think anything I could plan would allow us to defeat Tellerous. I'm not even sure how I'm supposed to do that, especially since I have to do it alone. I know rage clouds my judgment, not allowing me to think straight. I do it anyway.

The heavy footsteps of my hearties rushing after me trails close behind. I stop abruptly at the mouth of the cave, and we all stand there, our feet glued to the ground. Nobody knows what to do next. Least of all me.

There he is. A tall man turns around, his lips in a thin line I take to be a grin with an evil tilt. His emerald green eyes match mine, but instead of fiery red hair his is auburn. He's dressed in black from head to toe, but despite the darkness he almost looks as if he's glowing. I breathe heavily as I study my father for the very first time. I'd always imagined what he would be like, and this isn't it. On the way up here, I had planned to just attack. I don't know if it's the control of the magic or something more human deep inside of me, but I can't move. I hold my breath.

I thought he was talking to other people, but all around him stand creatures that look like shadows. They hold human forms, but no identifying features. I look at their faceless heads and gulp. I open my mouth, but no words come out.

"Serena," Tellerous says suddenly, his voice the kindest I've heard it, something warm taking his breath away. "You look just like your mother."

There is almost—*almost*—something like sentiment in his tone.

My crewmates stare, paralyzed, as he walks over to me. They're waiting for my signal, waiting for me to *do* something. Tellerous opens his mouth, but Jack steps in front of me, the orb in his hand like a weapon.

"Get away from her," he orders. Then he presses his finger to the brightest star, and the magic that erupts from the orb sends Tellerous flying into the cave wall.

It's like everyone needed the prince's shout to be struck with a moment of clarity. My crew surges forward. It should have be an easy fight: there are only three shadow men when we enter the cave. But as swords swing, they multiply. I rush through the chaos for my father, but a shadow blocks my path, then another and another. I'm surrounded. Through the space between them I glare at Tellerous, who stands among the fighting unbothered, a sinister glint in his eyes. I swing my sword through the shadows, but it's like sticking my cutlass through a cloud.

"You should make this easier on yourself, Princess," one of the shadows says.

Princess? Who the hell are they calling Princess?

The shadow who spoke raises his hand and I brace myself, recognizing the movement from when Ian used his elemental magic. The magic never hits; a bright green shield protects me and I stare down, dumbfounded, at the Dissometer around my neck. Flashes of green appear all around me as my crew fights the increasing shadows and their magic. Once they realize we all have Dissometers, they form swords of their own with their powers, and the fighting continues.

It's pointless. None of us can actually kill the damn creatures. But I need to get to my father to wipe that smug grin off his face.

Through the grunts and cries of my hearties fighting Tellerous's minions, I push through the shadows. They continue to multiply, outnumbering us, some coming for me and others pinpointing on the orb in Jack's hand. I curse my thoughtlessness. I couldn't have known they wanted the orb before we came upon this cave, but I'd known my father wanted me. And I'd delivered it and myself to him in one place.

The prince shouts, the shadows too many. He throws the orb and Nadia catches it with one hand, using her other to block a blow with her sword. I look away to dodge a swing, and every time I look back someone different has the orb in their possession like they're playing a game of hot potato.

But the struggle to keep the orb in the right hands grows more challenging. The chaotic shouts from my crewmates increase as Alexia trips and the orb falls from her hands. One of the shadows scoops it up, lifting it and targeting the closest person to him. Alina flies out of the cave, landing in a heap outside the mouth.

It wasn't funny, but I still have to hold back a laugh.

I dodge the swing of a shadow and leap to its other side. I duck when it tries to strike me again. I charge forward, and the shadow with the orb blasts me to the ground. I slide halfway across the cave, the rock tearing at the bandages on my back, making the Flipperfore's work on my skin bleed again. Gritting my teeth against the ache, I roll over my shoulder and climb to my feet, tackling the shadow before it can turn the orb's magic on me again.

The moment I snatch the magical item out of its hands, I slap my hand on it, hoping for the best. The magic glows, shooting out and striking the shadow. It disintegrates in a blink, leaving behind an echo of his scream but nothing else.

I smile. Now this is something I can do.

"Serena!"

I turn and aim at a shadow standing over Ben, his sword raised. It vanishes, and I swing the orb's magic around to the one attacking Nadia, then I use it to protect myself as well.

Again and again, the shadows' numbers fade, the tide finally shifting.

"Look out!"

I turn too slowly. A shadow catches me by surprise, knocking the orb out of my hands before I can turn the magic on it. The orb hits the ground and rolls, and we both reach for it, the shadow's hands closer.

"No!" I lunge and take the orb in my hand.

The cave fades. I hit the ground, my body curled over the orb, but when I look around I realize I haven't imagined it. The cave walls are gone, my surroundings changed into a bright white room. Everything around me has disappeared.

I spin. "Hello?" I call out. Then I shout, "Hello!" My voice echoes off the walls.

I run in circles, pressing my hands to the walls, looking for any possible exit. But I'm trapped. There's no way out, no doors and no windows. My eyes sting, my heart beating faster as I start to panic, as my hands curl to fists and I punch the walls, screaming.

I know I'm not alone even before I hear the voice.

"Hello, my little daisy."

19

a too familiar voice, right behind me. Calling me "little daisy" because daisies were her favorite flower. She'd told me that I reminded her of daisies because they were beautiful, like me.

I turn around and freeze. My mother—my supposed-to-be-deceased mother—stands right in front of me. I almost don't believe it. I shouldn't believe it. But she looks so real and three years of grief bubbles up inside of me, and I can't help myself.

I bolt into her arms and squeeze her tightly. I don't want to let her go. I've missed her so much, and seeing her again —just one more time—is something I always wished for. Now, it's like she's never been gone. She's wearing the same thing she'd worn the day she and Lennard left on their last voyage: a knee-length dress with a rose-red, ruffled skirt. The top of the dress is white, with loose sleeves that drape down to her wrists. There's a black belt around her waist and a black lace choker with a ruby in the middle. Her black boots reach up to her calves, the foldover brown. Her fiery red hair is gathered in a messy braid over her right shoulder.

I study every detail, looking for signs this is a hoax. But it can't be—she's perfect.

"What are you doing here?" I ask, smiling through my tears as she takes my face in her hands.

"I'm here for you, of course," she says, meeting my grin with her own. "Serena, I have come to talk some sense into you."

I breathe in, trying to calm my sobs, my shaking shoulders. "I have so many questions . . . the book, Mother, why did you give me—"

"Hush, Serena, we needn't rehash the past. Listen to what I am saying now." She puts her hands on my shoulders, leaning down just slightly so she can look in my eyes. "You know you can trust me. And you can trust your father."

I blink. "What?"

My mother only smiles. "He was always a wonderful man, and I could not be more thrilled that you have finally found him."

I shake my head, trying to step away. But my mother holds me firm. "What? But Elias told me that—"

"Don't listen to that old man, little daisy. Listen to me, your mother who loves you so much." She tucks my hair behind my ear. I shiver at her touch. Something isn't right.

"But, Mother—"

"And Tellerous," she continues. "After all, he knows me better than anyone. He knows a whole other side of me that I cannot wait for him to share with you. Once you're gifted the Cretion magic you'll be the most powerful being in the world. Don't you want that? You'll make me proud."

No, stop . . . this isn't her. I look around and the walls are fading again, crumbling into a cloud of black around us. This is what I saw in one of my visions.

"No," I breathe. "You're not real, are you? None of this is real!"

I tear away from my mother's grasp, back away as that smile remains fixed on her face. I look around, searching the cloud for an escape.

"Let me out!" I shout. Someone has to hear me.

But there is only silence.

"Let me out!" I scream again.

More silence.

But just like that, the white walls disappear and I'm back in the cave. The orb is still in my hand and I'm standing directly in front of Tellerous. But I can't move. Chains made from the pulsing black magic loop around my wrists to stop me from using the weapon against him. They wrap around my arms and my torso, biting into my skin, keeping me from moving. I crane my head to look behind me. My whole crew is there, but they aren't fighting. Five of Tellerous's shadows guard them.

"Oh, but it was real, Serena."

I swing my head around and look at my father, disgust flashing through me.

"At least, the message was," he says. "Your mind is much sharper than I thought it would be. No wonder it's taken longer than I expected for the magic to affect you. I suppose I just have to wait a little longer."

"Enough games," I snap. "Where the hell did you take me?" My mother's memory haunts me. She'd felt so real. He knows what she means to me, and using her is a testament to the cruelty that lives in him.

For a moment, I'd truly thought she was here with me.

Tellerous's gaze doesn't soften. "I simply created new surroundings for you, so you could focus. You're welcome, by the way. I know how much you miss her."

"Well, I wouldn't need to miss her if *you* hadn't killed her!" I yell, squirming in the chains.

He sighs. "I only did what I had to do. You have no idea how much it hurt me to create that storm." But there is no remorse in his voice.

"Don't act like the victim," I spit. "Don't you dare pretend to be so innocent. You murdered her!"

"I know it seems as if I am a monster, but one day you will understand." He reaches out then, as if to take my hands. I flinch away. "I am doing all of this for you."

I roll my eyes.

"Your mother was right, you know," he says.

"About what?"

"What she told you, about me and her. I know a side of her you never knew. I have so much I can tell you, so many stories . . . I'd be more than happy to share them with you."

I stare at Tellerous, not sure how to respond. The prince calls my name, and Nadia and Ben and the rest of my hearties try to get to me. Try to talk me out of it. It should have been easy: I know my mother, I know who she was. She was a fearsome pirate, she taught me the stars, she baked the best cinnamon buns in the realm.

But part of me craves to know what my mother was like before she had me. Before she met Lennard. Why she cried at night. What Tellerous did to change her.

I play with the orb in my palm, a thousand questions bouncing around inside my head. "What happens if I say yes?" I ask.

Tellerous smiles softly. "You'll come with me to my—*our* home. I have a lovely room waiting for you."

I nearly laugh. Something is off about this. There is more to what he wants from me, his plan much more complex than I originally believed, than even Elias had told me. He's a terrible liar; the corners of his lips inch into a smirk. Part of him isn't entirely human anymore, and that means I don't know how intelligent his next move is going to be. But I know it's going to be big. Right here, right now, he can just take the orb from me and take us both to the Dark Realm.

No way in hell.

But he doesn't. He's waiting, and something tells me it's about more than the magic spell stretching far enough into the sky.

"Don't you want to make Kat proud?" Tellerous asks, trying to provoke me.

Nobody has ever called my mother Kat before. Not even Lennard. He's dangling my mother in front of me. Using her. And it's working. "I—"

Stop it! He's using her to mess with you.

He wants to play mind games, but I can't allow him to get to me. He knows mentioning my mother will bring out a weakness in me. Maybe it does, but I am nobody's puppet, and I refuse to stand here while my hearties are in danger, when they're here because they fought for their lives—and mine.

I think of everything I hate about Tellerous. The magic, the darkness, the deaths he's caused. The way he wants to own me. How the way he said "Kat" got under my skin. He's going to pay for what he's doing to this realm, and he'll pay for what he did to my mother and Lennard—my *real* father.

Despite the chains, I can breathe again. I feel like the calm before a storm, and I say one word: "No."

Rage flows in my veins, more than I have ever felt in my entire life. I look up at Tellerous and clench my fists, relishing the uncertainty in his eyes, the doubt. The darkness calls to me, and this time instead of pushing it away, I welcome it. I close my eyes, focusing, and for a moment I become a different person. Someone I don't know.

Someone who terrifies me as the pressure builds in my veins.

When I open my eyes, I see my reflection in Tellerous's. My eyes glow with power, my face twists into a snarl of anger and destruction. I pull against my chains and this time they fall from my body. Tellerous steps back.

I don't have the magic inside of me, yet I have the strength to almost control it. It sticks to me like glue, washing through me like a wave of electricity, swarming through my palms. It attaches itself to me, and in that moment, I have never felt stronger.

The magic begs me to use it, the whispers growing, compelling me to listen. The power in the orb swirls in violent circles against the power radiating from my hands. Like the orb is amplifying it. Like the dark magic in me wants to use it.

"This is for my real father," I say, my voice not sounding like my own. Tellerous takes another step back, shock and something like pride breaking through his veil of fear. "And this is for my mother."

I place my finger on the brightest star on the orb, and the whole cave flashes with a bright light. It funnels toward my father, and I watch as a clump of the black Cretion magic clutching my hand exits the palm that holds the orb and slams into him.

When he disappears into nothingness, so do the remaining shadows.

20

I drop the orb and stare at my palms, breathing heavily.

Did I just do that?

As my hearties help each other climb to their feet, I bolt to the mouth of the cave and look up at the clear blue sky. The black cloud is gone. A weight lifts from my shoulders.

Nadia embraces me, and I slump into her, exhausted. "You did it!" she yells. Behind us, the crew and Alina cheer.

My face is wet, and I realize I'm crying. "Y-yeah . . . I guess I did."

"I told you that you were a hero." Ben rushes over and wraps his arms around me. I force a smile on my face and hug him back, though I'm still shaking. *Believe me, I don't feel like one. I am not one.*

If I'm a hero—if I really did kill Tellerous—then why do I have this odd feeling in my stomach? Something is . . . incomplete. Maybe I'm in shock from being able to control the magic—it was the strangest feeling. Or maybe I'm still reeling about my mother, how Tellerous used her against me, made me see her again as some kind of cruel trick.

Queen Iana was right. Cretion magic is more powerful than I could have imagined.

All around me, my crew celebrates. They pull me into the middle of their circle, surrounding me and cheering, chanting different songs as they bask in the glow of our apparent victory.

So why don't I feel victorious?

I make my way out of the circle, congested and out of air. The prince stands outside of it, too, picking the orb up off the floor and placing it in his satchel.

"Why the long face?" he asks, his smile wavering as he senses my anxiety. "You did it."

"Did I?" I try to think on the bright side: My time with Prince Charming is over. He'll return home and find a way to return the orb to Queen Iana, and I'll be back on the sea with my hearties, getting as far away from here as possible.

So why am I disappointed?

"I don't feel like I did anything," I admit. "It was too easy. Something tells me that this was all a set up. A small portion of a larger plan."

Because this feeling can't be about Jack. It's about Tellerous. The magic in the sky looks gone, but it's still here, surrounding me and messing with me.

"I think you're just tired," Jack offers. "Maybe in a state of shock. You've been exhausted from the visions and our journey, and you met your father for the very first time and had to kill him. But, Serena, look," he says, guiding me back to the mouth of the cave and pointing. "The cloud in the sky is gone, and we all saw Tellerous disappear. He's gone."

"I'm serious, Jack." I shove him away. "I'm terrified that this was just an act."

"Did you just call me by my first name?" he asks smugly, ignoring my concern.

"Don't get used to it," I grumble.

But when I look at him in the normal light of day, his marble gray eyes are clear, the sun beating down on us and making them shine through the cave like a spotlight. For the very first time, I don't see an irritating, arrogant prince. I only see a friend.

"You have nothing to fear. We did it. It's all over now," Jack assures me.

I truly wish that I believe him. But I can't, not with that same energy surge rattling my bones, my veins clenching, begging the damn power to flood my system and take over. I wasn't me, Serena, when I wielded it. I don't want to feel it ever again. Maybe I can believe this sensation will disappear after a bit of time. Maybe this has to be in my head.

"So what now, Captain?" Adam asks.

I shrug off my uncertainty. With everyone else believing Tellerous is gone, there's no excuse for me not to lead them. "Back to the *Tigerlily*, I suppose."

Sawyer cheers. "Finally!"

As the crew trickles out of the cave, continuing their celebrations, I see James approaching. I walk around him, unable to face him and how he's been with Alina, how I need to admit there's nothing between us. Is there? I don't have the strength to deal with him. I've had to deal with enough.

"Wait!" Jack says, not only to me, but to everyone. "Please, come to the castle with me. I promised you a reward." He looks at me. "You must claim it. And my parents will be pleased to know that you stopped the darkness."

Joseph laughs. "You want *us* to go to the castle with you? *And* meet the king and queen? No thanks."

"You can just pay us when we get back to the *Tigerlily*," Adam adds.

"I have a sister to get back to," Alina reminds us, already ahead of everyone.

"Absolutely," Jack says, but I can see him scrambling for an excuse. "You can all go your separate ways, just—I want my parents and the Olovian people to know what you did for the kingdom and the realm."

My crew looks at me, and I mirror their uncertainty. I really would rather sail as far away from Olovia as I can possibly get, and never turn back. There's nothing here for me anymore. No Will, and now the lure of Tellerous had soured whatever had been left. Maybe the only reason I still feel the connection to the magic is because I'm in Olovia, the origin of Tellerous's spell.

I'm too late to say anything. Adam stands straighter and says, "I refuse to step foot anywhere near the palace. I'm going back to the ship."

Nadia places her hand on my shoulder. When she speaks, it's to me only, her eyes pleading. "We did our part. More than our part. It's time to head back to the *Tigerlily*."

I nod and take her hand. "You're right."

Jack either overhears or knows just from the look in my eyes. He nods, disappointed. "I just—thank you all for coming with me. You have done the kingdom and the realm a great kindness. I will have your payment sent your way."

We flood the woods, some of the crew still cheering and some of us—well, me—realizing this is the end. I lag behind to walk with Jack, and I hold out my hand. "So, I guess this is it," I say awkwardly. "You, uh—you did good."

"Likewise." He shakes it, but he doesn't let go. "What will you do—"

Before he finishes, someone from the brush yanks my other arm so hard I think it might come out of my socket. A stranger pulls me into a chokehold, their sword pressing into my neck.

"Get away from him, pirate filth!" the man shouts.

"Woah, woah, woah! Let her go, she's a friend!" Jack yells, attempting to intervene. Up ahead, my entire crew halts their tracks and they rush back, already leering for another fight.

I struggle to get out of the guard's strong hold. I stomp on his foot and his grip weakens enough for me to pull free. I spin around and kick him in the groin, and by the time he falls to his knees I have my cutlass pressed against his neck.

"Everybody stop!" Jack yells, his voice shaking the trees and his arms spread wide, one to halt the group of guards and the other to halt my crew. "Enough, there has been a huge misunderstanding." He turns to his guards. "They helped me destroy the source of the magic in the sky."

The guards all laugh in his face, and I wonder if that's actually an acceptable way to treat one's prince and royal charge.

"Prince Jack, do you take us for fools?" The man who attempted to kill me stands. "What have these pirates brain-washed you with? We were told you were visiting a family friend."

"I had no other choice. My parents wouldn't have let me out if I told them the truth. I promise, they are not the enemy here," Jack replies.

They stare at their prince, the doubt unanimous between them. But the longer they look at Jack—and the longer my crew refrains from attacking them, at his word—the more they seem to realize he's telling the truth.

The one who grabbed me finally nods and sheaths his sword. "Very well, Your Highness. But we need to take you back to the castle. You must explain this to the king and queen."

I can see where this is going, and I step away. "Good luck with that. If you'll excuse us, we'll just be going."

"Wait," Jack hisses, taking my hand. "Please, come with me. You have to come now. You deserve the recognition, which will be difficult to receive if you're traveling on the *Tigerlily*."

"Captain," Adam says, his eagerness to return to the ship clear. He crosses his arms.

I pause. There's a nagging pit in my stomach urging me to go. I turn back to my crew.

"Those who are opposed to going to the castle, go back to the *Tigerlily* and wait for further instruction," I order. "Get ready to sail upon my return."

More than half of my crew happily vanish into the trees. Aside from Ben, Nadia, and James, only Sawyer and John, and Alina, Freya, and Alexia, remain put.

The guards seem to relax once most of the crew leave. I turn to Jack, questioning my decision. "Jack, are you sure your parents would even want us there?"

"Don't worry about them," he says, and he motions to his guards.

With one hesitant sigh, we follow Jack out of the woods.

The farther we walk, the more nervous I become, a familiar feeling lately. Like at Queen Iana's, I know I won't belong. Pirates have no place in a castle. I also have no right celebrating the end of our mission until I know for sure that Tellerous is gone. I eye Jack carefully as he walks next to me. He looks genuinely content, thrilled at our accomplishment and overjoyed to return home. But I can't share his relief until this feeling goes away, and I can't tell Jack about it because he already dismissed me. The physical evidence of

Tellerous's presence has vanished, and that's enough for him.

But cloud disappearing doesn't mean Tellerous isn't hiding in plain sight, waiting for the right moment to enact the remainder of his plan.

If the visions return, that will be a sure sign my father is still alive. Not that I want to have one. Elias said they'll only continue to get worse. Until I have that kind of proof, though, I'll have to be incredibly careful and aware of my surroundings. Only the gods know if or when Tellerous might strike again.

"Are you all right?" Jack asks.

"I'm fine," I lie.

"You look petrified."

"Everything feels out of my control." It's as close as I can get to a confession. "It makes me feel so helpless, which is a feeling I utterly despise. Also, your guards keep death-staring me."

Jack looks around at the guards trailing behind us, then the ones way ahead of us leading the way. Then he shrugs. "Just ignore them. What's out of your control that you're worried about?"

I can't tell him about the feeling I have. "Nothing, just forget about it."

"Come on, you can tell me," he presses. "I can clearly see something is bothering you still."

"Ugh, stop making assumptions about me." Even if, I realize, they're usually right. "I hate when you do that."

"Huh. You sure hate a lot of things, don't you?"

"Yes."

"Okay, well what don't you hate?" he asks.

I consider the question for a moment. "Ben, Nadia, the

color blue, rubies, daisies, money, bread—gods, I love bread —rum . . . are you going to make me continue?"

He chuckles. "Uh, no. No, I'm done."

"What?"

"Everything you told me is either already obvious or completely typical of a pirate. Is it so bad that I want to get to know the real you, not the person you pretend to be to everyone else?"

I look at him, confused. "Why would you ever want that?"

"Like I told you, I think we should have an understanding of one another," he reminds me. "At least until we part ways."

I suppose it's better than walking in silence until we arrive at his castle. Better than thinking about this leftover feeling, or the guards glaring at me. "Um, okay. What do you want to know?" I ask reluctantly.

"Everything," Jack replies, holding a branch aside for me.

"Too broad," I say quickly, shutting him down.

"Fine . . . tell me your biggest fear."

"Losing Ben." Of course, I have some new fears in addition to that, but those are better kept a secret for now, or forever.

Jack nods. "I understand that. Okay, how do you—"

"No, no, no, slow down, Prince Charming. If you're going to get to know things about me, then I need to know a few things about you."

"Fine, ask away."

"What's *your* greatest fear?" I ask, realizing I don't have any of my own questions lined up.

"That's easy. Letting down the kingdom when it's my turn to become king."

I want to tell him that isn't possible, but I keep my mouth shut. Jack being king won't affect me. I'm leaving as soon as I know for sure Tellerous is gone. I don't have a reason to come back anymore.

"Why do you love rubies so much?" Jack asks.

"It was my mother's favorite stone. It also happened to be her birthstone." I pull her necklace partway from my pocket, just enough to show him. "She gave this to me before she died. She told me that she wants me to always have a piece of her, no matter where either of us are in the realm."

"My grandfather, the one who gave me the translator book, passed away when I was thirteen," Jack offers. "He practically raised me until I was about ten. After that, he left to go travel the world and I got passed off to tutors. I was incredibly close with him, and when I found out he died I was devastated. That's why I carry the book with me everywhere. It was one of the first things he sent me from his travels."

"I'm sorry."

"It's not your doing," he says, then he changes the subject. "So, what was your first impression of me?" He tries to lighten his voice, but the pain is still evident.

"I thought you were selfish, arrogant, and exceedingly irritating," I answer honestly.

"And now?"

I smirk. "Just irritating."

He laughs.

Curious, I repeat the question, "What was your impression of me?"

"From that first day I met you on the *Tigerlily*, I was intimidated. You looked as tough as I heard you were. Same thing when I approached you at Will's tavern."

"And now?"

"I greatly respect you. You're unlike anyone I have ever met before."

I smile. "Likewise, Prince Charming."

I think the conversation is over then. We're nearing the castle, and the crew keeps looking over their shoulders like they're wondering why we're so far behind.

"What is it with you and James?" Jack asks suddenly. "Every time he tries to talk to you lately you turn away."

I nearly trip over my own feet. Something in his voice is urgent, like he's been waiting a long time to ask me, though I don't know why. "Have you been watching me that closely?" I ask, more embarrassed than alarmed. "Nothing is going on between us. At least, not anymore. From the moment she came on board, he's been all over Alina. He keeps on denying it, but I have known him my entire life. I always know when he's being untruthful, even to himself." I didn't realize how much it would hurt saying it out loud. Alina is cruel. A murderer. "He thinks he's in love with me because he thinks he should be."

"And how do you feel about that?"

"What kind of question is that? Obviously I'm upset. I should never have let my guard down with him. As usual, I got hurt."

James can tell me all of the lies he wants. It's not going to change my mind. Alina definitely isn't trying to hide how she feels about him, and I can't even blame her, not for this. I blame myself. I should have told James how I feel ages ago. I should have admitted it to myself. Maybe things would be different.

"I'm sorry," Jack says. "I know how it feels to have your heart broken."

"Tell me about Mallory." Anything to get my mind off James.

"Mallory Mae," Jack says without hesitation. "She was the most beautiful girl I had ever seen. I had a crush on her before I even got to know her. Much like you and James, we were childhood friends. We had just about everything in common, and she was my best friend. I was completely surprised when she kissed me for the first time, and I was devastated when she left me.

"But now I have been starting to wonder if it was actually love. When you love someone, or even just have strong feelings for them, then it should be as if you are the only two people in the room when you're together, or time should stand still. I never felt like that with her."

I've never thought about love in that way before. Then again, I've never been in love either. I never felt that way with James.

Before I can respond, Ben calls out to Jack. We both look up, and Ben waves him over. "We need you to settle a bet."

Jack shoots me an apologetic glance and jogs to catch up. Hardly two seconds later, James falls behind. He walks beside me, glancing at me every few steps. I remain silent, waiting for him to finally say what's on his mind.

"What were you guys talking about?" he asks.

"Nothing important." We're silent again, but I can't take it. "Out with it, what do you want?"

He shifts awkwardly. "Look, I just wanted to apologize. If you thought that Alina and I . . . whatever you thought, it's incorrect."

"I don't believe you."

"Why?"

I sigh. "I saw you two together. Whether you have feelings for her or not, she clearly has an interest in you. And I think you like her. I'm not mad, James. And the last thing I want to deal with is this." I motion with my hand at the air between us.

James exhales heavily. "But you will deal with anything involving the prince."

"What? No. *No*! This has nothing to do with him," I protest.

"I don't believe you," he replies, using my own words against me. "Why are we really going to the castle?"

I stop in my tracks to face him. "You need to drop this. Whatever we had before, it doesn't exist, okay? Not anymore." I leave him standing there, hoping he won't follow me.

He doesn't. As my anger grows, my veins tingle. It leaves an unsettling feeling in my stomach. I try to ignore it but it won't go away. I play with the ruby necklace in my pocket as I walk alone behind Jack and Ben, as the castle gates take shape before us.

21

I regret coming as we move closer to the palace.

"Before we move any farther, there are a few things that you should know," Jack says, raising his voice so everyone can hear. "Never speak rudely to my mother and father. They are very kind, but lately their patience has thinned. They may be a bit upset with me at first, but stay calm. And do not try to fight the guards if they come near you. I'm sure once my mother and father know what you did, they will act more . . . welcoming."

He looks at me for that last part about fighting. Why do I care?

Alina's the only one who nods along. "Got it," she replies. Suck up.

The palace gates are rusted silver. Two marble gargoyle statues stand on each side, as well as two guards standing between them. Behind them, the palace itself rises into the sky in a rose-gold color, stretching ten stories high.

The guards at the gate bow and let us through. On either side of the stone path to the door is a field of roses, all kinds: red, white, and pink. Through all of the darkness and chaos, the roses had remained luminous. Jack's face lights up as we make our way into his home.

Inside the palace, the foyer is even more impressive. The white walls make the room seem even more massive, and in the center is a giant plant in a white stone pot with beautiful hot pink flowers on the leaves. A door straight ahead leads to the back of the palace, and an enormous white marble staircase rises in the middle of the room. To the right is a large breakfront, and paintings of the different Olovian gods hang all over the walls. Above our heads is a ginormous crystal chandelier, fully lit.

"Hello?" calls a voice from upstairs.

"Mother, I'm home!" Jack announces. His voice echoes in the great room.

When the queen comes down the stairs, I see no resemblance between her and the prince. Her honey blonde hair is in a braid that coils into a side bun, and she's wearing a white gown with a floral design and sparkling silver high heels. A ruby hangs from her neck on a silver chain, and a sapphire from a bracelet on her left wrist. An emerald ring on her right hand matches her evergreen eyes. A small diamond tiara rests on top of her head, held in place by the braid.

The queen lifts her gown as she rushes down the stairs to greet her son. "Thank the gods you are alive! I was so worried about you!" She sighs with relief as she hugs Jack. "You told us you were going to stay with the Hartley family. When we contacted them they told us they had no idea what we were talking about! I was so worried you were hurt!"

"I'm all right, Mother, really," Jack replies gently.

That's when she finally notices our presence.

"What are they doing here?" she asks sharply, the

warmth from her voice vanishing, replaced with what seems to be anger and fear. She looks from me to Jack, sees the blood on his face. "Did they hurt you? Oh, Jack, what have they done to you? Guards!"

"Mother, relax!"

The guards surround us and my hand strays to my cutlass; my crew mirrors me. But the guards halt when the queen holds up her hand, and she listens as Jack explains everything that happened since he stepped foot in Will's tavern—minus the detail that Tellerous is my father. The queen looks at him as if he's gone mad, and when he finishes she turns her attention to us and just stares.

"Mother, let me introduce you," Jack offers. He points to everyone in turn, getting to me last. "And this is Serena Jones."

The queen's eyes widen. "She is *the* Serena Jones?"

Jack smiles. "Indeed."

"Huh." The queen studies me closely. "You are much different than I thought you would be."

"Um, thank you?" I say. Then I remember the manners I assume are expected. "It's an honor, Your Majesty." I bow, not that I actually mean it.

She forces a smile on her face. At least we're both making an effort.

"Well, I believe I owe you all a debt of gratitude," she says, turning her gaze to the others finally and motioning to all of us. "Thank you so much, for enduring such a dangerous journey for Olovia. It truly means a great deal to me that you would do this. And Jack, you may have defied my and your father's orders, but in doing so you saved an entire realm. So, I am not upset with you." She looks at me, then, and bows her head. "Anything you want, anything at all, please let me know."

I almost tell her about the payment Jack promised us, but we're interrupted by a voice booming from around the corner. "Son!"

The king. He rounds the corner of the hallway, a spitting reflection of Jack, though older. Same dark brown hair, the bright gray eyes.

"You had me so worried!" he yells, his voice getting louder. "What happened to you? Where have you been? I thought you—" He turns to us, and like his wife a flash of hatred comes through him, as if we're aliens invading his own personal planet.

But when his eyes land on me, they widen. He freezes, mouth opening like he wants to say something, then closing. I don't know how to take his reaction to my presence, but it definitely makes me uncomfortable. I look away.

"Darling," the queen swoops in, "these uh, *wonderful* people went with Jack to the Realm of Magic. They're the reason the cloud in the sky has vanished." She places her hand on his shoulder, which seems to spur him back into motion.

King Archer looks at his wife in disbelief. "Is that so? Well, thank you all very much. How very . . . very brave and noble of you."

The queen gasps—a happy, cheerful gasp. "We should have a celebration, Archer! We should have a ball, and the whole kingdom can attend!"

That's when Alina steps forward, the only one of us with any sense. "That's a great idea, Queen Helena. If you don't mind us, we'll just be getting out of your hair—" She turns to leave.

"Wait!" Jack says. "Mother, can't they stay? They deserve to celebrate with us. Without them I wouldn't have been able to rid the realm of the treachery we were trapped in." His eyes, again, land on me.

The queen, for her part, at least tries to look apologetic. "Oh, my sweet boy, I don't really think that they—"

"Mother, please? If it wasn't for Serena . . . any of them, the sky would not be blue right now, and so many more people would be dying."

"Jack, it's okay, really," Nadia says kindly. "We don't need to stay." We don't *want* to stay either.

"No, you deserve to celebrate too," Jack replies.

Queen Helena's sigh is like a gust of wind. "Fine," she gives in. "You may stay. What a . . . wonderful idea, Jack."

"Yes, *wonderful*," King Archer agrees. A moment ago he hadn't been able to take his eyes from me. Now, he won't look in my direction at all. "That's the word that first comes to my mind as well." He coughs. "If you will excuse me . . ." He doesn't finish his sentence. He squeezes his son's shoulder and then leaves the room.

The queen, too, looks ready to be gone. "If you will excuse me as well, I have much work to do to prepare. Shaya!" she yells. A young woman appears from behind the doorway. "Please show these people to their rooms." Then the queen makes her exit, albeit more gracefully than her husband.

Without any other choice, we follow the servant, Shaya. Jack insists we should relax, but then he disappears like his parents. The hallway the servant leads the rest of us down is wide, with many doors. Portraits of royal families from centuries ago hang all over the cream-colored walls, and Shaya opens rooms for Alina and her colleagues, Ben and James. Finally, Nadia and I are shown to two rooms on the third floor, right next to each other.

"Apologies for not housing you closer," Shaya says with a curtsey. "At such short notice—"

"It's fine," I tell her. I nod my head and offer her a smile, and she leaves me.

I walk through the double doors and enter a breathtaking room. The bed is in the middle of the room, the wooden headboard pressed to the wall and the yellow silk comforter adorned with pink flowers. The canopy is the same design as the bedspread, as well as the chair to the left of the bed. To the right is a nightstand, and against the wall next to that is a tall wooden dresser. Directly across from the bed stands a wooden wardrobe in a dark shade, resting against the light yellow walls and next to a large desk. Light streams through the curtains of a large window twice as tall as I am on the far end of the room.

I sit on the bed—which is extremely comfortable. As I look around the room in awe of its splendor and consider taking a nap, I hear a knock on my door.

"Come in."

Jack enters the room and sits down on the bed next to me.

"How do you like the room?" he asks. "Are you all right? You and your crew seemed stunned."

"Yeah, I'm fine. Your parents just seem so thrilled to have us here," I reply sarcastically.

"They were just taken aback by your presence. My mother is much more open-minded than my father, that's for sure. But I told you about my father and the pirate he met, and the treatment of pirates in the kingdom was his idea. I suppose seeing you and your crew just brought back those old memories."

"I just wasn't expecting your mother to say yes to keeping us here."

He chuckles. "Well, she's been looking for an excuse to have a ball for a while now. Will you and your crew be attending?"

"No way. They didn't want to stay, and they won't want to go to something this pretentious."

He laughs again.

I keep a straight face. Now that I'm mostly alone, I find myself still thinking about Tellerous, more certain now that I didn't kill him. I know I didn't.

"What is it?" Jack asks.

I shake my head, but the prince keeps prodding so I finally break down. I explain my hunch, my doubts.

"That's impossible," he argues. "Serena, we all saw him disappear. I told you, he's gone."

"But I still feel the magic trying to become a part of me." Even now. I clench and unclench my hands and they tingle, a phantom pulse in their center. Jack is looking at me, so I lift my head and meet his eyes. I need him to believe me, and I think he's starting to.

He reaches up slowly and wipes the tears off my face, his eyes never leaving mine. "I will have more guards scope out the kingdom, and Gurellia too," he says. "But I truly believe he is gone."

"No." I stand. "You have to tell your mother to cancel the ball." What's the queen thinking? Having the ball is a horrible idea. What if it's a trap? What if Tellerous is just waiting for us to lower our guard?

Jack stands as well. "Serena, why?"

"You may not think he is alive, but I know he is. I'm not wrong on this. Tellerous will hear about the party. He'll *know*, and he'll attack."

"Serena, that's ridiculous—"

"Is it?" I ask, pacing. "Because the last time I checked,

Tellerous basically has the powers of a god. Elias said it himself, that the orb wouldn't be enough to defeat him. It was too easy, the fight in the cave. This is all a part of his plan."

I begin cursing in the old Olovian tongue: my stupidity, this ball, Tellerous.

"Serena, stop. . . . Hey, hey! Serena, look at me." Jack puts his hands on my shoulders. "You have nothing to worry about, Serena, it's all in your head. You've hardly given yourself time to recover from the last few days. You're exhausted, you're paranoid . . . but Tellerous is dead."

He sounds so certain. So why am I so certain about the opposite? "I don't want to be like him," I say, my voice trembling. "I can't be like him, Jack. But I still feel it, and whenever I get the sensation that the magic is calling me, I feel like I am becoming my father."

"You are nothing like him, I promise you. You're kind, loyal, strong, and you make one hell of a captain."

I stop crying and laugh, wiping my face with my hands and cursing, once again, my tears. But Jack's hands remain on my shoulders, and I meet his eyes. Neither of us look away. He leans in and I find myself doing the same. But before our faces get too close, I pull away.

Jack's face reddens, and he turns around. "I, um . . . I should go," he says, and he quickly exits the room, leaving me alone with my fears and my embarrassment.

What just happened?

22

*W*e're all invited to dinner that night, but I tell everyone who comes to my door that I'm not feeling well. I need to be alone to think about what almost happened with Jack. Josie, one of the maids, brings dinner to my room, though I don't eat it. I lie in bed, pretending to have a headache.

Ben, Nadia, and James continue to check on me throughout the evening. After sundown, Ben comes into my room to lie with me for a while before he goes to sleep. He doesn't speak, and his company alone is enough to calm me and put me at ease.

Of course, I'm not going to tell him what happened between Jack and I. I'm not planning on telling anybody. It would just complicate things. I am still moving on from James, and I have to make sure that my father is actually dead. But not only that, I can't admit to myself what I'm feeling. A pirate and a prince? After the ball we're going our separate ways for good, and I refuse to participate in any more emotional games.

I barely sleep that night, but what else is new?

Josie wakes me up at sunrise. She brings me breakfast in bed, then tells me the ball has been scheduled for the very next day and it's time to start getting ready. I protest, but I'm silenced when Queen Helena enters the room.

"Good morning, Serena," she says with a smile, looking beautiful in the morning light. "Jack insists that you try on a gown my niece wore here a couple of months ago, when she was staying at the palace. Come now."

She gestures briefly, and I scramble to catch up with her as she leads me to her seamstress's room, just one floor above where I'm staying.

"This is Rose." A young girl sits at a desk surrounded by piles of colored fabric, needles, and thread. Her raven black hair is pulled back in a bun and she wears a plain, navy blue dress. When she notices our presence she rises and comes over to greet me. Up close, I realize she's even younger than I'd imagined; maybe younger than me.

Queen Helena must see my surprise. "Her mother just passed away, and Rose took over her role as our royal designer. She's quite talented."

Not knowing what else to do, I shake her hand. "Hi, I'm Serena."

"Nice to meet you," she says politely, then she turns to the queen. "What am I designing, Your Majesty?"

"Nothing new, Rose. Well"—the queen purses her lips—"maybe make some modifications to the blue dress that Vivian wore to Jack's birthday ball. My son is insisting she wear it, but I'm not certain it would fit as-is." There's clear disappointment in her voice.

"It would be my pleasure." Rose bows her head to the queen before turning her attention to me. "We best get started, then."

The queen gracefully leaves us. And quickly.

Rose takes my hand and leads me to the platform in front of a triple mirror. A tape measure appears from somewhere within her bodice and she holds it up to me.

"My goodness," she tuts. "You have such a tiny little waist. But you have a very nice shape." It's a compliment. I think.

"Um, thank you?"

She stands on her toes to lift up my hair, which goes all the way down my back. She considers it with such thought, and then her nose pinches. "Have you ever considered a haircut?"

"No," I reply quickly, reaching for it. "I am perfectly content with the length it is at."

"Fine," Rose sighs. "But we are going to have to do something with it." She drops my hair, then grabs my face in her palm and turns it to each side. "Such a pretty face, but incredibly pale. This calls for some serious blush."

I really don't know how she can manage to compliment and insult me all in the same sentence.

Rose measures my height, the size of my waist, the circumference of my breast area and torso. Her eyes widen with surprise with the last.

"You're about three sizes smaller than Vivian." She waves her hand, as if to rid herself of the shock. "But never fear, I just need to make a few alterations to the dress. Now, you are free to leave while I work. This may take a while."

I walk back to my room alone, extremely uncomfortable from the physical assessment and feeling small being alone in the castle hallways. When I turn the corner, I hear the queen's voice, cheerful and proud. The door at the very end of the hallway that leads back to the stairs is open. I peer inside, where Jack stands on a platform in front of a mirror, similar to the room I'd just left. The queen is reflected in the mirror, her face a picture of awe at how handsome he looks, tears in her eyes looking at her precious prince.

I stand there, hiding in the corner of the doorway. For the first time, I see Jack for who he really is: a prince. And boy, does he look the part. He's dashingly regal, all dressed in a navy suit with gold epaulets. The sleeves are tight, showing the shape of his muscular arms. His chestnut-brown hair is pushed back, and his smile never leaves his face. His shoulders are squared, his back straight, his head raised in a way that says *king*. I can't look away from him.

"He's a good-looking guy, isn't he?"

I spin around to see Alina standing infuriatingly close to me, smirking at nearly scaring the living daylights out of me.

"Huh?" I say stupidly. "Oh, yes, he's—I—goodbye." I'm flustered and embarrassed, and I still never want to be alone with Alina. I pull away.

"Serena, wait."

"I have nothing to say to you." I look over my shoulder as I keep walking. The thing is, any anger I have is no longer aimed at her, though a part of me knows it should. I should hate her still, and I do, I just don't have it in me to want to kill her any more. I just want to be away.

"Please!" she says, jogging after me. I stop suddenly when she darts into my path. "I need to say this."

The itch to not harm her fades. I wait, trying to keep my expression blank.

"I . . . about Will, I . . ." she exhales and drops her eyes. "I never planned to hurt him. I didn't even know who Will was to you until James told me."

"That doesn't make up for what you did." I try to move around her.

Alina stops me again. "Look, I know we loathe each

other, but if I'd known who he was, I—I wouldn't do anything like that to anyone, not even you."

"Yeah?" I narrow my eyes. "Why should I believe you?"

I push her, and this time she doesn't stop me from leaving. Instead, her voice echoes down the corridor. "My mother killed my father."

I stop walking, and when I turn around she's panting, like admitting it exhausted her. "Did you know that I had to watch it?" she asks. "I know what it's like to lose somebody close at the hands of another. I know the feeling, and I wouldn't wish it on anyone. I just . . . I didn't know."

Is that supposed to be an apology?

She continues, the words pouring from her now. "I know we're enemies, and we'll never be anything more than that. But you saved my sister, and for that I do need to thank you."

I almost don't know what to say. I despise Alina, I always have. I despise her even more for what she did to William, that will never change. But this is a side of her I've never seen. It almost frightens me.

I close my eyes and take a deep breath, bracing myself. "I will never—and I mean *never*—forgive you for what you did," I say. Then I open my eyes and make myself face her. "But, you're welcome."

With that last word, I walk away. Alina lets me. Never in a million years did I think an actual apology would come out of Alina Ortega's mouth, let alone one that sounded so genuine. Am I hallucinating? I must have been more tired than I thought.

As I finish the walk back to my room, I pass the king. I bow my head, not really knowing what else I'm supposed to do, but when I raise it again he's staring at me the same way he did when I first arrived: surprised, shocked. But oddly enough, there's a look of familiarity in his eyes. An intimate familiarity. It reminds me of the way Iana looked at me, and I wonder if there's more he isn't telling anyone.

I finally look in his eyes, but the moment I do so a sharp pain strikes my body. I scream and fall to the ground, my hands gripping the carpeted floor, tearing at the fibers.

A horrid ringing sound floods my ears, the noise deafening. I clench my fists, a terrible ache creeping through my bones. My sight blurs. The room above me spins and my head feels ready to split in two. The voice of the magic tells me to give in. Its eerie whisper echoes in my head.

I close my eyes. The darkness is in me—that's what it feels like. This time in my vision, I see me. I'm surrounded by Cretion magic, and when I turn around my eyes are black and I'm radiating power with that same glow I saw in Tellerous.

And just like that, everything goes black.

I wake up in my room with everyone standing over me. The orb is in Jack's hand, and I can still imagine the magical item's warmth on my skin. The prince smiles as I sit up.

"Another vision?" Ben asks.

I nod.

"I thought those would have stopped once we killed Tellerous," Nadia says.

I look at Jack. "That's what I've been trying to tell you."

"What are you saying?" Alina asks, suspicion darkening her words. "That you killing him was an act?"

"Not on my part. It was too easy," I confirm. "I think he's still out there."

"I wouldn't have believed it if this hadn't happened," James replies.

"Me either," Ben says, nodding.

Jack paces, running his hands over his head as he thinks. "I will have extra guards surrounding the palace tomorrow. I still think Tellerous is gone—maybe this is just the magic itself now—but just in case we will take precautions."

"Having the ball is a horrendous idea," I say, shooting to my feet before anyone could stop me. "Jack, if Tellerous comes—"

"It's too late to cancel it." Jack looks for all the world like he's trying to apologize. "My family is arriving tonight." He sighs and looks away. "I'm glad you're okay. I have to go."

I want to go after him. We haven't spoken since the almost-kiss, and I don't like that things are so awkward between us.

James must realize something happened between us too. "We should all go," he says, eyeing me, something petty shining through his tone. "Serena needs her space. She's been needing a lot of that lately."

When the others leave, Nadia stays. I have a suspicion it's because she senses the weirdness and wants to get to the bottom of it, but she doesn't pry, only stares at me while I avoid her gaze.

Suddenly, she playfully punches me in the arm.

"Ow! What was that for?" I ask.

"For not telling me right away!"

"I didn't tell you—or anyone—because it's not a big deal," I tell her.

"Yes, it is! You and the prince?" she laughs. "I definitely didn't see that one coming."

"Wait, really?"

She punches me again. "No, I totally called it from the

beginning." She dodges my own strike and collapses onto the bed. "So, when are you going to tell him how you feel? Has he told you how he feels?"

I sigh and climb into bed next to her. "No. Last night was a slipup. Nothing actually happened, and it will never happen again. Especially if I'm right about my father . . . there is too much happening right now for me to focus on something so selfish. I have to focus on being ready to face Tellerous again."

Nadia drops her eyes sadly. "But, Serena, you can't just push aside your feelings."

I take the hand she offers and squeeze it. "I can sure as hell try."

23

That night, Jack's family arrives. I sit on the balcony of my room, watching them all filter into the castle. I can see Jack, elated to see his little brother again. The younger prince looks just like him, and he runs to Jack, begging for a ride on the older prince's back. Not long after, I retreat into my room and stay there all night. I don't belong out there. I'm sure Queen Helena and King Archer would agree to that.

The next morning Josie forces me to wake up bright and early again. After eating the breakfast she brings to my room, I'm buffeted around, helping get things ready for the ball and trying to also prepare myself. I search for Jack when I can, finally assuming he'll be in the room I saw him in yesterday for a final fitting.

He is. Alone in the room with a quiet tailor, he looks at my reflection at the doorway but doesn't turn around.

"Where's the orb?" I ask.

"In my room," he says. "It's hidden, and it's safe."

I nod at his clipped tone. He sounds even more unsure

than I do, but I remind myself this isn't the time or place. "Bring it to the ball, just in case."

Jack looks at me as if I've gone mad, but after a moment he agrees. I don't give him the chance to change his mind or say anything else before I walk away.

I don't want to talk or even think about what almost happened between us. Luckily, Rose is the perfect distraction. Josie fetches me, and I grudgingly follow behind her. I've always loathed dresses, but I have to admit this one takes my breath away. It's absolutely stunning. Rose holds it up so I can take a good look at it.

It's a light, sky-blue color and it reaches all the way to the floor. The sleeves are made of a lace that pops off my shoulders, and the lace bodice is decorated with a floral design embroidered on the top and bottom, and a few flowers are scattered on the skirt as well.

"Rose, it's beautiful," I tell her. "But I can't wear it."

"Nonsense!" Rose says. She takes my hand and leads me to the platform in front of the triple mirror. "Prince Jack chose this dress for a reason. It will look lovely on you. Now, come. It is time to get ready."

I put the petticoat on first. It's thick and heavy and I want to take it off, but Rose is already slipping the corset over the top and tying it incredibly tight.

"Okay, Rose—"

She cuts me off when she pulls again.

"Rose, I cannot breathe."

"Beauty takes pain," she replies.

I roll my eyes and clench my fists as she pulls tighter, then layers more and more of the dress over me. Finally, after what seems like an eternity, I'm wearing the heavy dress. When I look into the mirror, I almost don't recognize myself.

Rose gives me a diamond necklace to match, along with small diamond earrings. Silver heels wait for me next to the platform, reminding me of the ones the queen had worn when I'd met her. I look at them disdainfully; I never learned how to walk in them.

"That looks incredible on you, if I do say so myself," Rose says, beaming. "Now, I must do something with this mop on your head you call hair."

What a sweet girl she is.

Although she's starting to get on my nerves, I have to admit Rose is very talented. She gathers my hair into a side bun and braids a section of it to curl around my head like a headband. She adds blush to my cheeks until they look naturally rosy, then applies the silver eye makeup.

Once she's completely done, I put on the heels. I stumble just getting into them, then I nearly break the mirror trying to hold onto it when I attempt to walk and then fall.

Rose laughs at my sad attempts as she helps me regain my balance in these damn shoes. It's much harder than it looks.

"Excuse me," a servant interrupts. "The gates will be opening in approximately ten minutes. The other guests of honor are already at the ballroom doors, waiting to be presented."

"Off you go then," Rose says, flapping her hands as she waves me away with a huge grin on her face.

I nervously grin back before walking out of the room. I look around the hallway, making sure I'm alone and grateful the servant who'd announced the ball hadn't stayed behind. Before joining the others, I walk as fast as I can in the heavy dress and heels up to the room I'm staying in. Right next to my bed rests my cutlass, waiting for me in its belt. I wrap my

Dissometer around the handle, then buckle my sword belt over my dress and head off to go find the ballroom. Jack might think me paranoid, but I want to be ready.

"There you are," Nadia says, appearing behind me. "I've been looking for you. You look beautiful!"

"Thank you," I reply, my cheeks going red. "So do you."

Nadia's dress is silver, and it reaches the floor like mine. White stars pattern the fabric, as well as the cape pinned to her sleeves. Her wavy raven hair is woven into a braided crown, with a few pieces perfectly curled and hanging by her face.

Nadia twirls. "Thank you. This is one of the queen's niece's dresses. Serena, why are you wearing your sword belt over a ball gown?"

"I am preparing in case Tellerous attacks," I huff.

"I think you're being paranoid now." Chuckling, Nadia waves at the skirt. "At least put the belt under your dress."

I play with the layers of puffy fabric. "And how do you suggest I shove it under this mop?"

Nadia rolls her eyes and chuckles. She holds up my dress and helps me wrap my belt underneath the skirt, around the bottom of the corset. Then she takes my shaking hand and leads me to the ballroom on the first floor of the castle.

A wide, long hallway leads to the two wooden doors that many others were waiting in front of. The royal family is nowhere to be seen, but their royal relatives crowd the double doors leading into the grand room. When the gates open to the people, I can only imagine how much worse the looks are going to get. Not all of his kin and court look at me with perplexity and disgust; some of them just look confounded by my presence. They cast the same look at Alina, though it's difficult not to look at her in that strapless, pastel pink gown with its ruffled skirt. The top of the dress is covered with sparkling silver gems, and half of her curly hair is arranged in a waterfall braid. She looks surprisingly resplendent. It nearly hurts my eyes, but enemy or not, she does look pretty.

James looks like he thinks the same. Despite his jealousy toward me and the prince, he looks astonished by her beauty, and even though I'm moving on, it still burns me to see.

I look up, avoiding their gazes, and realize the ceiling is painted like the sky, the pretty blue surrounded by clouds. While we wait, I study the eight portraits of the Olovian gods and goddesses. I stare at them and wonder about the power they held, the choices they made. The choice I'll have to make, if I'm right and my father isn't dead.

"Serena, is that really you?" Ben's voice reaches me through the surrounding din. "I cannot believe *my* sister is wearing a ball gown."

I squirm in the outfit and punch him in the arm. "Don't get used to it. The dress weighs a ton and I'm pretty sure I'm already getting blisters from these annoying shoes."

Thank the gods, the queen's assistant pulls our focus away from me and this dress.

"May I have your attention, please! Friends, nobility, family, and . . . distinguished guests, welcome! The gates have officially opened and the remaining guests are flooding in through the other entrance. Daniel will be announcing you. The Olovian Royal Family is already inside, ready for your presentation." She nods to the two guards in front of the doors, and suddenly the two doors swing open.

I didn't agree to this. Why do they have to announce the high-class citizens to the regular people in Olovia? Is that really necessary? Not only that, but the way she said "distinguished guests" just reminds me all the more that my friends and I don't belong, and nobody wants us here.

Nadia grabs my hand. "Are you ready?" she asks, smiling ear to ear and happier than I've seen her in a while. I shrug and force myself to smile too. Maybe some of us do need this.

We go to the very back of the line, not ready to face the people, but the closer we get to the open doors of the ballroom, the stronger the magic's whispers get, pressing against my nerves, begging me to allow it into myself, offering to pull me away from my discomfort. I shake off the feeling as Nadia and I reach the front of the line, the last to enter the room together, side by side.

We step onto a landing positioned between a double, white marble staircase. I stare at the grand room in awe. Two enormous windows on the left side of the room allow moonlight to shine through. The rest of the lighting is provided by the lanterns lining walls, making the area look more spacious, and there are round tables in sections all around the room with empty plates and champagne glasses covering them.

"And finally," the man I take to be Daniel announces, "presenting Serena Jones and Nadia Renona!"

Nadia and I walk forward, hands clutched tight.

The moment he announces my name, the room goes silent. Some gasp and others just stare. But I'm not paying attention to my fellow Olovians. When my eyes scan the room, they stop once they find Jack. Straight at the back of the room, four blue velvet thrones with gold outlining sit on a slightly raised platform. Jack sits with his parents and brother. The moment we lock eyes, I don't look away. Neither does he.

But when Nadia and I reach the edge of the landing, and

more people fill the room and movement becomes frequent again, we lose sight of each other. I stop looking for him. I can't help but feel as if I ruined things between us. Apparently, ruining things is my specialty. But even if that's the case, I hope he listened to me about the orb. I hope he gave me that much.

Nadia spies the others and I follow her to a table in the back corner of the room. "Is that who I think it is? What is she doing here?" someone asks as I pass. It doesn't surprise me people are perplexed by my presence. Some people recognize Alina as well, but it's me they'll whisper about and give dirty looks to. It bothers me more than I care to admit; I suppose it always has. But as my annoyance grows, the darkness grows, too, its infuriating voice still bouncing around my head. Keeping myself calm is no easy task, especially in this atmosphere.

I try to ignore all of the stares. It's like a thousand tiny daggers are shooting out of each persons' eyes into my back. And my dress is so tight that I can barely breathe, which doesn't exactly help in this situation.

At the table, I move the lilac tablecloth away from my chair to sit down. I meet Alina's eyes and realize the attention is making her uncomfortable as well. Alexia and Freya aren't seemingly as bothered by the looks they're given, laughing and talking with each other, almost inviting the ire of the other guests. I roll my eyes and rest my head in my palm, leaning my elbow on the table when I see the way James is staring at Alina. Is he just trying to make me jealous, or is he truly interested in moving on? I don't know which is preferable.

A loud instrument interrupts my thoughts, a horn bellowing into the air around us.

"Presenting, Queen Helena and King Archer of Olovia!" a servant shouts.

Everyone in the room stands and bows. We copy them as the king and queen come forward, no longer at their thrones but at the top of those double staircases.

The queen smiles and waits for the applause to end. "Thank you all for coming here tonight. I know that for the past few weeks, horrid, sinister things have been happening in the kingdom. But I am elated to say that the source of these terribly heinous acts has been discovered and eliminated!" She waits again as the audience claps and cheers. "I am deeply sorry to anyone who has lost a loved one due to the dark magic. You have our condolences. We will be offering services to those who are in need. But right now I would like to focus on the person that is responsible for the sky clearing again. Prince Jack, my son, risked his life in order to save the realm. He is brave and noble, and I know he will make a fine king. Please, everyone, rise and congratulate our wondrous prince."

Jack stands from his throne, awkwardly waving and smiling. Of course the queen gave him all of the credit.

Then he waves for the noise to die down, and in a loud, confident voice, he says, "Thank you, but it isn't just me that deserves your thanks. Without Serena Jones and her pirate crew, and Alina Ortega and her crew, I wouldn't have been able to bring the realm to its former glory. Please, everyone, give your thanks to my guests of honor: Nadia and Sawyer Renona, Freya Hill, Alexia Lucca, John Markus, James Ferris, and Benjamin and Serena Jones!" He sits back in his throne, sitting up completely straight, looking princely as ever.

All movement and talking comes to a halt. The audience looks to us and hesitates before they start clapping. And though I thought I wanted the acknowledgment, suddenly I'm not so sure.

I turn my gaze to the king, whose face is stolid, like he's trying to keep all of his emotions inside. But what? Anger? Fear? Embarrassment? It looks as if it's making him sick, his skin fading from tan to pale.

I know what it looks like when someone's keeping secrets. The king is hiding something, but I just don't know what. He dons a smile when the queen elbows him to say something, appearing embarrassed, herself, at the attention her son has foisted onto us, but she forces a smile on her face

"Prince Jack is a most honest man," King Archer announces to the crowd grudgingly. "These very . . . honorable heroes deserve your thanks."

They make a toast, and in front of everyone they share a kiss. Jack leaves his throne to join his parents, and he hugs his mother. His gray eyes shimmer under the bright light of the ballroom, and even as the members of the royal family make their way into the congested room and begin to speak with the people, I watch Jack, studying him in his true element for the first time.

It's quite impressive. I know most of the people here are his family, but he's wonderful with them. Everything from his posture to his tone is so regal and genuine. His laugh is so infectious that it brings out a smile in me. He talks with everyone, not skipping over a soul, spending minutes at a time with each one. This is where he belongs. Here, in the castle. Not on the ship, not battling traps in a magical tower, not hiking through the woods to defeat my father. Here.

I, on the other hand, don't belong. I stick out like a sore thumb. Seeing Jack in his natural habitat makes me question everything about myself, about how I'd let myself wind up here. I should be on the *Tigerlily*, at sea. To make matters worse, the tingly feeling in my veins is getting worse. I have to curl my fingers into my palms to muffle it.

"Serena!"

I turn to Nadia. "Hm? What?"

"You're staring."

"No."

"Yes, you were. I was just watching you do that. What's on your mind?" she asks, though from the glimmer in her eye she already knows.

"I was not staring. I was just thinking," I repeat.

"Uh-huh. Well, did you not hear the queen? They are all about to dance."

"No. . . . besides, you know I have two left feet."

As if on cue, James leans over to Alina. "Will you do me the honor of being my dance partner?"

Alina beams. "I would love to."

James takes her hand and leads her to the center of the room, where many other couples have already congregated as the music starts to play.

All around us, people happily make their way to the dance floor. Husbands and wives, fathers and daughters, mothers and sons.

"Do you want to dance with me?" Ben asks Nadia.

She giggles at his question before agreeing to go. John finds a dance partner at the table behind us, leaving me alone at our table. I stare out into the sea of people, looking at the happiness on their faces. As far as they know, all of their problems are gone.

I don't know when the last time I felt like that was. It's been too long.

"I'm gonna go out on a limb and guess this isn't your usual scene?" a new voice asks.

I turn my head to find a gorgeous girl around my age sitting down next to me. She's wearing a strapless, sparkly silver dress. Her strawberry blonde hair is pulled into a braid hanging off her shoulder and her ice-blue eyes shine as bright as the sun. She, out of everyone, does not look happy.

I laugh, relieved. "How did you know?"

"Just a hunch," she replies, smiling gently.

"I'm Serena," I offer, not wanting to appear rude

"I know who you are," she says, placing her hand out in front of her for me to shake it. "I'm Mallory, Duchess of Thomolia."

24

*T*his is the girl who broke Jack's heart.

So what's she doing *here*?

"*You're* Mallory? What are you doing here?" I ask.

"I was invited. Well, my husband and I were," she says with little excitement.

"Why say it like that?"

She drops her eyes, fingers fluttering across the table for an un-drunk glass of champagne. "The life of a duchess is not what I thought it would be," she admits. "My husband isn't who I thought he'd be. But I mean, I wouldn't even be with Kingston—the Duke—if Jack had actually cared about me."

"What are you talking about? *You* cheated on *him*," I remind her.

Mallory sighs. "I felt suffocated in that relationship. All Jack ever talked about was his precious kingdom. All he ever did was work. We never saw each other, and whenever we did it always felt so one-sided." She paused, her eyes to the ceiling. "But how do you even know about that?"

Flustered, I look at my lap. "Jack told me."

"Oh, right. Well, I arrived last night. Queen Helena told me all about your little adventure with Jack. You know, I saw the way your eyes lit up when I said his name. Good for you, a pirate who actually has feelings. I knew he always had a thing for redheads. Just take my word and be careful."

I look at her. "What do you mean?"

"If your relationship with Jack gets a bit . . . friendlier," she confirms.

I backpedal. "Oh no, it's not like that at all." I mean, sure, I'm not actually certain how I feel, but I don't want to have this conversation, and definitely not with her.

But Mallory presses. "I think it is. Like I said, just be careful. Sure, he's handsome and kind, and he's very good at making you feel like you matter. But he'll get bored of you."

"I think you have the wrong idea." Jack isn't like that at all.

"Oh, you poor, poor dear," the duchess coos. "Serena, I have known him my entire life. I know him better than most people. Once he gets back to running the kingdom, you won't even exist to him because he won't have time for you. He will always choose his people over anything else."

"Like I said, you have no idea what you're talking about." I stand to walk away, but Mallory takes my arm, squeezing tight.

"And like *I* said, I know him better than most people. Just don't make the same mistake that I did." Her eyes flick over my shoulder. "Oh, look."

Jack is heading our way. I yank my arm from Mallory's grip, but it's too late to leave. I wipe my palms on my dress and cough to cover the sound of my pounding heart. I'm not really sure what to even say to him.

He looks bewildered at Mallory's presence. "Mallory," he says stiffly, not succeeding in covering his surprise. "What are you doing here?"

"Good to see you, too, Jack," Mallory says, smiling coyly. "You look nice. Kingston and I were invited by Helena."

"Oh, that's—wonderful. Um, you as well. Shouldn't you be dancing with your husband, then?"

Mallory doesn't take the bait. "He's busy chugging champagne. How have you been?"

"Fine, thanks." He looks between us pointedly. With a glint in her eye, Mallory finally stands, smoothing out the folds of her dress.

"I should go, and give you two some privacy." But as she finally walks away, she places her hand on my shoulder and whispers, "Just remember what I said."

I look after her as she disappears into the crowd.

"So," Jack says awkwardly, "would you like to dance?"

On impulse, I say, "Yes."

He takes my hand and leads me to the middle of the dance floor.

"I don't know how to do this sort of thing," I warn him.

He grins as he starts to move to the music. "Just follow my lead." He pulls me close to his chest.

I get the hang of it pretty quickly, even with the heels. Even so, it's much too obvious I'm out of my comfort zone. I'm too stiff, too worried. But as we sway and move our feet, Jack whispers encouragement, just enough until my shoulders relax and I finally stop thinking about the steps to this odd dance.

"So, you actually know how to do whatever this is called?" I ask.

"It is called a waltz. I learned how to do it ages ago. You

might not realize this, but as a prince I have been to many events like this in my life. You look stunning, by the way."

"Thank you. You do as well."

He chuckles. "Thank you. I hope Mallory wasn't too much of a bother to you. What was she saying, anyway?"

I hesitate before filling him in, not wanting to appear nervous about Mallory's accusation. This is trivial court gossip, that's all. Not for me.

Jack's brow furrows, confusion and anger making his grip on me tighten. "Of course she'd say that," he mutters. "I hope you don't believe her. I do care about my kingdom, but our relationship's downfall was the moment she kissed someone else," he explains.

"Yeah, I didn't think she was telling the truth. But I told her there was nothing to worry about, since there is nothing going on between us." The words are out before I'm certain, but I realize upon saying them I've made up my mind. I know that everything that came out of Mallory's doltish mouth is bogus. But, what if it isn't? What if she's right and things wouldn't work between us after all? I mean, I'm a pirate and Jack's going to be king. I am not monarch material, and I don't want to be.

I don't belong here. I will never fit in, and I don't want to. The two of us just wouldn't work.

Jack is silent after my proclamation. Slowly, he says "Actually, about that . . . what about the other night?"

"As far as I am concerned, that night never happened," I answer quickly.

"Why?" he asks.

"We're too different, Jack," I insist. "It would never work. Besides, with Tellerous still—"

"There's another reason you are pulling away from me," he says, "and you just aren't telling me. It has nothing to do with Tellerous either." He lets me out of his embrace. The sudden distance between us is cold.

"That isn't true. There is nothing between us, and there can't be," I reply. "That's it."

He stares at me, plaintive. Then he lets out a sigh that's a massive understatement.

"All right," he says, his voice lowered and almost lost beneath the music and the swirl of guests around us. "I understand. We were just partners, and the job is done now so we're parting ways, anyway. Serena, I would never force you into anything you don't want."

The song ends, and he turns his back on me.

I go after him. "Jack, wait! I didn't mean to—" I freeze when the king rushes in front of me and grabs his son's arm.

"Father, what are you doing?" Jack asks.

King Archer looks between us. Something isn't right. There's a sheen of sweat on his brow and panic has dilated his eyes. "Son, there is something that I must tell you—"

"Well can't it wait?" Jack asks, looking around at the guests. But if anyone notices the king's appearance among them, they haven't reacted.

Ignoring Jack's protest, the king's gaze settles on me. "Serena, you as well . . . I should have told you earlier, but I—"

The candles in the ballroom abruptly go out and we're surrounded by utter darkness. A gust of wind brushes through the room, and in the growing silence comes a collection of hushed screams and gasps. My chest tightening, I wrestle with my poofy dress to take out my sword, cursing Nadia for suggesting it go under my skirt and cursing myself for letting her convince me it was a good idea.

The candles flare suddenly, but the room is much fuller

than it had been before, the shadows moving and the guests screaming as the shadows dart around like demonic bats, charging at person after person, swords in their hands and the air thick with the crackle of magic.

Tellerous's shadow soldiers are here.

25

A wide panic breaks out among the crowd. I race through them, most of them stampeding for the exits but some already dead on the floor. I search the mass of faces, seeing the queen and the young prince being escorted out of the chaotic room.

My father set us up. I knew I was right, that there was something ominous about his sudden disappearance in the cave. He knew this would be the perfect time to strike. There's no time to enjoy this train of thought, though. I hop on one foot, struggling to grab my cutlass and tearing at the fabric of my dress as I try to stay out of sight.

I finally reach the handle of my cutlass. My grip confident, a wave of rage washes through me and I run toward the attackers. From the corner of my eye, I see my hearties bolt to grab swords from the fallen guards.

The shadows lock their focus on me, and as I raise my cutlass they raise their hands. A surge of magic strikes me and I hit the wall. Ignoring the bump on my head, I get up and try to get back to the middle of the room, to my crew. The same shadow tries to hit me again, and I hold my cutlass in front of me to block it. Elias's Dissometer glows green as it deflects the magic, but the force is massive. I push and push against the strength of his powers.

The green fades, creating a beam of blue and black light that's almost blinding as Elias's charm clashes with the powers of the shadow. My hands shake. I dig my feet in those stupid heels into the floor, refusing to be pushed back. With a final burst, the beam breaks. The shadow flies backward across the room, slamming into a table, and I stand victorious.

But like in the cave, there are so many of them. Another of my father's minions comes up behind me, and I turn around and swing my sword at him. The magic on my cutlass gets him before he gets me.

I search the foray. Alina stands a few feet away from me, as well as Nadia. Jack is fighting alongside his father—King Archer being surprisingly good with a sword. But as I spin, I realize Ben and James are completely out of sight. I panic. "Ben!"

But I'm a fool to allow myself to be distracted. I'm knocked to the ground and my sword flies out of my hands. I land just inches in front of one of the creatures, my head hitting the ground hard.

"Careful," it barks to the others. "Sire wants her alive, you imbecile!"

I blink, horribly dizzy as blood drips from my nose and somewhere on my head. As I struggle to my feet, the layers and layers of my dress tangle in my legs.

The shadow in front of me leans down. Though there are no features, I can hear him smiling. "Make this easier on yourself, Princess," it hisses.

Grimacing, I reply, "You must not be speaking to *me*."

It presses closer. I lean back, falling back on my hands as

it continues, "Tellerous is King of the Dark Realm, which makes you a princess. *Our* princess. King Tellerous will not be stopped, but if you come with us now, everyone in this room will live."

Breathing heavily, I scramble back. My hand touches the handle of my cutlass, and I grin. "That offer is truly tempting, but I think I'll go with no." I lunge at him with my cutlass.

He meets me with a surge of black magic. I block it with my sword and roll to my feet, continuing to swing at him until we stand face-to-face. I strike him through the heart with my blade and nearly tip right through him. He doesn't die; stabbing him is like poking my sword through mist.

Horrified, I recall the same thing happening in the cave. "What are you?"

A rumbling sound emerges from him, and I realize he's laughing. "You have much to learn, princess."

"Stop calling me that!" I try to hit him again, which is, admittedly, just foolish of me.

Clearly we can't beat these things with our swords, and they're not going to stop until they get what my father wants. These shadows, or whatever they are, aren't here for just me. Tellerous knows we have the orb, the only item capable of weakening his powers.

So where is it? I don't think Jack listened to me when I asked him to bring it, and I'm not exactly in a position to find him and ask him.

"One more chance," the shadow hisses, pressing toward me. "Come with us willingly, or have the blood of your friends on your hands."

I pause, not knowing what I'm supposed to do. I can't kill him, or even escape from him.

"Have you made up your mind?" he asks, impatient.

I have. "Something you and my father should know about me is that I never give up. Ever. So the answer to your question is, once again, *no*."

"Have it your way, then. But something *you* should know that Tellerous never gives up either."

His magic hits my hand, burning my skin. My cutlass falls, sliding across the room into the chaos around me. I dodge another blast and run after it. This magic isn't the Cretion magic my father used—none of the magic they're using resembles it. Tellerous's magic looks like black lightning; this is a shimmering black smoke that leaves the air hard to see through.

I locate my sword near a column, but as I leap for it I miscalculate and jump right into the waiting shadow's magic.

He knocks me to the ground, the force pushing my breath from my lungs. Smoke gathers around my wrists, solidifying into chains. I struggle to release myself as he approaches me, and though I try kicking out at him, the dress softens all of my blows. The shadow reaches out and picks me up, slinging me over his shoulder. Though I squirm, his grip is too tight.

"Let me go!" I shout, hitting his back with my chained hands. It's like he doesn't even feel them.

"I got her," he cheers to the shadows around him. But as he makes his way to the exit, we're unexpectedly tackled to the ground. He drops me and I roll away, sitting up in time to see Alina wrestling with the shadow, trying to keep him pinned to the ground. It appears we'd had the same idea: her Dissometer is wrapped around her hand, using it to land blow after blow against the shadow. The chains on my wrist disappear as the shadow loses control, and I bolt to get my cutlass.

I nearly have it when someone else reaches it first. I sigh when I follow the hand to the person holding it and see Ben.

I hug him tightly, relief spreading a huge grin on my face.

"I was so worried about you, are you all right?" I ask as I hold his face in my palms, pressing my thumbs to the cuts on his face.

He doesn't have time to respond. A blast of magic tears between us, missing our heads by an inch. Ben tosses my cutlass to me, and as if on cue, Jack bolts into the ballroom holding the orb in his hands. He swiftly darts around the grand space, shooting the orb's magic at the shadowy creatures. Some of them are able to dodge it, others disappear into thin air.

The remaining shadows surge on me. I fight against them, Ben by my side, and my attention wavers. I have to protect Ben and keep the shadows from us; I have to watch Jack and make sure he's all right. There can't be anything between us, but I need him to be okay.

Jack shouts, pain lacing his voice. I kick off a shadow who comes too close and dive through a gap in their bodies, scooping up the orb from where Jack dropped it. The shadows are right behind me, surges of magic bursting over my shoulder as I weave through the ballroom, leaping over chairs, rolling over tables, hopping over broken glass—all while in heels.

I run up the stairs to the balcony, but when I reach the top I find myself blocked in. I look at the railing and take a leap of faith.

"Catch!" I scream to Alina before I jump off.

I roll onto the ground, my shoulder smacking onto the white marble floor. I get back up on my feet, ignoring the aching pain of my entire body.

"What am I supposed to do with this?" Alina asks.

"Use it, you idiot!" I answer.

She looks at me if I have three heads, and when the shadows converge on her she tosses it to Nadia, who is standing a few feet away from her.

As the shadows multiply, Nadia fumbles with the orb, struggling to use it on my father's increasing forces. I stand behind her, fighting off as many as I can, never able to kill them, only knock them back. They separate us, but as more shadows come forward, she tosses me the orb. "Not it!"

I use it on every shadow that comes toward me, loving the sensation of the energy the light magic radiates. But there are too many of them, and now everything they want is in one place.

I don't see the shadow who tried to take me earlier. He sneaks behind me and knocks me to the ground, his hands reaching for the orb. It rolls out of my hand, under a table cloth. As I scramble for it, he uses his magic to grab me and yank me back, sliding me across the room.

When I crash into a table, I hear two arguing voices. I looked up and I realize I'm right behind Jack and his father.

"Son, I need you to listen to me—"

"Now's not the time!" Jack yells back, dodging a bit of magic that comes his way.

"There's no other time!" King Archer yells. "I-I have been w—" He's interrupted when he's struck with magic, flying into the middle of the staircase, crashing down hard.

Jack hesitates, but at my nod he darts to help his father. The king's lips move, still trying to tell Jack something that must be important. But he can't get the words out. There is no room for conversation in the middle of battle.

The orb. I look for it across the room, fearing the shadows have gotten it, but it's Ben holding it in his hands, aiming it at the shadows as they group and reform, holding back as if they're planning something, or re-planning. The shadow who'd come after me is larger than the others; I find him in a smaller group and point, and Ben shoots the orb's magic in their direction. Only one of them vanishes.

"Ben, look out!"

He glances behind him and runs, chased by at least twenty figures who each use their magic against the orb. The magic hits him, sending him flying across the room. The orb falls back into the chaos.

I look around me. Half of Jack's soldiers are dead and the other half are doing their best to drive the shadows away, even trying to protect Ben and my hearties. They and Alina and her two crewmates group together, fighting off the endless onslaught of my father's minions.

This isn't working. It isn't going to work.

"Jack, what—what I was trying to say is that I haven't been honest with you," the king says behind me, louder over the battle, desperate to be heard. I spin around. He's standing now, Jack's arm holding him up. "I am so sorry for what I am about to say, Jack, but the truth is, I—"

He's cut off, his words vanishing in a pained gurgle and the point of the shadowy sword sticking out of his chest.

"Father!" Jack cries.

The shadowy figures appear out of nowhere, next to the king. They vanish just as quickly. Jack fights the blood pouring from his father's chest, collapsing under the king's dead weight. I look over my shoulder at all of the shadows, who pull back and disappear in a cloud of smoke.

The last to leave is the tall one, who'd called me "princess." He holds the orb in his hand, and he seems to tip his head to me before he, too, vanishes.

26

*J*ack sits over his father's lifeless body, a stream of steady tears falling. He rests his head on his father's chest, the image of him mourning his loved one too familiar. I know exactly how he feels. The fight over, I collapse as a tear of empathy runs down my cheek. I look down at the ground, paying my respects to the king, wishing Jack had listened to me in the first place.

Ben, Alina, Nadia, and James rush over to us. They stand over the fallen king, out of breath. The guards who are still alive each take a knee. Nadia grabs onto Sawyer as she closes her eyes, and I know she's remembering the feeling from when she lost her parents. So am I.

The air is thick, filled with blood and the salt of sweat and tears. I stand and walk over to Jack, and I lean down to his level as I put my hand on his shoulder.

"Jack, I am so sorry. I know—"

"I don't want your pity," he snaps, turning his head enough that I can see the hardness of his eyes. "You have *no idea* how I'm feeling. Do us both a favor and leave me alone."

"*Jack*," Nadia snaps back at him, tears in her eyes.

I pull away, stung. "No, Nadia. It's fine. If you'll excuse me." I run from the ballroom, thankfully holding off until I'm away from everyone for the grief to pour from me.

I had to leave the room. I didn't want to seem selfish, to sit there and argue that I do relate to what's happened to Jack. Jack's pain is fresh, and right now it's so much more intense than mine. I may not have had to watch my parents die, but the fact is that they *were* killed. They were killed, and for years I never knew the truth of what happened to them. I lost my parents to Tellerous, I lost William to the pirate who'd saved me during this very battle.

But right now I'm hurt because I've ruined things between us, before the fight and now after, and I don't think there is any way I can fix it.

"Serena, wait!" Nadia calls after me from the hallway, barely catching up to me when I enter my room. She bursts through the door and sits down next to me on the bed.

"I'm so sorry about what he said," she says gently. There are tracks on her face marking the tears she'd shed, smearing the makeup around her eyes. "I know losing your parents was the most difficult thing you have ever gone through. It was for me, too, and then you find out that it was because Tellerous—" she breaks off and shakes her head. "Well, that is like the cherry on top of worst experiences."

"What happened to the king is worse," I admit. "But I do know how he feels. We all do. And I am not sitting here bawling my eyes out because of what he said . . . I think I messed things up, and there is nothing I can do to fix it. This is all my fault, and he hates me now, and he has every right to."

"From what it sounds like, don't think he loathes you," Nadia assures me. "I think he's just hurt, now more than ever. He will forgive you, though, that I know."

Maybe. But we have other problems to deal with too. "The orb's been taken. I don't know what to do. Nadia, what am I supposed to do? I don't know how to—"

"Okay, slow down before you pass out from talking too fast," Nadia says, chuckling through her grief. "Breathe. We are going to find the orb."

"Yeah? And just how are we going to do that?"

"I don't know, but we will figure it out. For right now, we need to get out of these clothes and go back to the ballroom, okay? We need to be there for Jack and Queen Helena and the younger prince. We will figure out a plan there." Nadia wipes off my running mascara. "Come on, let's get out of these dresses."

It's a job that takes all of our concentration, taking us maybe fifteen minutes in total to get free of those gowns. I remove the jewelry, let down my hair, and wipe off all of my makeup. I'm much more comfortable back in what I was wearing when I arrived at the castle, but the most relief comes when I put my boots on in place of those heels. We walk back to the ballroom together, finding it filled with castle workers and the remainder of the royal family.

Jack is holding his mother and little brother in his arms. The king's body is already being taken away, along with the others. Too many others. Many of the injured guards are being carried away on gurneys, some of them still dripping blood that stains the floor. But the horrid pain still lingers. More than anything in the world, I want to comfort Jack. I don't know how I am going to make things better, but it physically hurts knowing he's angry with me, knowing he's in an endless kind of grief that I know will never pass.

I put my arm around Ben as we listen to the people in the castle grieve over their tremendous loss, but I can't look away from the royal family. The expression on the queen's face breaks my heart. She looks as if everything has been ripped away from her, and I remember the day Will told me that my mother and Lennard would not be returning home. I had collapsed to the ground. I didn't stop bawling for days. My entire world came crumbling down. I drowned in my sorrows, unable to eat, or sleep, or even get out of bed. For months it continued, and it wasn't until I saw the immense amount of pain my little brother was in, and the other children of my parents' crewmates, that I pulled myself together. That's where my crew came from—the grief and rage of our loss.

That's when I decided to shut off my emotions. They make you weak. They nearly destroyed me.

"In a way, this reminds me of Mother and Father's funeral," Ben whispers.

"It does," I agree.

"I wish there was something we could do. How are we going to get the orb back?" Ben asks.

"We'll figure it out," I hesitate to say.

Because we need to figure something out. This is all my fault. Tellerous sent his men to the palace to get the orb, to get me . . . and to kill the king? There is no mistaking their retreat after the king's death. But why? What did King Archer have to do with my father? He'd wanted to tell me and Jack something important, he was desperate to.

As I stand quietly, my arm linked in Ben's, I remember something Tellerous said when we met him in the cave—Southwest Hillins Island. That's where he is now, and as an idea strikes me I make my way through the crowd over to Queen Helena. Tellerous needs a wake-up call, and I'm going to give it to him.

"Your Majesty," I say softly. "I'm truly sorry for your loss.

I promise you, the man who is responsible for this will be gone for good this time. I know where to find him."

My hearties shoot their gazes to me when they hear the last part of my sentence, but the queen only looks at me with numbness in her swollen eyes. She glances over at Jack before looking at me once again, and this time there is a fire lit inside her that sends shivers down my spine.

"Then end him," she says.

27

"Don't give her false hope," Jack warns.

"I'm not. In the cave, remember? He said he was going to the Southwest Hillins Island."

James joins us, his arm wrapped around Alina. "So what are we waiting for?"

The queen looks over us all, but she hesitates when she sees the look on Jack's face. It's a determination that won't be argued, and I think she knows there's no stopping him.

"Please, be careful," she says to him. "I can't lose anyone else."

Jack hugs his mother. "I promise you, Mother, you will not lose me. And I swear on Father's grave I will make that disgusting excuse for a human being pay for what he did." The venom is clear, but when he pulls away and turns to a group of uninjured guards, it's gone. "I need every last one of you. Gather the ships, gather every available man, and sail to Southwest Hillins Island."

My crew filters from the room in a hurry. I take one last look at the queen before I follow them. We *are* getting that orb back, no matter the cost. And I am through playing games with my father. I'll kill him this time. It is now or never.

I pace as Nadia and I wait by the front door of the palace for Jack and the others to get ready. My hand slips into my pocket, my fingers finding the ruby necklace.

Soon, Jack storms down the stairs, followed by the rest of the crew. He pushes past me without stopping. "Let's go. I am not going to rest until Tellerous and every last one of those shadows is dead." I have never heard such rage from him.

We follow him out, and as we make our way back to the docks I speak to the others. "I know we're all tired and ready for this to be over, but we are so close to winning this—this war. So, Southwest Hillins Island, here we come." I grimace and turn to Alina specifically. "We won't make it if it's just my crew and Jack's army. Alina, we need as many people as we can get, that includes you two." I motion to Freya and Alexia.

Alina nods. There is a bruise on the side of her face, and a cut on her lip. "I will speak to my crew. They're waiting at the docks."

"Then let's give my father a taste of his own medicine."

Silence overcomes us as we exit the castle courtyard. I keep my eyes on Jack, marching ahead at the front of the group, his shoulders hunched and his hands curled into fists. "Why don't you just talk to him?" Nadia asks.

"Hm?" I reply, startled by her sudden presence next to me.

"You're staring at him. Longingly, I might add. You look like a sad, lost little puppy. Just go talk to him."

"He made it crystal clear that he doesn't want me to," I remind her. We pass under the castle gates.

She shrugs. "People say a lot of things in rage that they don't mean."

I pause in my tracks at her statement while she continues to walk. I think about it for a moment, but then continue down the path, into the woods that lead back to the docks.

Maybe she's right, but I don't want to risk making things worse between us. I nervously grip my cutlass as we head forward into the shadowed forest. Ben grabs onto my free hand as we walk farther, looking around urgently as if Tellerous's men will come back to finish us off. The whole time, I think about what the king had been trying to say to Jack. He wanted to tell him something important. He'd almost looked guilty.

Maybe that is why the shadows killed him. It's obvious that his death was orchestrated by my father, but I'm desperate to understand why. What would Tellerous gain from killing King Archer? The shadow man had told me that all of my questions would be answered soon, but clearly not soon enough.

My veins clench as we continued forward. The magic is near, and during the battle at the ballroom I'd almost forgotten about it. But the more worked up I get in my head, the more noticeable those powers become. The blood in my veins flows rapidly, and that tingling is no longer confined to my hands; it's all throughout my body.

I'm terrified of what Elias told me, terrified that whatever awaits us at the island will lead to the choice I have to make. I still haven't said a word to anyone, not wanting to alarm them.

"Why the long face? Pretty boy still not talking to you?" Alina questions.

"What are you talking about?"

"I overheard your conversation with Nadia."

Of course you did. I sigh, not in the mood to argue. "Can we please just talk about anything else?"

"Sure, like what?"

"Like, what's with you and James?" I ask, remembering the way he'd had his arm around her at the castle. I try to sound excited, but given who I'm talking to—and about— it's hard.

Alina blushes. "Honestly, I don't know. We're *just* getting to know each other, and I really like him, more than I've ever liked anyone in a long time, and I think he likes me, too . . . but there is too much going on right now to do anything. And there's you and me, and James feels quite loyal to you . . ."

That's a relief. "I completely understand that."

And just like that I'm back to thinking about Jack. But my situation with Jack is much different than the one between Alina and James. At least James is actually speaking to her. I want to talk to Jack, so very badly, but I don't know exactly what to say and I don't think he wants to hear it right now. From anyone.

We haven't known each other long, and he's a massive pain, and things are so different now than they had been before. But I have lost so many people and I can't lose him too. I need him. Facing my father is going to be no easy task, and I don't think I'm mentally ready for it.

What I want more than anything is for this to be over, and as terrified as I am, going to Southwest Hillins Island is the only way to do that. But I'm not ready. I'm not ready to figure out which outcome of the prophecy is going to come true. Maybe I should tell someone about it. Definitely not Ben, and one-hundred percent not James. Nadia? Maybe. I just don't want to cause any panic. They're too close to me. If I tell Jack, then—no. I can't.

I can't. When it comes to the prophecy, I'm alone.

As soon as I realize this, I freeze. I can't move, or think, or speak. Then I feel it. Magic already coursing through my veins, sending raging, throbbing bursts of pain all throughout my body. I scream as I fall on one knee, and I clamp my mouth shut, gritting my teeth, as I place my left hand on the ground and wrap my right arm around my stomach. As if I can physically hold the magic inside of me.

"Serena?" Alina says, dropping to my side.

Then there's someone else. "Hey, hey, hey. It's okay," Jack says. "The magic is starting to affect you again, isn't it?" he stupidly asks. I crack my eyes open enough to watch him slide on his knees to my level. He places his hand on my back.

I squeeze my eyes tightly shut as another wave of pain rolls through me, and I nod. I can't trust myself to open my mouth.

"What are we supposed to do?" Ben asks, panicking.

I hear the others speak over each other, but my vision goes dark as the agony spikes. I'm holding the magic back, but I can't do it for long. And then what?

"Jack, help her up. We need to move fast," Nadia orders.

Jack hesitantly places his arm around my waist and assists me in standing back up. The move shakes my vision clear, and I look up at Nadia, who winks, smirking. Although the pain still lingers in my body, I force myself to walk and hold on to Jack, who keeps me standing. Alina and Nadia walk ahead of us, and the others go on with them, leaving the two of us in awkward silence.

"How are you? You know, with everything with your father," I bite out each word, unable to take the deafening silence.

"It's the same thing with you and William," he says. "I can't dwell on it. That won't get us anywhere. I'll be fine once we kill Tellerous. Maybe then I'll know what my father was going to tell me. I asked my mother and she was just as clueless as I was."

"I'm sure you'll find out soon."

"I would certainly hope so."

Just as I open my mouth, I immediately close it, abstaining myself from saying anything I'll possibly regret.

But Jack sees it. "What were you going to say?"

"Nothing." I lie.

"With you, it's never nothing. Just tell me what you wanted to say."

"No, this time it really is nothing," I assure him.

"Fine." He gives up.

I had the words all ready to come out of my mouth, but I physically can't say them. And my inability to speak has made him pull away from me again.

Ben calls his name, and he's more than thrilled to go to him. Nadia takes his place, her arm around my waist, and I place my hands on my face, despairing at my ability to push people away.

"What's wrong?" Nadia asks, pulling my hands from my face. "And don't say 'nothing.' That might work with Jack, but you know it won't with me."

I groan. "I am not very articulate when it comes to saying how I feel, which just is driving him away."

"Well, that makes sense. You're nervous," she concludes.

"No, no I don't get nervous. It's just, whenever he looks at me or speaks to me, I get this odd feeling in my stomach, like I'm gonna pass out."

"Yeah, *that feeling* is called butterflies, and you just contradicted your own argument," she replies.

"It's just the magic—"

"*Serena.*"

"Damn it, I know." I lean my head back, frustrated.

Nadia chuckles.

"I don't get it, Nadia. What is happening to me? I mean, have you ever seen me like this before?"

"No, not even with James. That's why I think you should just tell Jack how you feel. I know it's easier said than done, but I have known you for most of my life and so I know that you are fearless," she tells me.

"I always thought so. But look at me now. What happened to me?" I ask.

Nadia smiles. "Something my mother always used to tell me is that there is always going to be a person who comes into your life and completely changes everything. For me it was you. You saved me and my brother from living life alone as orphans on the streets. For you, though, it's him."

So much about me has changed since I met Jack. I suppose I haven't given much thought about that, but Nadia isn't wrong.

"So, what do I do?" I ask.

Nadia laughs. "My answer is the same: When the time is right, just tell him," she answered.

"Thank you," I reply softly as she grabs my hand.

How is it that I faced Allensway's ship with only my twenty crewmates on my side, and I'm more afraid to tell Jack what I really think of him?

What am I going to even say?

We're approaching the docks, the streets empty in the

late night and the ships imposing against the midnight sky. I need to be one-hundred percent focused on what lay ahead, but as we reach William's tavern, I pause in my tracks and stare at the building. The glowing moonlight beats down on the tavern, almost highlighting the building. The air is thick, filled with fog and salt from the sea. A chill runs down my spine. I'd promised I'd kill Alina, and it takes everything I have to not turn around and make her pay for what she's done, accident or not.

Tears form in my eyes. I jump when someone's arm loops over my shoulder. I look up and there's Jack, and I know I'm safe. I glance over at Alina, who's also staring at the tavern, trembling with guilt.

"Come on," Jack says, "we should be getting ready to leave." He grabs my hand and pulls me along, and I realize that at his touch the magic softens. It's easier to fight away, almost painless now.

I send Nadia to the *Tigerlily* to give the crew an update and prepare them for what's next. I tell her to give them a choice of journeying with us or not. We desperately need all the help we can get, but I don't want to put my crew in any more danger. Tellerous is not the same as pirating; Tellerous is nothing we'd trained for.

Meanwhile, I follow Alina to her ship. She's already speaking to her crew, and it isn't going well.

"I am not going anywhere with a pertinacious prince and our sworn enemy," one girl says, crossing her arms.

"Rachel, please," Alina begs. "We need you."

"But of all people," another girl says, "why should we work with *them*?"

Alexia steps up then. "Because we don't have a choice. The man who cast the spell is not dead, and until we kill him, none of us are safe. We will never be able to set sail safely again." On Alina's other side, Freya nods.

The all-female crew still looks apathetic about it. I can't say I blame them.

Alina sighs. "I told you to dock here and wait for further instruction. Now, I am giving you instruction. I'm the captain, and I am giving you orders."

Ben appears behind me, to tell me something or just to watch, I'm not sure. The girl named Rachel notices the movement, and she looks over at Ben, causing him to blush. "You know what?" she says. "Fine, I'll join you. I suppose you're right, and as our captain we should all stick by your side."

I roll my eyes and cross my arms, stepping directly in front of my brother, blocking Rachel's view of Ben.

The other girl who'd objected isn't as easily swayed. "I still stand by my answer," she says.

Alina's shoulders pull back, and I recognize the signs of a captain about to explode. "You know what, Emilia?" she says, her voice frighteningly calm. "Fine. You're off my ship. Get out. I don't want to see you here again." Alina points her finger to the town.

"As if that's some kind of punishment? I would have thought you could do much better than that," Emilia laughs.

"You're absolutely right. I can do *much* better." In a flash, Alina is in front of her, her cutlass out and a thin cut on her crew member's arm, just big enough to draw blood. Then she nods to Freya and Alexia, who take Emilia's arms and pull her toward the sea, shimmering in the moonlight. "I'll have you swim with the sharks. Don't worry, Em, once they smell blood, it will be quick and easy. You won't feel a thing."

Emilia panics, struggling to get out of their grasp. But

she's powerless, and as the edge of the dock nears, her eyes widen.

"Okay, okay, okay! Get off! I'll join you. We all will." At the admission, Freya and Alexia let her go. Emilia pushes them away from her.

And with that, Alina grins. Alexia climbs back onto their ship to ready the crew to join mine, and the rest of the girls glare, blaming me for their unwanted fight. This won't be an easy alliance, but what choice do any of us have?

We wait for Alina's crew to climb aboard the *Tigerlily*. I hear many shouts—annoyed, angered shouts—coming from her crewmates. But she somehow convinces them, and I wonder how many more threats to join the fish she'd had to give. My crew objects as well, but with the exception of two boys who abandon us among the chaos, they know that there is no other option. This isn't about gold or power or being the best anymore. Knots tie in my stomach, my body becoming more and more tense as we prepare to set sail.

I have done my best to neglect the feeling of the dark magic, but it's still lingering throughout my body, making me dizzy. I push through, helping the combined crew raise the sails and prepare to meet my father at the island.

As I pace the deck, multitasking to get things done, Ben comes to my side. Whatever he wanted to say to me earlier is about to bubble out of him. "Serena, um, can I ask you something?"

"I'm sorry, Ben, can it wait?" I ask.

"No," he answers firmly.

"Okay, what is it?"

"Do you think that we're going to survive?"

I pause, my eyes widening at his question. I have no idea how to answer that. I really don't know what's going to happen. I don't know what outcome Elias warned me about would come true.

Something about his tone, though, suggests he already has the answer, and it isn't good. I can't lie to him, but I have to come up with something at least semi-positive.

"I think so," I say, fibbing just a little.

"How can you be sure?" he asks, his voice wavering

"I'm not. I just have faith." I smile at him and nudge his shoulder. "Don't be thinking about this now. We need to focus on actually making it to the island first." I direct him to John and Sawyer, trying to distract his thoughts.

"Right." He nods before he walks away, anxiously playing with the end of his green doublet coat.

He could probably see right through my fake, upbeat tone. I just want to give him something to hold on to. Maybe for this specific battle, he shouldn't come with us. But without William, he'll have nobody to take care of him. He's not a baby, he's thirteen. But he's my brother. I practically raised him, and he was so young when our parents died.

"James?" I call out. It takes him a moment, but he comes rushing over to me.

"What is it, Captain?"

I stare after my brother. "At all costs, I need you to help me protect Ben."

"Why do you already sound like something is going to happen?" he asks.

"I'm just trying to prepare," I reply. What I don't tell him is that I need him to take care of Ben in case either of Elias's predictions comes true.

James looks uncertain, like he wants to argue with me. Then he nods. "I will protect him with my life."

No matter what happens to me, I just want to make sure Ben is okay. I want to give him the best life possible, even if all of his blood-related kin are all gone. Even if I'm gone. James would be captain, and I know Ben would always be taken care of.

"Thank you," I breathe. "Get everything ready to set sail. I need to take care of something."

I don't give James a chance to reply before I leave the ship on a whim. There's one last thing I need to do before we leave.

I head to the tavern, ignoring the sound of my mates' voices calling after me as I pause in front of the building, staring. It feels colder than it used to. I shove open the doors and walk inside the empty room, look around at the bar, at all of the tables and chairs and the stone fireplace in the corner. When my parents died, I spent a lot of time here. I sat in the corner with Will and he gave me these delicious pastries as he told me stories of adventures he went on when he was a kid. Whether he made them up or not, I still didn't care. There's a blocked-off staircase in the left corner, where his apartment was. Ben and I lived there for a time. Will would sit with me on my bed until I fell asleep.

Shivering, I pull out a chair and sit down, resting my hands in my lap, leaning over and staring at the ground. The burning guilt was bubbling up in my throat—my secret of Elias's predictions, my knowledge of possible future events. I know keeping it a secret is the best idea, but I am afraid of what will happen when my crew—my friends, my family— find out I lied to them. My head pounds, my chest aches, and everything around me spins. It wasn't a good idea to come here, I realize. Working myself up is not helping anything, but I can't help myself. The more and more upset I get, the worse I feel physically.

I give myself five minutes with Will's ghost, but we're on a time crunch. I have to leave.

"Wish me luck, Will. I love you," I whisper before exiting the tavern for the last time.

Out in the open, the pain intensifies. All I can see this time is a black dusty cloud, but nothing else surrounds it. Not me, not anyone. Everything around me disappears, my breath caught in my throat, and I hit the ground. This time, I know what the vision means.

My father knows we're coming, and this time he isn't leaving until he gets what he wants.

28

I pass out. Again.

Just like the last time, I can hear everything going on around me, but I just cannot move. It seems everyone's getting used to it. Jack carries me to my sleeping chamber, and I feel safe in the comfort of his arms.

I'm relieved when the pain vanishes, but my body still aches with fear. Elias and Queen Iana's words play on repeat in my brain and I can't get them to stop.

"What are we supposed to do now?" Ben asks as Jack places me on my bed. "It's getting worse."

"Just get Joseph to start sailing the ship. Nadia, make sure the two crews don't kill each other. I'll figure out how to wake her up without the orb," Jack responds.

They don't reply, but I hear them exit the room. I try so hard to force myself to move, but no matter how much effort I put into it my body won't budge. I can't just lie here, completely useless. I need to be on my feet at all times for the upcoming battle.

I focus, more desperate than I've ever been. I carefully imagine myself moving, and I take in a deep breath and focus on Jack's presence nearby, at the sound of his breathing, the sudden sensation of him taking my hand. I clench my fists tightly, sending a sensation of powerful energy through my bloodstream. Not dark magic, just . . . me.

I open my eyes, slightly grinning at my accomplishment, and slowly sit up. I rub my eyes before attempting to get out of my bed, but Jack pressed me back down, his face a mask of shock.

"No, no, no, lie back down. You need to recover. That vision looked incredibly painful, more so than the last. What did you see?" he asks.

I explain what I saw and what I felt down to the last detail. "He's ready for us, Jack," I say.

"Did you think he wouldn't be?" he asks. He sighs and leans back in his chair. "But you—are you okay? How did you wake up on your own?"

"I am okay now," I say, realizing I'm still grasping his hand. I let go of it, my face heating up. "I-I don't know how I woke myself up."

"Jack!" a muffled voice calls out from the deck.

"Get some rest," Jack says softly, curling the fingers of his hand gently. "I'll be right back."

I put my hands over my face, easing my pounding head. The majority of my anguish had disappeared—and I don't know how—but my body still trembles with pain. Elias warned me these visions would keep getting worse and worse, and I am honestly terrified of what will happen the next time I experience a vision. This one was from my father; he wants me to know he's waiting, and I don't think he intended for me to remain unconscious.

I can't dwell on it long. Nadia bursts into my room. "Hey, how are you doing?"

"I'm a physical and mental mess," I say, counting on my

fingers, "and I'm just spiraling deeper." I sit up and bury my face into my shaking palms.

"What do you mean?" Nadia asks as she sits next to me, placing her hand on my back.

I explain the feeling of the darkness and how horrified I am.

"That's just called being human. This is the first time you've experienced true fear, and you've learned the truth about the many mysteries of your past. That's never easy," she says, rubbing my back. "Fighting off the darkness cannot be easy. But Serena, you don't have to do it alone."

I ignore that last part. "I just . . . what if we fail? What if my father's army outnumbers us? What happens if we all—"

"Okay, slow down. I feel the exact same way as you. But you have to take things one day at a time. Step by step. We're not even at the island yet, but even so, I don't think we'll fail. With Jack's army, Alina's irritating crew, and us, I think we have a good chance." She stands and turns to me, hands on her hips. "Now, what I want is for you to get some rest. You haven't fully slept in days. Once you recharge yourself, you'll be ready to fight."

I give her a soft, sly grin before she gives me one last gentle pat on the back and leaves my quarters. I take a deep breath in and dramatically slam my body back down onto my bed. Then I close my eyes, doing my best to listen to Nadia's advice.

In just two short days, we'll arrive at the island to find my father and try to kill him . . . if it's even possible. I really, truly hope it is. In all of my nineteen years, I have always wondered what my father is like. Growing up, even with my mother telling me how horrible he was, I secretly pictured him as some kind of benevolent hero. I always just assumed my mother meant that he'd hurt her.

When I was much, much younger, I used to think that one day he would come back into my life. When I met him, I was going to give him the biggest hug and warmest smile. As I got older I realized that my naïve thoughts were probably incorrect, but I never expected him to be a nefarious sorcerer intent on wiping out millions of innocent lives so he could be king.

I am absolutely, utterly petrified. If the magic doesn't kill me, if the other outcome Elias predicted comes true, then what will Tellerous do with me?

Could I even get back to Ben? A montage of possible scenarios plays in my head, sending a chill down my spine and terror through my veins, and I realize I'm angry with my mother, angry with her for not giving me some kind of warning about him. I understand why she didn't, but maybe things would be different if I'd known who he was in advance.

I'm not just unprepared for the upcoming fight, I am unprepared to stand face-to-face with Tellerous a second time. I don't know how I am going to make it through that. How am I supposed to look at the face that killed my parents, nearly murdered half the people in my kingdom, and plans to rule the realms with an iron fist?

He's mad. I can't help but suspect I am leading my crew into a fight that is being set up for us to lose. They deserve a better captain, a better leader. A lump appears in my throat the more I think about it. No matter how much I want to sleep, I just can't. There's too much chaos in my mind keeping me awake. But when the sun finally rises, I sleep like a baby, having tired myself out from panicking in my head.

I wake up quite late, feeling well-rested for the first time in a long time. I brush my hair and get dressed, then walk out to the deck, happily enduring the warm sunshine of the early afternoon and staring at the shimmering water as if I never will again. Maybe I won't.

I take control of the wheel from Joseph and stare out at the shining blue water ahead of me. Given our situation, sailing my ship is the only order I have. I tighten my grip on the wheel and swallow the lump in my throat as my worry grows again, knowing we're sailing closer to a place I won't return from.

"Captain?" I jump at Adam's sudden presence. "What happened to you? And what, exactly, are we going up against when we arrive?"

I hesitate to answer. Honestly, I really don't know. I assume more shadow creatures, but only the gods know what's going on in my father's deeply twisted mind.

"You know what we're up against, Adam. You were there when we faced Tellerous at the cave. He has magnificent power, an army of shadow creatures with a handful of magical elements to help them, and now he has the orb. If you didn't want to be here in the first place, you should have stayed in Olovia with Oliver and Whilmer," I snap fearfully, not truly meaning to say any of that.

He looks incredulous, months of the struggle between us reaching the boiling point thanks to the last week. "We need better leadership," he says suddenly, though discreetly. "You are an unfit captain."

"Adam—"

"What kind of captain leads their crew into shark-infested waters?" he asks.

I drop my hands from the wheel and face him. Nadia, who has been sitting behind me, jumps up quickly and takes the wheel.

I approach Adam slowly, daring him to stand up to me,

more and more infuriated as his features go from confident to terrified. I grab my cutlass with one hand and grip his shirt with the other as I push him against the ship's railing.

I hold my weapon up to his neck, for I have no control over the wave of anger that comes over me.

"Listen, and listen good," I whisper to him. "I can kill you, right now, without anybody even knowing. But I won't. I am not doing this to bring you all into danger, but to keep you from it. Once my father is dead, we can carry on with our normal lives. If you didn't want to be a part of this, the time to say so has passed. If one more insult about me comes out of your mouth, you won't live to see the light of day. Is that clear?"

"Yes, Captain," he says sharply, though there is no denying his voice is cracked with fear. "Sorry, Captain. I don't know what I was thinking."

I give him a grin before I release my hold on him and allow him to go free. I place my sword back in its sheath and take the wheel from Nadia, who looks uncertain.

"Serena, I know we're all on edge here, but what's with you? I don't think I have ever seen you do something remotely close to that to a crew member," she says. "Maybe you need more rest."

But I don't need rest. I know it's the magic affecting me, but how am I supposed to control it?

"Nothing is the matter with me, Nadia. I am perfectly fine. You know how I get when people insult me," I remind her.

"Yes, but you—never mind." She drops the subject, though I can tell she doesn't think I'm telling the truth. After putting Adam back in his place, I feel fine. Obviously still anxious, but I'm no longer fuming with rage.

· · ·

That night, like every other night, sleep does not choose to take over my body. I toss and turn until I decide to escape onto the deck. My coat hangs on the handle of my miniature, wooden wardrobe, and though I leave it, I grab my mother's necklace from the pocket.

I sit down on the wooden floor of the deck, hugging my knees. The air is crisp and cool, the moonlight seemingly iridescent. I hold the ruby in my right palm, rubbing my thumb over it, and look up at the shining stars that paint the sky.

"I miss you so much, Mother," I say softly. "I really wish you were still here. I am terrified. I am terrified to face my father again, I am terrified of what the magic is already doing to me, and I—I am terrified that Elias's prediction will come true. I'm not used to this feeling. I don't know how to handle this. I just really need a hug from my mother right about now . . . but you're not here." I confess everything to her and more as tears pour out of me like a stream. I thought I'd be done crying by now; I guess not.

Once I start, I just can't stop. I hope Joseph doesn't hear me. I don't want anyone in my crew to know about any of my doubts and concerns about the upcoming situation. I just need to pull myself together and get back on track. I need to go back to my room to muffle the sounds of my sobs. But as I open the door that leads to the hallway of our quarters, I bump into Nadia headfirst.

"I thought I heard someone out here," she says, her voice softening when she sees my face. "What's wrong?"

"Nothing, I'm good." I wipe the tears off of my skin and attempt to go back to my quarters.

"Woah, woah, woah. Stop. Serena, I am not a complete imbecile. Come here." She pulls me into her embrace.

I allow myself to sob on Nadia's shoulder, bare from the

nightgown that's slipped from it. I always thought I was invincible. Nothing could penetrate the walls that I put up. But now those walls are down and I am more vulnerable than I have ever been in my entire life.

I don't understand how this happened. I want to be angry with the person responsible for their fall, but I can't. I don't know how he managed to do it, but the formerly vexatious prince has gotten past my barriers.

I hate it. I hate the feeling of vulnerability. Instead of complaining, I should just deal with it.

And I will. By sunset tomorrow, we will be on Southwest Hillins Island facing my father, as well as the army of mindless followers he calls soldiers.

So this will be the last night of shedding tears. I refuse to be unguarded. When I face my father, he won't meet the frightened, defenseless little girl he saw in the cave. He will meet the confident, vicious, cunning captain that I have always been, no matter which outcome of the prophecy comes true. I want to surprise him. I want—I *need* him to know that he holds no power over me.

As I shed the last of my tears, my fear leaves me. I'm only angry. And I can use that to my advantage.

Tellerous will never know what hit him.

29

———

The next morning, I wake up foolishly believing everything is going to be calm, at least for a little while. The ship rocks a little more than usual, but the seas are unpredictable. I'm in the middle of brushing my hair when Nadia barges into my room.

"There's a little problem."

I toss my hairbrush on my bed. "How little?" I question, trying not to sound too worried.

Nadia drags me by my wrist out onto the deck, pointing to the front of the ship. The sky in front of us is no longer blue. It's filled with dark gray clouds, some of them almost completely black, with hard edges. In all my years of sailing through storms, I have never seen clouds like these before, and I can't help but wonder if this is Tellerous messing with us again. The clouds are already beginning to block out the sun. Alina stands next to me, her mouth dropping slightly open as she stares at the sky above us.

"Joseph," I say, "we've got the wheel from here. I need you to tell the crews to batten down the hatches and get ready for a bumpy ride. There is no way this storm isn't going to be severe."

"Yes, Captain." He nods before he leaves the wheel to me.

"How much time do you think we have?" Nadia asks.

"Minutes," Alina answers, still standing next to me. At my look, she adds, "You're going to need help sailing through this storm. I am not leaving your side."

"I can handle this myself," I assure her.

"This is no ordinary storm. You're going to need my help navigating through this. Nadia's, too, probably."

"I don't need help—"

"I'm not taking no for an answer," she snaps.

I pause before sighing, giving in to Alina. I hate to think she's right. Nadia goes to help the crews prepare for the storm, and I wait, helpless and nervous, as the first sound of thunder rumbles around us and the first strike of lightning lights up the sky.

Within minutes, rain starts to fall. At first, it's a light sprinkle. But seconds later it's like the sky is pouring down buckets of water on us. The rain is like rocks as it hits the wooden deck of my ship. The waves grow rougher and the sky turns black. The wind that blows by is rough, and I'm afraid if I don't hold on to the wheel tighter, I might actually blow away.

The rain soaks through my clothes and weakens my grip on the wheel. Angry waves toss themselves over the sides of the ship, growing larger. Alina takes the wheel by my side as it threatens to tear from my grasp, but I'm still powerless, my arms screaming against the resistance of the storm. It grows and grows as seconds fly by, creating chaos and discord on the entire ship. I hear the shouts and arguments from the others on board, their cries booming through the entire ship as they tie themselves down to keep from falling overboard.

One giant crash into a wave would mean sudden death for everyone on the *Tigerlily*.

Alina and I work together to keep the ship on course, but it's more and more difficult with each second. I think about Ben. I wonder if this was how my mother and Lennard felt right before their ship went down. Alina rolls up her puffy, aqua-colored sleeves before tightening her grip to get better control. My doublet coat flies in the wind along with my hair.

I can barely see as the raindrops cloud my eyes. We struggle to keep the ship on track—more like from crashing into a giant wave or small group of the rocks that fill these parts of the waters. My boots slip on the watery deck.

I lose hope as the minutes fly by. Every time it thunders the noise rattles the world itself. The lightning blinds us, the wind wages its war against our stand. This isn't just a storm —it's a hurricane.

And the worst part is that the darkness is flaring in my bones as we continue to sail on.

Goddess Clary, please have mercy on us.

Alina and I keep sharing glances at each other, always with the same expression on our faces. She wants to know what my plan is, and all the while I hope she has an idea. Knowing what to do during, before, and after a storm are crucial to survival. There is always a point in a cloudburst when you can tell it is almost over, but as far as I can see, we haven't reached that point, and I'm more and more certain that we won't.

I wish I knew what my mother did before her ship went down. I always believed that if I was going to die, it would be because of an enemy striking me back. But this is not what I expected at all. I have seen many a storm in my lifetime, but nothing like this, and it seems Alina hasn't either. Her face is drawn with fear, draining of confidence.

"The waves are getting too high!" Alina shouts over all of the noise. "I don't know if this vessel can handle that large amount of impact!"

"Maybe not," I admit, "but what else can we do?" The wheel fights us. My hands keep slipping off of the soaking wet, wooden holds.

"I don't know! But if the waves continue to show us no quarter then we are going to capsize!"

"Are you just going to keep pointing out the obvious, or are you going to say something helpful?" I snap.

"For starters, you could lose the attitude! After all, I am the one who is helping you steer this cursed thing!"

Before either of us can say anything else, an enormous wave hits the front of the *Tigerlily*. It crashes over the entire ship, as if the ocean has personally slapped us. Water shoots up my nose and enters my throat. The wounds on my back and arm from the Flipperfore—what feels like so long ago—stings from the salt. I cough up water as I peel myself off the soaking wet floor.

Alina's right. One more enormous wave would sink us. We're so incredibly close to already going down, as well as almost drowning. I help Alina off of the deck, one hand on the wheel, one lifting her up.

"Is everyone okay?" she screams, not really expecting an answer.

I turn to the deck, barely making out the faces of my crew in the misty light. James, Sawyer, Adam, and Nadia are running up the steps toward me. But Ben—is Ben okay?

"Nadia, where's Ben?" I ask as she rounds the corner to

us, her hair plastered to her head and neck. She looks at me, surprised, and then to the others. She shakes her head.

"I don't—"

"Alina, I'll be right back," I say, already leaving her. "I have to go find Ben."

"No! You can't let me do this alone!"

"Alina, I have to find him!" I shout urgently before running down to the deck.

"Serena! Serena!" she screams.

If Ben's hurt, I need to find him fast. My stomach churns at the thought of something happening to him. Alina's grip had been right on the wheel before I left her; she'll be fine. As I quickly make my way to the back of the ship, I pass Alexia, who is kneeling down with a girl from Alina's crew. The girl is hurt and they're huddled together, their faces screwed up tight and bodies tense. My crew is trying to keep everything together and help those who were injured by the crash. I run my hand through my drenched hair as I slide through the giant puddle of water that floods the deck. Ben's nowhere in sight.

Just as I'm about to turn the corner to enter the hallway where the chambers are, I slip on the puddle of water and fall. Someone grabs me by the arm and hoists me back up, and I spin around to see Jack's face through the storm's rage. As our eyes lock, my heartbeat increases. I almost forget about all of the chaos around me. I can't help myself, and I don't think he can either. Because it's now or never. I press my lips against his.

This kiss is much different than the one I shared with James. It's much deeper, much longer. I can't pull myself away. I don't want to pull myself away. But the storm is raging and I have a job to do. I swallow my disappointment when the kiss ends, and we both share a grin.

Jack brushes my hair behind my ear. "You have no idea how long I have waited to do that," he says, having to shout above the storm. "It's you."

"What?"

"You are the most beautiful thing I have ever seen."

"That is the sweetest and cheesiest thing I have ever heard," I reply, chuckling. "I am sorry about what I said in the ballroom. I didn't mean it. I was just scared." I lean forward to kiss him again, but that's when Nadia interrupts us by clearing her throat.

"Hi, yeah. Don't get me wrong, I am all for this—I *love* this—but maybe this can wait until, oh, I don't know? When we're *not* about to die?"

James and I both fail to stutter out a good response. Instead, he goes in one direction and I continue down the hallway, a huge smile on my face despite the situation as I rush to Ben's chambers. There he is, swaying with the ship and digging through all of his shelves and the drawers in his desk, throwing papers and books behind him, including one that hits me right in the middle of my face.

"*What* are you doing?" I snap, throwing the book back at him. Ben ignores me, so I yell louder. "What the hell are you doing in here?" Water is flooding the floor, soaking the books and pages and filling my boots.

Ben spins around, panic striking through his features. "I —nothing. I thought I left something important in here."

He's always been the worst liar, especially to me. But I don't have time to interrogate him.

"Come on, we have to get out of here. It's dangerous down here." It's dangerous everywhere. Still, I drag him out the door. By the time we make it back on deck, the rain has somehow gotten worse, the wind more relentless.

"Stay here," I order when I find James.

249

Ben crosses his arms. "I'm not a child, Serena. I can protect myself while helping the others on deck."

"Well, right now you certainly sound like a child," I snap. "I don't have time to argue with you about this."

I slide across the deck, making my way back to Alina and Nadia as they continue to struggle against the cloudburst's conditions.

"We only have a few miles left until we reach the island," Nadia shouts. "If we can keep the ship on course, we might be able to make it out alive!"

I place my hands back on the wheel, gritting my teeth when it tries to yank away from me. I refrain from saying it would take a miracle for us to get out of this unscathed.

As the three of us try to keep the ship upright, our eyes widen at the sight of the horrifyingly enormous waves heading our way. How are we supposed to survive that? My thoughts jumble together in my head, all leading up to one inevitable conclusion: death.

"We need to go around the waves," Alina says.

"What the bloody hell do you think we've been doing this entire damn time?" I holler.

"I know that, you buffoon! Just follow my lead!" She takes control of the wheel and turns the ship left, away from the upcoming wave. The turn is so sharp I think we'll never make it, but the worst of the wave hits to the right of us, rocking us but sending the worst of the water's force back into the ocean.

I chance a small smile. We can't completely avoid the waves, but if we pick them carefully we can get my ship away from the more fatal ones, steering it away just enough to avoid such a strong impact. Only a few miles left.

Just as I start to think we might actually make it through this, I hear a horrible ripping noise. The mizzenmast flies off its pole, nearly tangling in the other sails before landing in the water and being carried away by the massive waves.

Alina throws her hands up in frustration. "Oh, come on!"

"What do we do now?" Nadia asks. The ship is already beginning to falter. We can't get anywhere without that sail.

"Joseph!" I shout, hardly waiting for him to take my spot before I run down to deck. I grab John, James, and Sawyer and rush to the storage room, rummaging through the boxes and barrels to find the backup sail. Each of us grabbing an end, the four of us lug it back to the tall pole and begin climbing it together, our progress slow as we carry the ends of the heavy sail.

"Get back down here before you fall and crack your head open!" Ben yells.

I ignore the crews' cries and continue to climb the soaking wet, wooden pole.

"Please, be careful!" Jack shouts.

My foot slips and I fall, nearly dragging the others down with me. But I tighten my grip on the pole's handrails. I can do this. I climb these poles all the time. Plus, this is *my* ship. I know every bit of it. And if we don't fix this fast, none of us will be left alive.

We safely make it to the top of the pole. As I bark orders to James, John, and Sawyer, the four of us struggle to find our balance. The wind constantly attempts to smack us down. John, at the very edge, has the worst of it. But we can't wait any longer. We wrap our legs around the supports and tie the black and red sail into place, tugging the knots and taking hold of the extra lengths of rope.

"Down!" I command, and the boys jump, sliding and climbing down their lengths of rope that will drop them back down to the deck. Sawyer is the first, then John. James waits and I stand, holding on to the mast as the ship swerves, making sure they all made it down all right.

When it's my time, I take one step forward. A powerful wind blows my way, knocking me off of the platform. I scrabble for purchase, hanging on by my fingertips, swinging out over the raging water.

"Serena!" John shouts. He tries shimmying back up the pole, but James orders him down, rushing over to me himself. I'm hanging on by one hand, my other flailing about in the air. James grabs my hand, then my arm. He pulls me back up, and I'm halfway to my feet when a crash of thunder rattles the ship, the entire vessel shaking. James loses his grip on my arm and I fall into the ice cold water, screaming all the way down.

30

*M*y entire life flashes before my eyes the moment my body smacks the surface of the ocean.

I struggle to keep my head above the water, trying to swim toward the *Tigerlily* as the waves do their best to pull me under. The waves drag me beneath the freezing surface, salt water flooding my mouth and lungs and burning my wounds, making it all the more difficult to keep up with the angered sea. Salt burns my throat as I swallow heaps of water each time I sink underneath the waves. Under water, I scream.

I break the surface again, already foreseeing being pushed down again.

"Serena!" Jack's voice calls from the ship.

I struggle to keep myself from sinking too deep underwater. Jack throws a life saver at me, and I'm lucky his aim is so good. I grab it and cling to it, and he and Ben pull me back to the ship and yank me back up to safety.

On the deck of the *Tigerlily* finally, I collapse and cough up water. As I plop onto the floor, Jack, James, and Ben kneel down to my level while everyone else keeps trying to prevent the ship from going under.

I sit up and lean back into Jack's embrace as he helps me sit. He brushes the hair out of my face and lets out a sigh of relief. I shiver in his arms, and John comes over to me with a blue blanket. As they wrap the blanket around me and I fumble for it with my frozen fingers, I look up, noticing that the rain has begun to lighten up and the wind has stopped howling so forcefully. The waves stop crashing over the deck, and the black sky goes gray, already on its way to returning to the familiar bright blue color.

Ben and Jack help me stand. I'm still shivering. Though my pulse calms, my fingernails are purple. Nadia comes to my side—"Let's get you out of those clothes."—and with her help I change out of my wet clothes, fighting the lethargy in my arms and legs as I come back out to the deck.

The skies are clear, as if the storm had never happened.

Jack walks with me to the edge of the ship, and he puts his arm around me as we look out at the calmed ocean. Definitely not a normal storm. I lean into Jack, feeling warmer against his body, his embrace tight, as if refusing to release me. Safe.

"Leave it to you to find a way to almost die," he jokes. "The rest of us were never in any danger." I playfully elbow him in the stomach as a response.

We stand there for a few more minutes. My temperature rises, but I want to remain where I am as long as I can. "Serena, you are not cold anymore. Why are you trembling?" Jack asks.

"I am not trembling," I respond defensively.

"I can feel you doing it. It's okay to admit that you're afraid. At least, admit it to me."

I look around my ship, at how few we are. "My father

could have hundreds of his soldiers ready to fight us and we barely have forty people."

Like when I fell off the ship, there's that same helplessness.

Jack places a fallen strand of hair behind my ear, then puts his hands on my shoulders. "I promise you, my soldiers will come. We are going to defeat Tellerous and you will be free of your father. *The world* will be free of your father."

I kiss him one more time. Maybe I should just tell him my secret. He's going to find out eventually. "Jack, about that last part, I—"

"Pardon me, Captain, but there is a fleet of ships following us," John says, pointing. The storm had been good cover for them, but now they're clear, and close. "Give us the signal when you want us to attack."

"No, no, no wait," Jack says, squinting his eyes at the sight. He smiles. "Those sails have my family crest on them. Refrain from attacking those ships. They are here to help us."

John nods, visibly relieved, and walks away. Jack turns back to me. "What were you going to say?"

"Uh, nothing. It's not important." I lose my courage, and though I know Jack is watching me, knowing I'm hiding something, he remains silent. We wait as the shape in the distance takes the shape of Southwest Hillins Island. "We're finally here."

I walk away from Jack. As half of my crew drops anchor, the other half cleans up the ship. Alina's crew assists and helps those who were injured during the storm. Hours have passed, and the sun makes everything shine with a golden sheen.

After anchoring, we wait for Jack's ships to anchor in the sea behind us before we head for land. Not much of it is actually sand, only a small strip about five inches along the edge. Tide is high, and the rest of the island is nothing but a huge platform of gray rocks that seem to stretch for miles. There are no trees, no animals—nothing to hide behind.

And it looks deserted.

But the moment my boots hit the sand, the blood flow in my veins quickens and a shiver runs up my spine. A tingly sensation strikes me, as if the magic knows I have arrived. It's strong here. Jack must have noticed, because he takes my hand as we walk farther onto the island.

Ben walks directly behind me, holding onto Nadia. The quiet is thick, unsettling. The seconds tick by and I become more and more anxious, forgetting the vow of confidence I had made earlier.

Be strong. Show him who you really are.

But he isn't here.

Jack pulls away from me, squeezing my hand first. His army is behind us, and he barks orders at them, telling them to keep sharp, warning them of the shadows' incorporeal forms. In his absence, Ben takes my hand. I walk forward, staring around the island, skeptically staring into what looks like a pile of nothingness miles away from the shore. It's much too quiet still, dangerously silent, and my instincts tell me to be alert. My father will be coming. The magic is already here.

I turn around and share a glance with Jack before a vociferous ripping sound fills the air.

A black portal opens in front of us and hundreds of humans—humans, not shadows—jump out, clumps of them landing on the island all at once. When they charge at us, I release Ben's hand and grab my cutlass, catching sight of a bright glimmer in the horde.

The orb.

But before I can go for it, a young-looking guy comes right at me, using neither a sword nor magic. That's his first —and only—mistake. My sword cuts through his heart with ease.

I look around. They're human all right, engaging my crew and Jack's army with swords and magic and falling. Except the ones who come at me—nobody comes at me with magic or weapons, and each of them have the same look in their eyes.

It's the exact same look I had in my eyes before any of this happened. They know what they're doing, and they're content with themselves about it: leading a life into a death that's planned for them, and not by themselves. Mislead, naïve, and wholly believing they're in the right.

But who are these people, and what happened to the shadows—or whatever the hell they are?

They fall by the droves, but we aren't invincible. A few soldiers from Jack's army have fallen, though Alina's crew is overpowering anyone who comes near them.

I slash my way through the portal army. "John, look out!" he turns, but too late—one of my father's men cuts him down at the throat. I scream but force myself to look away, feeling my eyes sting with tears. I've known John since I was five. He was always coy and silent, but he was smart, skilled, and one of the best people on board. But then my sorrow turns into rage. I force myself to look at my fallen crewmate, and then I lock eyes with his killer. I go through five people to get to John's murderer, slicing and dodging and lunging, and I cut his head clean off.

It's easy, and it gets easier. The more people who fall under my blade, the more the dark magic calls me, encouraging me. It's egging me on, begging me to kill. Blood makes my grip on my cutlass slick and I hear the magic whisper, telling me to keep going. The feeling it gives me is amazing. It makes me believe that I'm invincible, that I'm safe. I don't care about anything except *kill, destroy, kill.*

A flash of bright light catches my attention. In all of the fray, Ben had stolen the orb back from my father's soldiers. I'm taken aback by his accomplishment, and though he's covered in sweat and dirt and blood, I grin at the sight. Maybe he's not so little anymore. I'm going to have to stop looking at him that way.

I fight to get to his side, dodging weapons and magic as I race toward the man sneaking up behind my brother, sword in hand. I tackle him to the ground and end him, more than ready to put down anyone else who gets in my way. I know that I'm under the influence of the dark magic, but the effect it has on me is not what I expected. Right now, I'm not compelled to give in to it. On the contrary, I've never felt stronger, and I have never run so fast in all of my nineteen years of life—my legs move *so incredibly fast*. It doesn't give me pain, it gives me power. It makes me furious, and it makes me a weapon. And it motivates me even more to beat Tellerous.

And we are. We still have Dissometers around our necks and swords, which protect us greatly. My father's soldiers fall in droves, far less experienced than the shadows we encountered earlier. But there are so many, and they just keep coming.

As I kill one, another of my father's boorish followers hits Ben with his magic. The black lightning strikes my brother and the orb goes flying, landing a few feet away from all of the chaos. The soldier and I share a look.

We race to the orb, both reaching for the magical arti-fact. I dodge his magic along the way, but it slows me down. He grabs the orb. I scramble to my feet and lunge at him, and we both fall, wrestling as we both continue to attempt to grab the magical object. I knee him in the groin, and when he goes limp, I grab the orb and toss it to Nadia, who's standing behind me, arms open. The man gets up from the fetal position, and he grunts in frustration when he sees Nadia running away with the orb.

Before he even gets a chance to go after her, I shove my cutlass through his middle.

We're starting to outnumber my father's soldiers thanks to Jack's royal guard. But our enemies don't seem bothered by the fact that we're beating them. There's a tension in the air, something ominous pulling at my senses.

Something just isn't right. My father's soldiers are here, but he isn't—yet. Maybe that's why they aren't worried. Once he comes, maybe—no. I can't think like that. Not yet.

"Well, well, well," a familiar voice rasps behind me. "Looks like we meet again, Princess."

It's the shadow I'd fought in the ballroom, only he isn't a shadow anymore. He's all flesh and bones: dark skin and raven black hair, yellow eyes. He stands in front of me, a smirk resting on his face.

My mouth falls open in shock, and I'm almost unable to close it. "What are you?" I ask him, frustrated and a little bit afraid.

He just laughs at me. *Laughs.*

"If I were you, I would make this easier on yourself. I have a message from your father: If you come with me now, your father will offer your crew double the reward the prince offered you. He will allow your brother to come with you, and he will give you the answers to all of your questions."

I scoff. "How many times are you going to make the same speech, thinking I'll actually agree to that? I don't care if he offers me a thousand treasure chests, a million piles of gold, and a damn unicorn. I will fight until my last breath."

"Suit yourself. You know, Tellerous just said not to kill you, he didn't say not to hurt you. When you wake up, you won't feel a thing. But you will know that you caused your friends' deaths. And—"

I stab him with my sword, laughing as he falls to the ground. I know I should kill him right then and there, but I want to fight him so he knows he isn't just dealing with any girl. I want him to feel the kind of continuous pain I've been feeling since the day I left the tavern.

I watch him peel himself off the ground, holding onto the open wound in his stomach. He looks at me with pure hatred, and suddenly I find myself falling deeper into my trance. This man will not leave the island alive.

I turn around. He can bleed out and die.

"You shouldn't have done that," he warns me. "You have no idea who you are dealing with."

"I'm trembling with fear," I reply.

Then he stands and blasts me across the ground with his magic, something more powerful than what he'd used in the ballroom. I roll to my feet on the rocky terrain, but then I'm unable to move, my feet trapped in a brick-like pile of magic, stuck to the ground. The man comes up to me, a ball of magic in his hand waiting to be released.

"Don't make me do this the hard way," he says.

Tiny bits of magic climb up my body, clinging to my skin, choking me. He knocks my sword out of my hand and yanks my hands behind my back, his magic crawling up my arms. It's bleeding into me, tightening around my veins, sucking the air out of me. I want to scream. I try to break free, but I'm unable to move.

"You have five seconds to decide before I make it worse," he says softly, voice in my ear. Then he counts. "Five . . ."

I'm not going to give in, not to him. I close my eyes and drown out all of my surroundings. By the time he reaches three, I'm filled with ire. My fingertips twitch, aware of the power, the heat, the unmatched strength. It takes all I have, but I sluggishly break free of his grasp on my wrists. I grab his arm, elbow him in the stomach, and flip him over my shoulder. When his head bounces against the rocky ground, the magic on my ankles vanishes.

I grab my cutlass from where it had fallen, and this time I shove it through his heart. Blood pours out of his chest, and he finally goes limp on the ground.

At his final breath, I exhale. I'm not even winded. The more blood I spill, the larger the power surge that sweeps over my body. It's inside me, growing stronger and stronger. A burst of energy unlike anything I've ever felt before.

I hear footsteps behind me. I turn and swing and bury my cutlass to the hilt in the soldier, then I look around. Most of my father's inexperienced men are dead. Those who aren't turn their attention to me and charge. I run to meet them, swinging my cutlass in front of me and shielding myself from the magic using Elias's gift. I'm digging myself deeper into the darkness. I don't care.

Because the thing is—I like it. I hate that I'm fond of it, but I can't help myself. Jack is protecting Ben, Nadia is holding her own. I hear a scream and look over my right shoulder. Alexia is on the ground, a man with fire covering his hands about to burn her to death. I run, but I'm not going to make it, the soldier is closing in—

Then something inhuman comes over me. I'm covering more ground than I should, almost unable to stop. I jump, and I launch ten feet in the air, my cutlass in both hands.

When I come down, the point of my sword runs down the soldier's back, splitting him open. Alexia kicks his lifeless body off of her and gets back on her feet, dusting herself off and looking at me with a little less hatred, and what seems to be awe—and fear.

I know that the magic is amplifying my every movement. And if I'm being perfectly honest, I don't hate it.

"Don't expect me to like you now," Alexia says.

"Oh, I wouldn't dream of it," I reply.

She nods before darting over to another of her crew. I run back into the fight, more confident, more certain that we're meant to win this, that we're being set up. If that really is the case, we can't not fight—but we'll have to figure something out.

I can figure it out. I always come up with solutions to problems. I just need to focus on this fight, right now. The magic pulls me deeper. I need to get out of the trance I seem to be in, but now that I've used the magic, however little, it won't leave me be.

The same ripping sound, and that flash of light appears again, more of my father's human soldiers coming out of a new portal. My crew is exhausted, we all are. Tellerous is waiting for the right moment to reveal himself, I know he is. But my fear is that once he does, we might be too exhausted to fight back. We'll be walking into a trap. What if we already have?

I fight the urge to just turn around and run. To call to my crew to retreat, to run away from this island, this darkness, the unknown, and all of the emotions that I don't exactly understand. But I can't. I am not a coward, and besides, we'll never get to the ships in time.

So I settle on being angry. I let my blood boil as I carry

through the chaos. It makes me stronger, my surroundings fading away.

I'm finally able to focus on what really matters: kicking my father's ass.

Four, five, six. I count the number of men who fly at me, desperation for my father's approval in their eyes. I crave the energy the darkness inside me gives me, and I lose sight of the danger it represents. We've been fighting for ages, never getting the chance to stop even once. My hearties are exhausted, and Alina's as well. Jack's army takes longer to run out of steam than my allies, but I can tell they want to give in, their movements growing sluggish in their armor.

But I'm never tired. I never run out of breath.

Soldiers with magic, soldiers without. I kill them all, blood spraying my face, staining my clothes. But it doesn't last for much longer. The air shimmers and turns black with smoke, and suddenly I'm surrounded by shadow soldiers, unable to get them off of me, my cutlass slicing right through them. One knocks my cutlass out of my hand with their magic. Another grabs my arm and twists it around my back. I manage to get my leg up to kick him in the face, but it hardly seems to faze him. Then the man standing next to him grabs my other arm. They hold me tight and drag me across the island.

I kick, scream, squirm, and even bite. I do everything in my power to escape, but they won't let go. I am feral; I am trapped.

It's only then I hear a familiar scream.

Ben.

31

*B*en's scream echoes across the battle.

I yell his name, unable to see him in the foray. My power surges again, feeding on my grief and fear, and I use it to break free of the two shadow soldiers, pushing them away from me as if they're solid, after all. I grab my cutlass and slice anyone who gets in my way. I jump up high in the air, my sword held over my head, and as I land on one knee I stab another shadow in the stomach. I kick the one coming at me to the ground and manage to cleave him to the brisket.

Finally, there he is.

Ben is lying on the ground in the shadow of a large rock, blood pumping from his body like a stream. James kneels by his side, fumbling to stop the bleeding. I rush over to them both, sliding down on my knees, neglecting the scrapes and holes in my black leggings. I fight the urge to start crying as I take in the blood, his stillness.

I place his head on my lap and put my hand over the open wound on his stomach, shoving James's hands away. Ben is completely pale, his breathing slow.

My other hand covers the first. I press, trying to stop him from bleeding out. I've always been there to protect him, and now I've failed.

"Ben?" I say, hoping he'll hear me. There's no indication he does. "No. No, no, no! Ben!" James is stuttering something, apologizing or trying to tell me how it happened. I'm not listening.

This will be it. This will be the single moment that will be the end of Serena Jones. I'm not broken anymore, I'm utterly shattered, my heart breaking. He isn't dead yet, but if I don't do something fast, he will be.

As his breathing slows even more, I press harder on the wound, unable to stop the waterfall of tears blurring my vision. How could I have let this happen? I promised him I would always protect him, and now he's dying.

I can't lose him. I just can't. He's my best friend and I'll be lost without him. Even if something happens to me, I can't have anything happen to him. He deserves so much better than this. My hands are covered in his blood.

"Ben? Come on, wake up. Please, come on," I cry. When he doesn't respond, I lean my head on his shoulder. "Ben, you can't leave me yet. I need you. Please."

Everything else fades, as if Ben and I are the only two people on the island. No James standing over us both, no battle, no soldiers. I want to scream at James for not keeping a better eye on him. I'm pissed at myself for not doing better.

His heartbeat is fading. I try to dive into the well of power inside me, but it's unresponsive. What good is it if it can't keep the one person I love from dying? I want him to open his eyelids, I want to see his sea-green eyes. I want him to sit up, to breathe normally, for the bleeding to stop.

I need him in my life.

"I am so sorry," I cry.

I don't deserve to be called captain. Adam was right about me. I knowingly led everyone I care about into shark-infested waters. It's my fault. All of this is my fault.

Then I hear an echo in my head. The Cretion magic is whispering again, telling me to give up, that I can't save him, that caring about him only makes me weak.

"Shut up, shut up, shut up!"

I don't care that we're beating my father's men. Nothing matters if Ben is gone. I hold on to him tightly, just in case it might be the last time I'd be able to actually do that.

"I love you, Ben," I tell him.

I lay my head down on his chest. I can't move, I can't breathe, I can't even think straight. I can't go back into battle like this. I disappointed my mother and Lennard. Mother made me promise to always keep Ben safe. I let her down. I let everyone I ever cared about down. And now I've lost the most important person in my life.

And the magic's voice is growing stronger.

You're weak and stupid. You are nothing, nothing, without me. You did this to him. It's your fault this little boy is deceased. I can take the pain away from you. You need me, you need my power to heal your wounds. Come, Serena. Aren't you tired of being weak? Helpless? You can be invincible. All you need to do is accept who you really are.

It's not completely wrong. I let this happen. I did this to Ben. To John. To all of the others. Ben is dying because I was not strong enough to keep him alive.

The magic's voice is painful to listen to. Its whisper makes my stomach churn. This is the first time it's truly spoken to me, and something about its tone makes me want to listen. Something else about it reminds me of my father.

No! Stop it, you moron! This is what he wants!

"Be quiet!" my voice echoes throughout the entire island.

"Serena!"

I look up, and through the sorrow in James's eyes, there's hope.

"I, uh, I think this may help." The orb is in his hand, and he holds it out to me. "You're not alone, Serena."

His words barely register. I snatch the orb from his hands and realize we really *aren't* alone. James, Joseph, Nadia, and Adam stand guard in front of us, shielding my brother and I from the fight as I press my finger to the brightest star and activate the orb's power. Within moments, the wound starts to close, almost like it was never there. As the skin seals, Ben opens his eyes. I scream with relief.

"Woah, woah, woah," I say through my tears after stopping him from trying to sit up. Jack scoops up the orb for use in battle, but that's okay. Ben is all right. "Stop. Come on, you can lay here for a minute. We have our defenses right there. What happened?"

He offers a shaky smile, but his voice stutters weakly as he speaks. "I was bested. I am not the best s-sword fighter. I don-don't know all of the defense techniques like you do."

"Once this is all over, I promise I'll teach you," I tell him. "I will work on it with you. I don't ever want to feel like this again, I don't ever want *you* to feel like this again."

"Thank you," he sighs. "I-I'm sorry I frightened you."

"What? No, don't be sorry, it's not your fault. I'm just glad you're alive."

He tries to laugh. "Likewise."

I need to focus on getting Ben back up on his feet and getting him somewhere safe where he can rest. Then I can concentrate on keeping my promise and teaching him more. I truly hope I can follow through on that promise. Once

Tellerous shows up, everything could change. Everything probably *will* change.

As I help Ben to his feet, he doubles over, making a series of groaning and moaning noises as he squirms around in my arms.

"Hey, hey, hey, what's going on?" I ask, tightening my grip around him.

"A little left over pain from the wound," he winces.

His wound might have healed, but his body is still weak.

"Okay, just breathe. This will all be over soon." I try to comfort him, but my eyes land on the fight around us. I need to be there. I need to be the one to single-handedly kill every one of my father's minions that comes in sight. I'm ready to. Looking around at everyone fighting, I am compelled to return, but Ben is my priority.

It's difficult to shield my anger from him as I do my best to comfort him, wanting so badly for his pain to go away—his pain makes my rage worse. I'm like a volcano, ready to erupt at any second.

"Y-you need-need to go," he manages.

"I—Ben, I am not leaving you," I force out of my mouth.

"You have to. G-go prove to everyone what I-I already know. Go-go be a hero."

"I am not a hero, I'm your sister. I can't just leave you here."

"I'll be okay. Go do what you do best: win."

I help him rest against the boulder, then I kiss him on the forehead and take one last look at him. I fight back the stupid tears forming in my eyes. I have to have faith that he'll be okay. But the amount of fury flowing through my veins outweighs the sorrow.

I stand slowly, every horrible thing that has happened since the day Jack came into the tavern playing on a loop in my head: the visions, learning the truth about my family, the Flipperfore, Alina killing Will, almost dying during the storm, nearly losing Ben. It's pain, and it's fuel. I pick up my cutlass and bolt back into this dark war.

"Nadia!" But I don't need to warn her. She cuts down one man in front of her and pivots cleanly to take out the soldier sneaking up from behind. Her movements are quick and swift, sharp and put-together. She rises from her stance and looks at me with a face that says "together?"

And I know I'm so lucky she is my best friend.

I nod and stand beside her. Fighting beside Nadia gives me a sense of comfort. Whenever the two of us work together, we are unstoppable. We both have numerous reasons why we *have* to win, and I can think of no greater warrior to fight beside me. Nadia never gives up on anything, ever. She is one of a kind. I remember what James said, when I thought Ben was dying: *You're not alone.*

"There are too many of them!" Nadia shouts from the ground as she fights off two attackers. They've formed a perimeter around us, some of them getting cut down by our allies, but most of them closing in. I can't respond; I'm busy myself, dodging their magic and their weak swings and swords.

"We're done for without that orb!" I scream.

"Jack!" she yells, but neither of us has any clue where he is, where the orb is, or if anyone can even hear us.

How would he even be able to get through all of this? We're surrounded, many soldiers deep.

And just like that, a bright light breaks through the circle of my father's soldiers. Half the royal guard breaks through the human barrier and frees us, pulling us from certain doom.

Jack lifts me off the ground, getting me back to my feet.

There's blood pouring from a deep gash on my arm, but it'll just have to wait to be tended to. I do my best to ignore the pain as he hands me the orb and lunges behind me, and I finally get the chance to do what I came here to do.

Jack and Nadia and Ben and the others, they can use the orb. But I know how it feels to not just use it, but make it stronger. I press my hands to its surface and pull at the magic in my veins like it's putty. The light grows, pocketed with black. I close my eyes as the orb burns my hands.

Then it's done. I open my eyes and my crew and Jack's guard are on the ground, ducking. Every last one of my father's men is dead.

I stumble to Nadia, hands on her knees and hunched over. I place my hand on her shoulder, comforting her as she tries to catch her breath.

And just when we all think everything is calm, there's a cloud of black smoke, similar to the one that had once covered the Olovian sky, and my father appears before all of us.

I place my free hand in my pocket, holding onto the ruby necklace.

My feet are frozen on the ground, unable to move. Chunks rise in my throat, taking the focus of the pain in my arm away. This is not how I expected to react to the sight of him, especially for the second time. I have a million questions I'm dying to ask, but I can't. We have to destroy him. Nadia looks between Tellerous and I.

"I am impressed with you, my child," he says, his voice echoing over us. "All of you actually, but mostly you. You are one incredible fighter."

A compliment. I have no words to respond with. Jack's royal guard charges him, but I already know that isn't going to be enough. It's time to take matters into my own hands.

All of the rage bubbles up inside of me. There he is, standing directly before me.

The orb's magic flows rapidly as I tighten my grip around it. Finally, he's here in person this time. It isn't an illusion like in the cave. I can ensure he dies this time. With one scowl, I activate the orb's magic again and flood it with every ounce of dark magic inside of me.

But he remains unharmed, the magic arcing around him harmlessly.

It didn't work. How could it not work?

With a wave of his hand, I'm no longer standing on the island.

32

*T*echnically, I *am* on the island, but everyone is gone: the living, the dead. Now it's just the two of us, my father and I. I stumble backward, my heart pounding, as he walks over to me.

"Well, well, well. It's good to see you again, Serena. Let me take a good look at you. You're my daughter, all right. You have no idea how long I have waited for this moment." He smiles.

"What did you do to everyone else?" I ask.

"Relax, everyone is fine. I simply created an alternate reality," he enlightens me. "One just for us."

"So now what?"

"No need to be so tense, darling. No harm will come to you."

"It's not me I'm worried about," I state firmly, trying to gather some of the confidence and bravery I'd had a moment ago.

"Your brother?" he asks. "Your friends? Your prince?" He chuckles. "You needn't worry yourself about such inferiors."

Inferiors. As if he has any say in their value to me.

Suddenly, all of my fear slips away. I take out my cutlass, prepared to fight.

"If you hurt them, I swear to you I'll—"

"You'll what? You are not powerful enough to harm me," he says, leaning his head back as he laughs. "You already tried."

With a wave of his hand, my sword disappears and I'm grasping at empty air. "I was told that my magic could be more powerful than yours," I taunt him, angry as I remember Elias's words.

"Maybe so, but look at you. You don't actually have any powers yet." He places his hand out, his palm facing up as he moves it up and down, motioning to my body, my weakness.

"No, I suppose I don't." This power is only a glimpse, and it isn't mine. "But I have questions that I need answers for," I reply, thinking that as long as Tellerous is here, with me, then he isn't able to hurt the others.

Tellerous nods. "Ask away."

"My mother," I begin. I have wondered this my entire life, since she wouldn't tell me. "How did you meet my mother, and why did you leave her?"

"I met your mother in a tavern," he says quickly, easily. He paces around me, speaking as if it happened yesterday. "This was right after I left Renayhem, which if you spoke to Iana I am sure she told you about. Katherine was the most beautiful woman I have ever seen. It was love at first sight. Within three months of us being together, my magic grew even stronger. It was too much to ignore."

He sighs. "She made me consider giving up my plan, but when she was pregnant with you, I had to accept the darkness. I knew I could follow through with my destiny. She knew what I had planned for you, and we fought and eventually went our separate ways. I never saw her again, though I knew we'd meet one day."

No wonder my mother never even mentioned his name. And though she never told me, she had the book. She knew what he was, and she wanted to prepare me. "So, you really were friends with Queen Iana?"

"Indeed. Elias too. He was more like an older brother. The three of us spent a lot of time together at Renayhem." He looks at the sky with an unsettling soft grin as he recalls the memories.

"And your soldiers?" I ask. "Those shadow things you sent in the ballroom? What are they, and why didn't you send them to the island too?"

"I am surprised Iana didn't go into much detail with you. The Dark Realm is where people go after they die, or if they are being punished for an unspeakable crime. Only souls are allowed in. I sent the souls, not *shadows,* into the ballroom that night."

"And now?" I ask, thinking of all of the blood and bodies.

"They can only re-enter the Human Realm in their given bodies if I allow them to do so," he says. "The people you saw on the island are my new recruits. I was testing them. I needed to see how they fight—to see if they are good enough to join my royal guard." He chuckles. "You made quick work of them."

He feels no remorse for their deaths. But the shadows—souls—knowing what they were made my interaction with them make more sense.

"You have more questions," Tellerous says thoughtfully. "You know I am the only one who can answer them."

Unfortunately, he's right. "How did this magic come to exist?"

"I inherited it from my grandfather. Our family is blessed with it. The first in our family received it hundreds of years ago. It was weaker then," he explains.

Blessed? He really just said *blessed*? "Why our family?"

"Your grandfather of many generations ago was experimenting with different types of magic. It was an accident, really, which resulted in an explosion of black dust—Cretion. But he absorbed the power, and a symbol appeared on his shoulder"—the symbol from the book, I gather—"and it took him years to figure out what it meant. Three more people in our family were to gain the magic. Legend has it the magic allowed him to see into the future. He wrote down the names of the three people he believed would obtain it." He pauses there. "You are last in line."

I gulp. "When did you realize you were next in line to obtain the magic?"

He circles me, using hand gestures as he carries on.

"I read every book and scroll in the school library. I already knew something felt strange, and none of my instructors or colleagues could determine the cause. My temper shortened greatly, and I could feel something happening *inside me*, inside my veins . . ." As he trails off, I put my fingers to my wrist, pressing against my pulse. "Then I found it," he says. "An old, old scroll tucked deep into the archives. I read about the prophecy and I read all of the myths about the Dark Realm, my grandfather's name, and his grandfather. It wasn't until after I left your mother that I found the portal at the ends of the Human Realm. I entered the Dark Realm, and I learned my grandfather was king at the time. After he died, I became king," he answered.

He says it so simply, all of it: the shadow souls, becoming king. "But for all of this to happen, you knew we'd meet one day, anyway. So why did my mother have to die?"

Tellerous stops moving. When he speaks, his voice is soft. "I had no choice, Serena. She was going to try to stop my plan, and I could not allow that to happen."

"Like that makes it any better."

"I *am* sorry, but I can't change who I am. I did what I had to do. You should understand that better than anyone, *Captain.* After all, you forgave Alina Ortega for killing William, your only friend on land. She did what she had to do to save the life of her sister, isn't that right?"

I shake my head. I don't know how he knows about them, how he knows what's been happening to me. But it doesn't matter. "This has nothing to do with either of them—"

"But it has everything to do with *you,*" Tellerous says, spinning around, leaning down so he can look me in the eyes. "Everything with how you *feel*, don't you see? I was just a boy when I first found out about my magic. Before the dark magic I had control of fire. I lived in an orphanage until I was seventeen, my parents having abandoned me—only later did I know it was because of the prophecy. I discovered my powers at a very young age, and it was very lonely and difficult concealing it from the outside world—the human world. The year I turned seventeen I lost control of my magic one night. The entire orphanage burned down. That guilt was *crushing*, Serena.

"I had read about Renayhem in the orphanage library. I was planning on leaving to go there, anyway, but after I burned down the entire building, authorities wanted me dead. So I ran away to Magia, angry and desperate and alone. Everything Cretion thrives on."

He's trying to get under my skin. Trying to create a connection between us. I look away, but I'm too desperate to learn more to say anything.

"I practiced at Renayhem as a student until I was twenty-three. The headmaster saw how well I was doing and asked me if I wanted to train to be a teacher. I was content there, so of course I said yes. Then, well, it wasn't long before I discovered the magic in me and met your mother."

"You already had your plan, though. Why do you need me?"

"Your grandfather's prediction was that I would have a daughter who would inherit my powers, maybe even becoming more powerful than me. The more I studied Cretion magic, the more I realized that if you and I combined our powers, we could take over each realm together. That's the only way it would work."

My mouth goes dry, horror creeping through me. "But why? Why do you want to do that?"

"Because of my magic, I was denied everything as a child. You've seen the Realm of Magic, how people like us must live apart. But I don't want to live in exile, living in fear of what would happen if someone found out about my powers. *Power* is not evil, my dear. People are."

"Is that why you want to kill half of every realm's world?" I question.

"Humans are leeches. They're all bad, in one way or another. If we have any hope of uniting the realms, we must be sure any resistance will fail."

I'm dumbstruck as he spreads his arms wide, as if motioning to the entire world. "All of this has been for you, Serena. For us. It's already happening, you are already so close. *You* destroyed my hologram in the cave, you even enhanced the orb's power and made it seep through the magic that projected my image. It hit me, burning part of my skin to a crisp. I lost control and the magic in the sky disappeared." He smiles. "That was *you*."

His grin drops. "But I cannot share everything with you just yet. You need to prove you can be trusted."

"I can be trusted," I tell him. Everything is falling into place, the pieces clicking together. Iana's and Elias's stories, the cave, the orb, the way the darkness revels in my rage and desperation. Everything except one thing. "But . . . why did you order the killing of the King of Olovia?"

Tellerous laughs. "Well, it doesn't surprise me that he didn't tell his son."

"Tell him what?"

"That he was working for me."

My skin goes cold.

Tellerous continues. "When Jack was born, I threatened to kill him if his father didn't agree to my deal. I needed him, his resources, to keep an eye out for you and to recommend possible new soldiers for my own army. In return, I allowed him, his son, and the kingdom to go unharmed until I was ready.

"He knew you were in the kingdom and didn't inform me. He had you in his home, and he still said nothing. He broke his deal, so I broke mine. He disobeyed me, so he forfeited his life."

His explanation hits me physically, and I nearly stumble with the force of his words. The king died protecting me . . . but why? He risked his son's life to save mine? Jack's going to be heartbroken. I am the reason his father is dead.

"Oh, don't give me that face," Tellerous says. "He is not as kind-hearted and innocent as he pretends to be. Archer never did what was best for the kingdom, he only did what was best for himself."

"You don't know anything about Olovia, or the king," I spit, fighting back the urge to break down.

"I grew up there, Serena," he replies. "Besides, I know

you don't give a rat's ass about the king. You just care about your precious prince. He'll get over it."

No, he won't. I haven't gotten over my mother's death, or Lennard's. Jack won't be moving on so quickly, either, especially when he finds out the truth, how deep Tellerous's treachery runs. He has the right to know what really happened, even if that means he'll hate me forever. He deserves the truth.

It's too much to take in. To tell Jack what really happened to his father, I need to get back to him first. How am I supposed to kill Tellerous and get out of this empty reality? I am completely powerless against him.

Tellerous continues. "Since you care about the prince so much, I am prepared to offer you a deal. You come back to the Dark Realm with me and help me carry out my plan. Your brother and your precious prince can come with us. I'll give your crew sanction and unlimited rewards, whatever they desire. I can make your crew the most ferocious pirate crew on the sea. In fact, I can make them the *only* pirates out there. But only if you accept what I have to offer for yourself."

I feel sick. "How could you even think that I would agree to that?"

"What other option do you have? It is inevitable that I will get my way. I have an unlimited army at my disposal, and you and your friends are mortal. You can stop all of that with one simple word."

What horrifies me more is that, honestly, I'm tempted to take his offer. I don't want Ben or anyone else I care about to suffer through all of this. I can guarantee their safety, their lives.

But what about each kingdom, and all of the realms? Millions of people I don't know. They don't deserve this.

Living under my father's rule is something nobody should have to suffer through—ever.

If I refuse, he'll kill everyone I care about and bring me to the Dark Realm, anyway; if I accept then I'll go to the Dark Realm, my friends will live, and millions of lives will still be ruined.

It's a lose–lose situation. I don't see what else I can do.

Think, Serena, think.

Not one idea pops into my head. I don't have time for a plan; the one I had hinged on me killing Tellerous, and that's not looking likely. I'll just have to improvise, I suppose, but I know one thing: just like my crew, I'm not giving up without a fight.

"Let's get one thing straight here," I say with more rage than fear, although I'm afraid of the aftermath of my answer. "I may come from you, but I will never be you. I will *never* go with you willingly."

He stares at me thoughtfully, studying the expression on my face, trying to see if I'll break. "Are you sure about that? You're already a killer, like me," he finally says.

"But it isn't for the twisted reasons you do it for."

"Twisted? No, no, I am doing the world a favor. Cleansing it of all of the wretchedness from its people," Tellerous replies.

I scoff. "You're mad."

"You call it mad, I call it ambitious. My dear child, you and I are more alike than you think. You've lost everyone you have ever cared about, you are misjudged and misunderstood. Who else understands that but me?"

"I may have lost people along the way, but I still have people I care about in my life," I assure him. "You can give me all of the information and empathy in the world, I already gave you my answer. It isn't going to change."

"What happened to you?" he asks, incredulous. "You were the fiercest, toughest, most ruthless person in the world, but it would appear that you've gone soft. And for what? I have to say, I'm disappointed."

I shake my head. "I know what you're doing, and it isn't going to work."

"I am having a conversation with my daughter. As we speak, I am leaving your friends alone. But since you asked me so many questions, I only see it fit that I return the favor. Tell me, Serena, tell me one thing: Why did you forgive Alina Ortega for killing William?" He circles me again.

"I haven't forgiven her," I say, but I know it's a lie even as I say the words. At some point, I did forgive her. "I, well—"

"If you come with me, I will fix your softness. You could take your revenge. I know you are exhausted, but the darkness will easily fix that mushiness holding you back."

But he's wrong. Maybe I haven't forgiven her, I just choose to try and move on because we have a common enemy. "Alina is an ally," I tell him firmly.

"The last time I checked, true allies don't betray each other like that," Tellerous concludes.

I roll my eyes. "You are such a hypocrite. *You* of all people don't have the right to talk about betrayal. Do I have to mention Iana? Elias? *My mother*?" I shoot back, crossing my arms, waiting for a response.

He sighs. "I don't think I've made myself clear. Serena—"

I cut him off. "Why don't you just get to the point? You've pulled me here, you've heard my answer . . . you're so desperate for me to accept you, but I won't. Why are we still here?"

"Because you don't understand the *magic*," he says. "With the dark magic, you can do anything. You will be invincible, think about it. You would have the ability to create anything imaginable, have an infinite energy source." Something lights up in his eyes when he speaks about the magic.

"Energy source?" I repeat.

"You never need to catch your breath, you will never grow tired. Didn't you feel that when you were fighting on the island?" He must see the look in my eyes. "The magic that you use will be more destructive than lightning, you will be stronger than any one person—or ten. Nobody will stand in your way."

I vaguely recall Queen Iana mentioning this power to me. But his tone is different than hers when he talks about it. He's obsessed with it.

"You see, Serena, I am not the villain here," Tellerous claims. "I am just trying to help you reach your full potential."

I laugh at his statement. Is he choosing to not see the damage he is doing to each realm, or is he really just that oblivious? Or that cold?

"Come," Tellerous says, holding out his hand, motioning for me to go to him. "I'll show you."

33

I hesitantly walk over to him, genuinely curious to see what's going on in his twisted, deranged mind. He turns me around, and with a blast of black lightning from his hands he creates an image in front of me.

It's Jack and I, sitting at a table on the balcony of an unfamiliar castle. We both look content as we stare into each other's eyes, savoring every moment. Daisies rest on the rim of the balcony and the golden sun shines down upon us. On the table are tea and pastries. As I lift my cup, I lean in closer to Jack, laughing at something he says. His marble gray eyes are iridescent in the sunlight. He places his arm around me and I rest my head on his shoulder.

It's so real. Jack's smile gives me a sense of comfort I long for. I can't pull my eyes away from him.

"If you take my offer, this image can be a reality. No harm will come to your prince," Tellerous tells me.

Looking at Jack's face now, I know I'll be completely shattered if anything happens to him. I know Tellerous is messing with my head, but this feeling is so incredibly difficult to snap out of.

I swallow, my mouth dry as cotton, as I continue to focus my gaze on the image. I'm mesmerized.

Tellerous says, "The way you feel about Jack is the way I felt about your mother. If you come with me, I can tell you more about her. I know how important the prince is to you, and I am giving you a chance to save him. If you accept me and the magic, you can have all of this and more."

I can't express in words how I feel about the prince. I like him. Maybe I love him. But this is the wrong time to work out my feelings. I need to get out of this headspace. As difficult as it is, I rip my focus away from the image and turn back around.

"Stop it! No amount of alternate realities is going to change my mind," I tell him firmly.

Tellerous begins to speak, but I ignore him. I spin around, looking around for a possible way out. There has to be a way to exit this place, somewhere.

Think. If there's a way in, there has to be a way out.

I am in an alternate reality right now. Maybe the only way to leave is by getting my father to break it. But how can I possibly get him to do that?

Magic. I need more information on this type of magic. Maybe if I learn more about it then I'll find a way to escape this alternate reality.

"I won't go anywhere with you until you explain to me how Cretion magic works," I say, turning back to him.

"And I won't tell you anything until you have proven to me you can be trusted," he replies.

You really couldn't have told me about this sooner so I could prepare, Mother?

The only way I know to break my father's power is with the orb, but I can't procure the orb from here. I'm at a loss for ideas, but I can't stay in here any longer. I can assume everyone on the other side is safe, but for all I know, Tellerous was lying and Ben and my entire crew, along with Alina's and Jack's guards, are dead.

I just wish I could see what's going on out there. I'm hoping they're putting up a good fight. I promise myself that as soon as I make it out of here, my father will pay for what he is doing to us.

"Serena?" Tellerous says, catching my attention.

"What?" I reply.

"I said, hold out your hand."

Uncertain, I do as he asks.

"Your palm must be facing upward. Good." He creates a ball of magic in his hand, black and thick and swirling. He tips it into mine, and I hear the whispers that I heard before, this time much louder and way closer. "This is what the magic feels like," he says, and I understand. He won't tell me how to create it, but he can taunt me with it. "Test it," he continues. "After all, it's calling you."

As the ball of black magic sits in my hand, my veins tighten, reaching, wanting the magic to be one with my body. I stare at the mesmerizing magic, shift it from palm to palm. It's so powerful; I feel invincible. I understand why it's so easy for Tellerous to give into the darkness. Something about the magic is so familiar, so comforting.

It doesn't really feel like darkness. It looks harmless, even. Looks can be deceiving, but as much as I try to remind myself what's really going on here, there's a part of me that doesn't care.

It's like the good half of myself and the bad half are playing tug-of-war with my brain. I'm so blinded by the security of the magic that I don't know what's right and wrong anymore. With it, I could be better, stronger. I could protect Ben. I could see Will again, be reunited with my mother and Lennard. It promises me everyone's safety . . . it promises me everything.

Most of all, the magic just makes me so—alive.

No. I flinch, coming back to myself. *They're dead. They can't come back. Nothing can change that, and only you can protect Ben. It's a rouse.*

I drop the ball of magic on the ground, and it disappears into nothingness.

"How did that feel?" Tellerous asks, but he already knows the answer.

I stare at my palms, afraid of what I might do—what I might become—if that happens to me again. I can't believe I allowed myself to dive in that deep.

"Deny it all you want, but I know you want that feeling to return to you again," my father claims, reading the want on my face.

I despise myself for feeling that way, but I can't help it. I can't control myself.

The longer Tellerous keeps me here, the more likely I am to dive so deep I won't be able to get out. I need to figure out how to get out of here *now*. My head and my heart each tell me not to give in, but the rest of my body wants so badly to feel that power again. I'm queasy, as if I might throw up at any moment.

I'm fighting my body's natural instincts, and I appear to be losing.

"You don't have to fight it, Serena. In the end, that will hurt you more than help you," Tellerous prods.

But even with a raging headache and an upset stomach, I can't give up, no matter how much I want to. Not just for me, but for all of the people in each realm whose lives are at stake.

That's a statement I never thought I'd say.

But what if that's what I'm destined to become? Pure darkness. I used to think I wanted to be like my mother, the good parts of her, but now I am not so sure. There has always been a darkness inside of me, a part that likes being in control and spilling blood and proving that I can't be touched. That part of me is a lot more powerful than I thought. I can't control what has been inside of me since the day I was born. The one thing I can control is how I choose to deal with it.

And maybe if I accept that darkness inside of me, I can actually defeat my father. Maybe I need it so I can use it for good instead of evil. Maybe I'm not doomed after all. I just need to figure out how to get the hell back to reality.

And if I remember right, Tellerous said that when he was hurt, he lost control. If hurting him is the only way to escape this, then so be it.

You can do this. Just, breathe.

"It's more than okay to want this power," Tellerous says. "I can see how much you truly desire to feel it again. Your mother may have denied it, but she did want this for you."

"And how would you know that?" I question in disbelief.

"When I first told her about my powers, she said she would love for her child to have magic. Look." Tellerous waves his hand, creating an image of my mother to my left.

Seeing her face brings back so many memories. I blink away the wetness in my eyes as I watch her and my father talk to each other in a tavern. He shows her his magic, and she loves it, smiling and laughing. I see how in love with him she was, and it amazes me, how love can turn to hate so easily.

He played her like a fool. She must have known that later. As much as I want to believe him, want to believe that this is what my mother had wanted, deep down I know this image wasn't real. There is no way my mother wanted this for me. She died because she was on her way to make sure this didn't happen to me. She was trying to protect me.

I wish she'd been honest with me. It would have been helpful, years ago, to know what had happened between them. If my mother was still here, she could have helped me through all of this. I have to get a hold on my anger, keep a calm mind. It's what she would have told me.

"Serena," my father says, "I am going to make this offer to you one last time: Accept the darkness, come with me to the Dark Realm, and nobody will get hurt. If you refuse, I will kill everybody you have ever cared about. I will leave you with nothing. I am giving you a chance to save them all. You and I will rule the three realms. We will have access to not only the most tremendous magic these worlds have ever known, but we will have the truly opulent power of the throne."

I shudder. Tellerous can't admit to himself that after everything he's done, everything he's trying to give me, I don't want it. The promises, the magic—he just has to make sure he gets his way at any cost, but I swore on my mother's grave that he'll pay for all of the damage he's caused, if it is the last thing I ever do.

"Once you accept my deal, no harm shall come to your crew, your brother, or your friends. Even the despicable Alina, who you for some reason choose to call a companion. Your crew can sail around the world, and Jack can still have his crown and castle." He leans in, his eyes pleading.

"But most importantly, you and I will be together, ruling over the realms, obtaining everything we have lost in our lives. Nobody will be able to take anything from us ever again. It is all up to you. You decide the fates of your beloved friends and brother."

I close my eyes. I'm out of time. I have to either go with something and pray that it works, or be forced into a deal that I can't get out of. Or I can do what I do best: panic.

I'm going to need some serious luck if I'm going to pull this off.

34

*I*n my panic, I can't control what will come out of my mouth. But I don't want to.

"As I told your ex-left-hand man before I stabbed him through the heart, I don't care if you offer me piles of gold, a thousand rubies, and a damn unicorn. I will never go with you willingly. You may have helped make me, and we may share the same genes, but you are not, you have never been, and you never will be my real father. I may come from you, but I will never be like you." I slam my hands into him, my anger getting the better of me.

"Why don't you get that into your head?" I ask, pushing him again. "I am not a puppet, and you can't control me or tell me what to do. You killed my mother, my stepfather, injured my brother, and threatened to kill everyone I care about. You are going to pay for that, one way or another."

Tellerous scowls, and for a moment I regret hitting him, yelling at him. I can't help the things I say in rage. It just flows out of me.

So I come to a conclusion: I am an actual idiot. I might hate him, but he holds all of the power.

"You ungrateful child," he says, his voice a warning. A bulging vein pops out of his neck, and I shiver, afraid, as I back up. "I am not going to play nice any longer."

I bolt away from him, faster than I have ever run before. My feet hit the rock of the island, slamming hard, my breath quick. I don't know where I'm going, but I sure as hell won't stop until I'm as far away from my rampaging father as possible. I come to the edge of a cliff, my father not too far behind. Below me, the ocean waters churn endlessly.

I'll be fine, right? It's an alternate reality.

I jump off the cliff and into the, hopefully, deep water below. It's definitely deeper than I thought. The cold washes over me, dragging me down, and I flail my arms, swimming to the surface. My head breaks into the air and I swim to shore, but the water around me swirls, carrying me with it. It rises until the damn water carries me all the way back to my father. Petrified of what he'll do to me, I try to escape, but I'm powerless.

"You are weak!" Tellerous screams, his voice echoing, booming over the entire rocky island. "You have the audacity to speak to me like that, then runaway instead of stand and fight?"

Only the gods know what he's going to do now. I made things a trillion times worse. It's going to be my fault if everyone fighting back in reality ends up getting killed. I made it way too easy for that to actually happen.

I squirm and kick as I try to escape the grasp of the water, which wraps itself tighter around my torso, squeezing the breath from my lungs. If it keeps tightening, I won't be able to breathe.

The water drops suddenly, but I don't hit the rocks—I land in a large meadow, surrounded by flowers—daisies, of course. A portal. Soaking wet and coughing, I sit up, shivering and looking around for any sign of Tellerous.

"I am not taking no for an answer," he hollers, his voice coming from everywhere and nowhere. "You should have accepted my offer the first time."

The ground beneath me vanishes. I scream as I fall again, this time landing face-first in a snowy field, next to a frozen river and glaciers that seem to stretch into the clouds. The water in my clothes freezes, my fingers grow stiff. My vision spins, my head pounds, and it's so cold I can already feel frostbite setting in.

"*I* am your real father! Lennard was a fraud and you know it!" Tellerous roars.

I'm in the middle of peeling myself off the ground when I fell through another portal, this time into a giant body of water. I swim for the surface, but the dark magic pushes me under the surface, not allowing me to come up for air. Then it wraps around me like a snake, rising up out of the water and crashing down again. My nose and mouth fill with water.

"Don't you ever—say those things—to me again—or your punishment—will be even worse!" Each time I come up from the water, he shouts more. I can hardly hear him, the crash of the water filling my ears, my lungs screaming for air.

Finally, the magic releases me. I fly onto the shore, gritty sand sticking to my wet skin. I roll, coughing up water, gasping for air as I struggle to my feet.

Lesson learned.

I'm still trying to drag air into my lungs when handcuffs appear around my wrists and waist, ensuring I can't escape again. I pull against them, yanking so hard the links bite into my skin. It's useless.

Then Tellerous appears in front of me. "Don't be so sure that was the end of it," he says. Then he snaps his fingers and everything goes black.

~

I don't remember anything from after Tellerous yelled at me. All I know is that my head is pounding and I'm sitting up, the lumps of a boulder digging into my back. Once my vision clears I realize I'm on the island, but without my father. I look down. I'm covered in blood.

My shirt, my hands, my neck—it's all stained red. My cutlass lies on the ground next to me, its blade black and dripping.

I scramble to my feet, shaking and staring at my hands, praying to the gods that I didn't hurt anybody. I look up, and I see a sea of bodies surrounding me on the rocky island.

Please, no.

I scan the bodies, my heart squeezing in agony when I pick out the form of a young boy, lying down on his side on the ground. Blood surrounds his lifeless body.

No.

I rush over to him and slide down on my knees. It's Ben. His sea-green eyes are open, still wide, petrified. Betrayed.

"No!" My scream rips out of me, the sound so loud and sharp I think my vocal cords might rip. Tears pour from me as I hold his body tight, trying to squeeze him back to life. "What have I done?"

This is my fault. If I had kept my rage under control, this never would have happened. It's my fault he's dead. Everything terrible happening in Olovia, everything that's going to happen . . . it's because of me.

I loathe myself for it, and I won't blame everyone else if they do as well.

"See what happens when you turn your back on your father?" Tellerous's voice appears. Everywhere, and nowhere.

The glimpse of doubt is a relief. I stare down at Ben's body, the blood that doesn't quite smell like iron. "Is this real?" I ask softly. I'm not sure it is. "Hello? Tellerous! Is this real?" I cry out.

He doesn't respond.

"Please!" I shout in anguish, my grip on Ben's body tightening.

I know he can hear me. He's torturing me, withholding the truth.

"Please," I say in defeat, softly. I bury my face into Ben's chest.

The ground beneath me vanishes abruptly. I fall through a portal, waking up in that meadow again. I look around, Ben's body gone and my vision thick with tears, and I realize I recognize this meadow. When my mother died, I had this reoccurring dream that I met her again in a meadow. *This* meadow. She always talked about how when she was a kid and she was training on land, she would sneak off to a meadow that was only a mile away from her home. She described everything about it to the last detail: the daisies, sunflowers, and daffodils that grew tall in the grass. The duck pond that shimmered under the sunlight and the butterflies that constantly flew by. Blue Jays and humming-birds flew aloft the trees, happily tweeting sweet tunes. She always told me that she meant to take me there one day, but we never got around to it.

I never told anyone, but that was the place I've wanted to

visit most in the world. I'd almost forgotten about it until now. I stand and look around, wiping away my tears, the blood on my hands gone. How did Tellerous know? I wonder if my mother ever told him about it. Or if she took him there.

I blink. Jack stands a couple yards away from me. He's still in the peace and quiet, then a smile spreads over his lips and his arms open wide, ready for me to run to him.

I can't help it. I bolt over to him, the familiar sight making me desperate after the vision of Ben's murder. But as I near him, a sword pierces his chest from behind and he falls. In his place, the soul of Tellerous's left-hand man.

"No!" I shut my eyes, my screams erupting from me. I drop to my knees, hugging them as Jack's blood stains the meadow's grass.

Is any of this real?

It doesn't matter if this is in the alternate reality or not. It's real enough. Ben, lifeless. I can't live without him, but it doesn't hit me until I watch Jack die that I don't want to live without him either.

He means everything to me, and if he's gone—and Ben —I don't know how I am supposed to just carry on.

"*It's not real,*" a voice whispers in my ears.

"Hello?" I call out.

Instead of a response, the reality changes. It's the balcony again, and Jack and I are sitting and laughing together.

"You could have had all of this and so much more." Tellerous's voice makes me cringe. "You could have been with him every day . . . day in and day out. You could have told him how you feel about him. He would have absolutely loved hearing that. But he is gone, because of you."

"No. It's not real. None of this is real!" I yell, trying to convince myself.

"Are you sure about that?"

I'm not sure of anything anymore. But until I have proof that they're actually dead, I can't believe him. I can't believe anything Tellerous is telling me. Ever since my father appeared on the island, nothing has been real. He wants me to believe it's real so I'll give into him. I have to get out of my own head.

This is a false reality.

"Enough!" I shout. I throw my hands up, and when they fall back down the magic presses against my palms. When I look up, Tellerous stands in front of me again, and I realize I somehow used the magic already around me to get me back to him.

"You're right, it wasn't real," he says, appearing mildly surprised. "But this is." He waves his hand, and he finally shows me what's happening in the real world.

While I've been here with Tellerous, he'd sent more of his minions out to the island. Ben is on the ground, his face full of pain. Alexia stands in front of him, protecting him from my father's soldiers as Ben's skin pales, losing the life in him as the seconds go by. Alina and Nadia fight side by side, struggling to keep each other alive. Jack is among his guards from home, but most of them have fallen. James bleeds in multiple different places, and I can see him struggle to move and swing his cutlass. But he continues to fight, knowing what horrid things will happen if he stops.

My father and I are yards away, on the hill. Guarded by his soldiers, I'm unconscious, my body floating in the air, surrounded by black smoke. The rest of Alina's crew is fighting to get to us, but it doesn't look like they're having much luck. Even with my own crew pressing in, my father's endless supply of soldiers is more powerful.

"You see how much they're struggling," Tellerous says. "I have more soldiers I can stick on them. But that is your choice, my child. You decide what happens next."

Crap.

I have all the faith in the world in the people on my side, but Tellerous's numbers will always win. I can't accept his sinister deal, but if I don't and any one of them dies, I will never be able to forgive myself. And right now, I don't know if they'll be able to make it out alive.

"Come on, Serena. All of your pain and suffering will go away."

With the wave of his hand, the window vanishes. William appears a few feet away from us. Without thinking, I run to him, surprised when he actually hugs me in return. I don't care that this isn't real. I *know* that it isn't real. But I'd give anything to see him one last time.

I suddenly fall forward, my arms closing around nothing as he disappears. I turn around and he's on the other side of the clearing. I approach him warily, and before I reach him, Alina appears. She turns to me and winks, then spins around and thrusts her blade through Will's body.

I close my eyes and clench my fists as tears roll down my cheeks. Knowing she killed Will is one thing, but seeing it is completely different. Even with the knowledge that this time it wasn't real, seeing it makes my blood boil. I never truly dealt with the grief from losing him because I was too busy trying to find a way to stop my father.

Alina isn't an ally. We had come to an understanding, but maybe Tellerous is right. Maybe it's weak of me to believe her. She apologized, she cried, and she understands me, but what she did to Will—

Stop. This is exactly what he wants.

I unclench my fists, leaving dents on my palms from my fingernails digging into my skin.

It's now or never. Mother, wish me luck.

35

*B*reaking free means hurting Tellerous. But I don't have my cutlass, and I won't get close enough to use my fists. I need to distract him, and so far there's only one way I know how to do that.

I run away again. Like he can read my thoughts, he catches me before I make it two steps. His magic sticks to me like glue, the smoke thick but strong. I can hardly move, my arms trapped at my side no matter how hard I try to break away.

"I am offering you the world, and you continue to insult and disobey me!" Tellerous shouts. The black smoke carries me to him. I glare at him, gritting my teeth and directing every ounce of hatred I have at him. He matches my gaze and leans in close. "If you won't willingly accept my offer, then I'll make you."

The magic shoots into the sky and swirls, cutting out the sun and leaving us in shadow. Tellerous raises his arms, and my stomach sinks as I realize I might actually be out of time. This is it.

Tellerous slams his arms down and hurls the magic right at me.

The magic weighs a ton. It's like standing under a waterfall, the pressure of the water slamming against my back and head, dragging me into the abyss with its relentless downpour. It floods my mouth, my nose, my ears; I can't see anything but the smoke, the particles thick, smothering my brain, sifting through my memories as if trying to alter them, trying to pull at my emotions to keep the rage and the pain.

I scream, the agony peaking. It toys with my insides, pins and needles climbing through me down to my bones.

I nearly pass out, but maybe that would be better. I'm completely helpless. I want to fight back, but I'm paralyzed.

But there's that voice, the one that told me these realities aren't real. I recognize it finally: my mother, telling me not to give up. The infusion isn't complete, or permanent, yet. Something can still be done.

And I realize that maybe I can use this.

All of the sudden, something inside me clicks. Underneath my skin, a spiral of energy bubbles up to the surface of my palms. I almost become a different person, like there's Serena and there's *this*. This body is filled with power as the magic sticks to my veins. I can take control of it.

I clench my fists, grab the smoke from the air, and pull, forcing it out of my body. It takes all of the strength that I have, but I yank it hard and fling it in front of me, hitting Tellerous and blasting him across the island, his head making a sharp sound when it hits a rock.

I gasp, my mouth falling open as I stand there in awe, processing what I'd done. I did it. I actually did it. And if I can continue to hurt him like that, then maybe I can break this aggravating alternate reality. Maybe I can defeat him.

The magic technically isn't a part of me, so I can't destroy it myself. My father has more of the power, but I still have control of the physical magic. I am not completely defenseless. Now, I can give Tellerous a taste of his own medicine. He's going to get exactly what he deserves, and I will make sure of that.

I am not afraid anymore, and I am not helpless.

I laugh. "Am I weak now, *Father*?"

Tellerous climbs to his feet and runs toward me, a cloud of black shooting from his hands. I raise my own hands and brace myself, catching it and sending it back to him.

"Enough!" he shouts. The entire island shakes, the booming echo of his voice lingering seconds after he screams. I freeze, waiting for whatever he'll throw at me next.

I fall, a portal appearing beneath my feet. Tellerous's favorite punishment, I realize as I fall into the meadow, the cold waters of the Tammerin Sea, the rough cobblestones in front of Will's tavern, the frozen and snowy field.

But he isn't the only one who's had enough. I told him I am not his puppet, and I meant it. The portals are predictable, and though I'm certain I'll black out soon from constantly falling on my face, a way out becomes clear. Just like in reality when I first got to the island, my anger fuels me.

I close my eyes, and as I fall again I reach out, calling the magic to me. Once I have it, I send it back through the top of the portal I've fallen into, making one out of two alternate realities disappear. The next time he tries to drop me, I grab onto the edge of the portal, using the magic to force it open. The portal struggles against me, trying to close, but I swing my leg up and over the portal's opening. Tellerous watches me, looking somewhat impressed—and maybe even slightly nervous.

I'm completely filled with rage, tired of being controlled by my father. And I know from the fight on the island that the more enraged I am, the more powerful I grow. I have much better control over the magic, probably because darkness and exasperation can go hand in hand. As long as it helps me defeat Tellerous, I'll take it.

I'm going to stop asking questions and just be grateful, exactly what Tellerous wants. Controlling these powers is incredible.

And the look on his face is the cherry on top. As victorious as I feel, his anger matches mine. This isn't going as planned, and the look in his eyes is something I have never seen before.

The next time he hits me with the magic, I fall, sliding across the rocky ground and splitting open my scabbed-over wounds. My confidence wavers as I mentally note all of the cuts and bruises forming on my back.

I roll over my shoulder and stand back up only to get knocked down again, my head slamming against the ground. I may have passed out for a moment, but I soon open my eyes and regain my composure.

Shaky, I finally get back on my feet.

"Yes," Tellerous says, smirking. "You are still quite weak."

"Don't be so smug," I spit back. "You haven't won yet."

I don't even think. I let the magic do the work, opening up my arms, closing my eyes, and focusing on the cloud over my head. The magic rushes toward me, and I send it back to Tellerous.

Though he stumbles back, he returns the favor. His blast sends me off the cliff, dropping me into the water. When I try to come up, I bump my head on a barrier, a forcefield over the surface of the water preventing me from coming up.

You have got to be kidding me.

Instead of fighting it, I sink to the sandy bottom of the ocean, trying to use my remaining energy on the oxygen in my lungs, my mouth. Tellerous won't let me die. But I'm less sure of that when I black out moments later.

When I wake up, I cough out the water in my lungs and see my father standing over me.

"You say nobody can control you?" he greets me warmly. "Think again."

I rub my aching head as I sit up.

"Look around, Serena. I've been controlling you this entire time. You are powerless against me. I told you that you should have accepted my offer the first time I made it, and now look at you. Still weak, on your knees."

I breathe hard, still working on gulping at the air. I turn over and press myself up, concentrating on one foot, then the other. "Yeah, look at me now," I stutter. My arms and legs shake, threatening not to hold me up. "I have come such a long way from when Jack first visited me in that tavern. I am definitely not the same girl as that time ago," I admit, straightening. "But now I finally know what I want. Thanks to Jack, and you, I've learned a few things."

Tellerous smirks, like he's catching me in a lie. "Like what?" he asks.

"People like you are too conceited and gullible to tell when they're being fooled." I clench my hand at my side.

Tellerous turns around, finally noticing the magic rushing toward us. Once I have it in my grasp, I blast him, sending him flying away as the island around me finally fades.

~

I fall flat on my back, knocking the wind from my lungs. I stand quickly, relief flooding through me as the pleasant aroma of fresh air fills my lungs. I can finally smell the salt from the ocean, blood in the air. I stare out over the island and I know this is real, the familiar sight of everyone I've been away from easing my anxiety, proof that everyone I love is still alive.

I pick up my cutlass, which had been abandoned at my side, and run it through the men guarding the way to me.

Nadia yells to me. I rush to her and pull her into my embrace, almost not wanting to let her go.

"Are you okay? What did he do to you?" she asks, her panic clear.

"I'm fine," I reply, hesitating to loosen my hold. "I will explain later, it's sort of a long story." I turn around to see Alina standing behind me, and instead of the anger my father had made me feel toward her, there is only relief.

I hug her, knowing that I will never forgive her. But I am grateful to be back.

"Serena!"

Jack's voice makes me pull away. I bolt over to him. He pulls me into his arms and spins me around, the two of us kissing before he places me back on the ground.

After believing he was dead, I don't want him to let go of me. But there are still more of my father's witless soldiers coming after us. We break away and I look around for Ben, who is still pale but sitting up, James having joined Alexia's side in protecting him.

The fight is still going strong, not too different from the window Tellerous had shown me, or even what it had looked like when I left. I wonder if time works differently in that alternate reality. It felt like I was there for hours, but it must have only been minutes. Most of Jack's soldiers and my crew are in the same position they were before Tellerous got to me. Though it's crystal clear the number of allies on my side has decreased.

Jack rejoins his soldiers and I return to Nadia and Alina to help them finish the fight. I'm exhausted, and starving, and everything hurts. But I can't just give up, especially now that I have pissed off my father to a level I didn't even know existed. I'm just glad to finally be back in reality. Tellerous is unconscious behind a wall of his men. Now is my chance to kill him.

I steal glances over at Ben, feeling guilty that I haven't spoken to him yet. As soon as I get the chance, he'll be the first person that I go to.

But right now, Nadia, Alina, and I are surrounded. As they close in on us, Alexia breaks through the crowd, the orb's bright light preceding her, killing all of the soldiers before us. Maybe Alexia isn't as terrible as I always presumed she was.

I look up at the sky. The cloud of magic is swirling. The time is coming, and soon. If I don't get to my father first, I'll have no chance in hell of escaping the clutches of the prophecy Elias warned me about. I bolt through what's left of Tellerous's goons, swinging my sword and ducking under a ray of magic coming straight toward me.

"Serena, look out!" Ben shouts, catching me by surprise.

I turn around to meet the sword raised for a fatal strike, but before the soldier brings it down Alexia jumps in front of me. The sword smoothly glides through her chest. She rolls to the ground, and I scoop up the orb and kill the man.

Alexia slumps to the ground, blood gushing out of her like a waterfall. I catch her before she lands, falling to my knees, and I sit with her with her head in my lap. I brush her hair out of her face with shaking fingers to see if she's breathing, then I place my hand over her wound.

This wound is much deeper, and bloodier, than Ben's. She's lost a significant amount of blood already. Her chest stills and I place my hand in front of her lips, searching for a breath. But she's dead.

Alina falls next to me as I carefully rest Alexia's head on the ground. James keeps her steady as she stares at her friend's lifeless body, her tears silent.

I don't know what to say. Alexia was one of the only people Alina had left. In all my years of knowing Alina, I always saw Alexia at her side. She was Alina's Nadia. And she's gone because she saved my life.

I put my arm around Alina and she rests her head in the crook of my neck, still sobbing over her tremendous loss. Ben stumbles over to us and takes Alina's hand, and James sits on her other side while the rest of our crews keep my father's remaining soldiers from us.

I toss Nadia the orb. Then I turn my focus back to Alina. She's still crying quietly, but she can hardly breathe, and I know Tellerous is wrong: There are so many reasons for Alina and I to hate each other, even more so with Will's blood on her hands. But Alexia laid down her life for mine, and I would have done the same.

"I am so sorry," I say. But I know I can't stay here. The clashing continues around us and the sky is darkening further. I turn around and see my father on that hill, just watching us. Because I stayed with Alina, I lost my chance to kill him. And now, I know what's coming next.

The secret that I had kept from Ben—that I'd kept from everyone—is simple. I can't kill my father on my own. I'd tried, and I'd failed, and I had the bodies of my allies to reckon with.

"There is something you must know," Elias had said in his hut. "The only real way to defeat your father if the orb fails is to take in the magic. Then, when you're in the Dark Realm, you'll have to use your magic to defeat him. Your magic has the potential to be more powerful than his. Once you receive the magic, he will have you train with it. Once you know how to use it, then you just might be able to kill him.

"But there is a catch. Since you will be obtaining a great deal of magic, the force and amount of the magic, especially since it's dark Cretion magic, might be too much for you to hold. So it may either kill you or become a part of you."

Now, it's time to test that theory.

36

Serena Jones, get ready to die.

      I've learned that family isn't just blood, it's the people you surround yourself with that love and support you unconditionally. Also, sometimes letting your guard down isn't always a bad thing. You never know what surprises await for you once you do. Not everybody who comes into your life is going to hurt you.

That's why I don't have a problem potentially dying for these people. This whole mess we're in is my fault. I have to be the one to fix it so their lives can return to normal.

My mother always used to say, "Your crew is your second family. Hold them close. Always follow the code and protect one another." She's right. While I had mixed emotions about Adam, he's still a part of my crew and he is a decently skilled sword fighter. I am doing this for him, and Nadia, and Sawyer, and James. For Ben and for Jack.

If I do end up dying, then at least I'll get to be with my mother and Lennard—Lennard, who is my real father, not Tellerous. Lennard raised me, he trained me, and he's the one who loved me. And I will also get to see Will, the most kind-hearted, innocent, friendliest man I have ever met in my life.

The only person that I need to worry about if I die is Ben.

He has the crew to take care of him, but a bond between a brother and a sister is different. I know that I treat him like a kid, but after my mother and Lennard died, I raised him. We spent every single day together after our parents' deaths. I made my mother a promise that I would always keep Ben safe, and if I break that promise, it will hurt my mother just as much as it would hurt me.

But if this prophecy is the only way to defeat Tellerous, then I have to try. Even if Tellerous kills me. Even if the magic does. As Queen Iana said, there is really no way of knowing until the moment arrives.

James manages to get Alina to her feet, but she doesn't need any help fighting. She uses her anger and grief to motivate her, and as the others strike ahead it's Alina I rush to.

It's time I tell someone about the prophecy.

"Why the hell would you keep this from us?" she asks.

"Because I knew what would happen if I didn't," I reply. "You'd try to interfere with the prophecy and end up getting yourselves into trouble with the gods."

Alina shakes her head, her tears still falling freely, cleaning tracks through the mud and blood on her cheeks. "I'm not letting you go through with this. I cannot lose anyone else today."

"Alina, please. This is the only way. And you might not lose me," I remind her.

"Aye, because that super-convincing statement changed my mind."

I grip her shoulders, hard. "This is the only way to ensure the Human and Magical Realms' security. I can't allow any more of you guys to die."

"Serena," she says, shaking her head, "if you do this . . . even if you do survive, the dark magic will completely change you forever. So yes, we will be losing you either way."

"That may not necessarily be true." But even I'm unconvinced by that statement.

"You're not exactly helping your case."

"I'm sorry. But if you truly do care about me, then you'll help me. Would you rather lose everyone and everything, or just me?" She opens her mouth to respond, but I cut her off. "Don't answer that question, the answer was implied. Please, Alina, just help me."

"And when Jack and Nadia find out, how do you expect me to stop them from going after you?"

"You'll just have to hold them back. Please, get Freya to help you."

She looks uncertain, her mouth opening and closing, no more excuses coming to her. She knows I won't back down. "Why are you telling me this now?" she asks. "You could have just gone."

I decide to be honest. "Because if something goes wrong, I need at least one person to know what happened to me. And if things go right, I need you to tell them what Elias told me about the Dark Realm."

Now, Alina shakes her head harder. "No. We're not having this conversation." She starts to walk away. I grab her wrist and yank her back.

"Alina, please. Look, I know it isn't the most ideal plan,

or even a good plan, but it's the only plan we have left. I need you," I beg.

She crosses her arms.

"I know I'm asking a lot," I continue, "but I promise you it will be worth it. If I die, Tellerous can't complete his plan. If I live, then I'll navigate through the darkness and use the magic to kill Tellerous. Besides, isn't this what you've always wanted, anyway?"

"I never hated you, Serena," Alina says, taking my hand. "Never. I was just envious, I—know we've never gotten along, but I can't—"

"Think of it as redemption. This is how you can start making up for Will's death," I bargain.

She pauses. "But when you're gone, that means I'll have to deal with Nadia and her feelings," she complains, and I know then she'll do what I asked.

I chuckle and pull her into an embrace. "Something tells me you'll be okay."

"You are so lucky I am such a good friend." She pushes me away from her and nods. "Go."

All I know about Nadia is that she'll be angry and shattered at the same time. Maybe I should have told her sooner. Jack's going to be pissed too. But this is all going to be worth it. This is my chance for vengeance. I have to do this, and not just for me.

I wish there's another option. If there is, I can't think of one. The orb failed, and I failed, so now it's time for the backup plan.

You can do this. It's now or never. Say goodbye and go. There is nothing else left to do.

I leave Alina to search for Ben and Jack, coming across Jack when I down a soldier trying to sneak up on him.

"Hey, there you are," I say.

He grins. "Here I am."

I pull him aside, and that's when his relief turns to bewilderment.

"I don't know how you managed to do it, but you somehow got me to care about you deeply," I say quickly. If I don't say it now, I might never. "And honestly, those feelings scared me at first. But I'm not so afraid anymore."

"I feel the exact same way," he replies. He pulls me close, and he kisses me. He doesn't know this might be the last time. "Serena, why are you saying this *now?*" he asks, motioning around to the battle around us and lunging behind me to block a blow to my head.

"Well . . ."

"Serena, what are you doing?" he asks.

I give him one more kiss, then I hug him for the last time. My eyes sting with tears. I refuse to cry. I'm done crying.

"Goodbye, Jack."

He tries to come after me, but the flow of the battle blocks his way. Over the sound of the fight, he continues to call out my name.

When I get to Ben, he pulls me into his arms. He knows. He somehow always knows. "Serena, what's going on?"

"I love you," I tell him. I take his face in my hands and make myself memorize every bit of it, then pull him into another hug.

"I love you too. . . . What are you—"

I walk away. When he tries coming after me, Alina holds him back, and I'm glad. Saying goodbye to him is much harder than I thought it would be. I can't bring myself to say goodbye to Nadia, to anyone else. I swallow the lump in my throat and fight back the tears forming in my eyes as I make my way over to the hill where Tellerous watches it all, his soldiers stepping aside for me.

"So you see now," Tellerous says as I come closer. "This is the only way. Are you ready now?"

"Yes," I reply.

"Good. Then it's time to reap what you deserve for all you've done." He points his magic in the direction of my crew, my friends. I'm afraid, and I do what I had to do back in the alternate reality.

I open my arms wide and close my eyes.

My body acts as a magnet, and the magic in the sky curves away from the others and naturally rushes over to me. The sky returns to its natural color. I brace myself to hold him off for as long as I can.

I hear Jack behind me. I turn my head to see Alina and Freya sitting on top of him, keeping him away from me. Nadia and Ben are shouting as well, and more of Alina's crewmates have to hold them all back. I know that I can't hold Tellerous off forever. I don't plan to.

The magic is either going to kill me or take over me in a matter of minutes. But the least I can do is keep the people I care about safe until it does.

"Listen to me! I swear to the gods, Serena, get out of there!" I heard Jack cry out. I hear the struggle to keep Jack on the ground. The fight against Tellerous's soldiers is over; this is a fight among themselves.

"Serena, if you can hear me, then please, listen to me! Stop! Please, don't do this!" Jack screams.

"You have to let her go!" James shouts, hesitation making his voice break.

The magic burns. The more I hear Jack calling out for me, the more difficult it is to keep fighting. But I don't have any other choice. I hope that he knows that. I hope he knows that I'm not choosing to leave him.

"Serena, please!" His voice fades. Now, he's finally breaking down.

He says something else, too, but it's muffled over the sound of the magic, the rush of it in my ears and in my veins. I weaken under the magic's power, as if it's pushing me along the ground. It's almost time to see which of the prophecy's outcomes will come true.

You did the right thing. You didn't have any other choice. They will know that soon.

I stop fighting, and so does Tellerous. He doesn't need to. The magic surrounds me like a tornado. This is what I saw in those visions. As it closes in on me, I anxiously await whatever happens next.

No matter what happens, I did what's right . . . right?

The smoke trickles against my skin. It's not so bad. Then it starts crawling into my skin, under it, peeling up the layers. And I scream.

As much as I'd thought about how much this would hurt, this pain is even more agonizing. It's worse than the visions, worse than when Tellerous tried to infuse the magic into me in the alternate reality. I don't fight it, and the magic shoots straight to my core.

It feels like my organs are slowly being ripped out of my body. It's in my head, striking to the center of my brain, squeezing and stretching.

When the magic starts to physically wrap itself around my veins, I know it's not going to kill me, as much as it feels like the pain will. I will live, and Tellerous will take me to the Dark Realm, and I will have to try to figure out a way to defeat my father.

The pain is numbing. My body shifts like clay, molding

as the magic flushes from my head. The more I focus, the more the pain retreats. I'm in complete control of it now. Well, just the darkness inside me. Outside, I'm still surrounded by a cloud of magic, everything left of what attempted to attach to me.

But now that I have the magic, I can learn how to harness it. I can use it to kill Tellerous. He needs to pay for the death of my parents, Alexia, and even William. For nearly killing Ben. Putting everyone I love in danger.

But most of all, I need him to pay for torturing me. For trying to break me.

He's going to find out just how dangerous and ruthless Serena Anne Jones can be. When I see him, I will give him no quarter.

To the Dark Realm it is.

The cloud of magic slowly vanishes, telling me that I officially have obtained the dark Cretion magic. But I am not the same. As the cloud fades, my body crumbles and everything goes black.

EPILOGUE

1—2—3.

I count the intervals of pauses between each heartbeat. My breathing is slow, and I struggle for air in each breath I take. My vision blurs, leaving me terrified in this unfamiliar place. My head is pounding. My entire body aches.

Through my blurred sight, I see the color of blood on my hands. I'm lying down face-first, blood seeping from my pores. The pain of the dark magic still lingers, and I'm sure that's what the blood is from. I attempt to push myself off of the ground. The air is thick, filled with dust and grime.

The last thing I remember before being forced into the Dark Realm is the cries of my crewmates and Ben. I was anxious about something, but I can't remember what. Was it about Jack? Whenever I think about him, my mind shuts down. I know what my task is, but I have no idea where I am or how to do what Elias told me. I don't even know how long I've been out. All I know is that something about me is different, and it isn't just the magic I obtained.

The pain worsens as I try to remember every detail,

every event of these past few weeks. I just want to get back to Ben, but even thinking about him makes it much worse. I can think about that later. Right now, I need a plan. I force my fluttering eyes to open wide, and my vision clears enough to see rusted metal bars in front of me. I'm next to a grimy brick wall on the sandy ground. My hand shakes as I place it on the wall to steady myself, my knees shaking as I rise. As far as I can tell, I'm the only one in here, wherever *here* is. The wounds on my body sting, stretching as I move, and I hunch over. I wrap my free arm around the bleeding wound on my stomach, not quite sure where it came from.

I look down at my hands, realizing I might be able to break free of these bars. I push off the wall but struggle to find my balance. Once I gain my composure, I focus on the cell doors in front of me, then throw my hands forward, flexing my palms. The Cretion magic floods from my hands with just a thought, just like black lightning, eager as it hits the bars. In that one moment, I am so powerful. I'm in awe of what I've done. But the second it touches the surface, the magic disappears into thin air, the bars remaining intact.

Of course. Magic proof.

I fall back to the ground, giving in to pain and despair. As I lie back on the sandy ground, cry. I left everything behind for *this*? This pain, this dungeon, this . . . fear. Tellerous needs my magic, but after I defied him he doesn't need *me*.

How could I be so stupid to come here willingly?

It's too much. I am completely and utterly helpless, lying here on the ground like a sitting duck, waiting for Tellerous to decide what he's going to do with me. What if I'm stuck here forever? What if I never get the chance to kill him? How am I going to save three whole realms when I can't even save myself?

I hear the muffled sound of a door being opened. As the footsteps grow louder, I know what's happening. It takes them a moment to find the right key, but once they do the cell door creaks open. I sluggishly look up, my head shaking. Above me stand two guards, both of their faces covered with black face shields which match their black armor.

"Tellerous is ready for you now."

THE GODS

Adara - the Fire Goddess
Arminia - the God of War
Arnav - the God of the Ocean
Carlisle - the God of the Wind
Clary - the Sky Goddess
Huntelmin - God of the Hunt.
Lucinda - the Creation Goddess
Rosalind - the Terrain Goddess

GLOSSARY

Abaft - the back of a ship

Avast Ye - pirate slang for an order to stop and pay attention.

Aye - yes, or something is being confirmed.

Batten Down the Hatches - prepare for a storm.

Celestial Magic - the magic of the gods and otherworldly beings. The orb is also said to defeat the source of the magic, not the actual magic itself.

Cleave to the Brisket - pirate slang for "nearly cut a man in half with a sword."

The Code - a system of rules and punishments that all pirates must follow

Cretion Magic - a type of magic that creates and destroys things.

Cutlass - a type of pirate sword.

Dark Realm - one of the three realms. It is a place where only souls can enter. People go to the Dark Realm if they are being punished or if they have died. It is ruled by Tellerous, Serena's father

Dissometer - a magic-proof shield that protects people without magic from people with magic.

Elias - Olovia's most powerful sorcerer.

Gurellia - Olovia's neighboring kingdom.

Human Realm - the realm that mortals live in, which is where Olovia is.

Iana - Queen of the Realm of Magic.

Landlubber - a person unfamiliar with the sea or sailing.

Lennard - Serena's stepfather, who raised her.

No Quarter - pirate slang for "showing no mercy."

Olovia - the kingdom that Serena lives in and was born in; ruled by Queen Helena and King Archer, Prince Jack's parents.

Orb - a magical item that is so powerful it can defeat sorcery and celestial magic, alongside many other abilities, like healing and fixing things.

Petticoat - a skirt-like undergarment that women wore under the skirt of their dresses.

Realm of Magic - the third and final realm that only people who possess magic can live in. Like the Dark Realm, it requires an entry portal to get in.

Scurvy Dog - pirate slang; specifically, an insult.

Sorcery - a type of magic that includes spells, which the orb is said to defeat

Tellerous - Serena's biological father who is the king of the Dark Realm. He wants to unite all three realms together and be the ruler.

Tigerlily - the name of Serena's ship.

Visions - side effects of Serena obtaining the dark magic, causing her to see, feel, and hear things.

William's Tavern - the tavern that Serena and her crew hang out at when they aren't on the Tigerlily.

ACKNOWLEDGMENTS

I'm grateful for the many resources online, like the Way of Pirates and the Your Dictionary Pirate Terms & Phrases for all of the amazing and helpful information about pirates for my book!

I want to thank my parents for helping me make my dream come true. I want to thank all of my friends and family for being so supportive and excited for this novel. I want to thank Briana Morgan for seeing potential in my book and for recommending me to my amazing editor, Rachel Oestreich, who has made an incredible difference in my life. She is talented, personable, and she's a great teacher. She has been patient and kind, and I have learned so much from her. I cannot wait to continue my journey with her, and she has become a role model of mine.

I also want to thank Christian Lindo, who is truly responsible for this book. He inspired me every day and that English class truly helped shape my writing into what it is today. He is one of the most impactful teachers I've ever had in my life. I want to thank Dale Mahfood for all of the helpful tips about publishing, for being so supportive in class (I love his class and he is a wonderful teacher!), and for recommending me to my awesome cover designer, Dusan Arsenic, who I also want to thank for designing my cover, which I absolutely love. I want to thank my band for giving me confidence; performing with them makes me feel so confident, content, and able, which inspired me to use that energy to continue working on my novel, even when I had writer's block.

Last, but most certainly not least, I want to thank my sister, Emma. My role model, my rock, and my number one fan. Without her support, love, and advice, I would have never been able to write this novel. I couldn't have asked for a better sister.

ABOUT THE AUTHOR

Abby Greenbaum is a sixteen-year-old junior who has been writing her entire life. When she's not writing more of Serena Jones's story, she loves spending time with musical theater, dance, Disney, Marvel, and playing music with her band. She loves writing, and it actually saved her life at one point. Abby wants to keep writing, improving her skills along the way. She hopes to go far with her writing career, maybe even one day becoming a screenwriter. She believes that books—particularly fantasy—have so much more meaning than people realize. She wants to capture that and help people escape from reality and take them to a whole other world.

 instagram.com/abbygbooks

Made in the USA
Columbia, SC
14 March 2021